ALSO BY PAUL LEVINE

Illegal

Trial & Error

Kill All the Lawyers

The Deep Blue Alibi

Solomon vs. Lord

9 Scorpions

Flesh & Bones

Fool Me Twice

Slashback

Mortal Sin

False Dawn

Night Vision

To Speak for the Dead

LASSITER

LASSITER

A NOVEL

Paul Levine

BANTAM BOOKS

NEW YORK

Copyright © 2011 by Nittany Valley Productions, Inc.

Published in the United States by Bantam Books, an imprint of The Random House Publishing Group, a division of Random House, Inc., New York.

BANTAM BOOKS and the rooster colophon are registered trademarks of Random House, Inc.

Library of Congress Cataloging-in-Publication Data
Levine, Paul (Paul J.)
Lassiter : a novel / Paul Levine.
p. cm.
ISBN 978-0-553-80674-8
eBook ISBN 978-0-440-42313-3
1. Lassiter, Jake (Fictitious character)—Fiction.   2. Stripteasers—Crimes against—
Fiction.   3. Sex-oriented businesses—Fiction.   4. Murder—Investigation—Fiction.
5. Miami (Fla.)—Fiction.   I. Title.
PS3562.E8995L37   2011
813'.54—dc22   2010054128

Printed in the United States of America on acid-free paper

www.bantamdell.com

9 8 7 6 5 4 3 2 1

First Edition

Book design by Caroline Cunningham

For the kids . . .

"For the kids" is the rallying cry of Penn State University's annual dance marathon on behalf of the Four Diamonds Fund, which supports cancer treatment and research at Hershey Children's Hospital.

"In the halls of justice, the only justice is in the halls."

—Lenny Bruce

LASSITER

Prologue

I presented my Florida Bar card at the security window and eased onto a metal bench that would likely throw my back out if the wait lasted more than a few minutes.

It did.

I stood, stretched, and studied the frescoes covering the cracks in the plaster walls. Island scenes of towering palms along a placid sea. Laughing mothers and hopscotching children in splashy Caribbean colors. The paintings made the place even more dreary, the inmates' lives even more hopeless.

Finally, a female guard brought my client from her cell. With her face scrubbed of makeup and her dark hair in a ponytail, Amy Larkin looked more like a college cheerleader than a woman charged with First Degree Murder.

"I didn't kill him, Jake," she blurted out. "Honest, I didn't."

"Hold that thought."

I settled into a straight-backed chair, and we faced each other across a table with cigarette scars from the days lawyers smoked in the visitors' room, just to cover the smells.

"Where were you last night?" I asked.

"Nowhere near Ziegler's."

An alibi? Attending Mass with a hundred witnesses would do just fine.

"I was with a man," Amy said.

Not as good as church, but better than the scene of the crime.

"Who's the lucky guy?"

"Can't tell you."

"Why the hell not?"

"It's too dangerous."

I gave her my big, dumb guy look. It's not much of a stretch. "What's that mean?"

"If he testified, his life would be in danger."

"What about *your* life?"

She fingered the opening of her jailhouse smock, flimsy as crepe paper. "He wants to help, but I won't let him."

"That's my decision, not yours. Give me his name."

"I can't."

My lower back was throbbing again. Too many blind-side hits had knocked a lumbar vertebra off-kilter.

"I'm thinking your alibi is bullshit."

"You just have to trust me, Jake."

"The hell I do."

I get my hands dirty for my clients. I fight prosecutors in court and occasionally in the alley behind the Reasonable Doubt tavern. I stand up to judges who threaten me with contempt and to Bar Association bigwigs who would love to pull my ticket. But I won't tote my briefcase across the street for a client who deceives me.

"Lie to your priest or your lover. But if you lie to me, I can't help you."

"I'm not! I wasn't at Ziegler's. I didn't shoot anyone."

I looked for the averted gaze, the tightened lips, the nervous twitch. Nothing.

"I'm innocent, Jake. Dammit, isn't that enough?"

"Innocence is irrelevant! All that matters is evidence. So give me your alibi, or the jury will give you life."

She took a moment to think it over before saying, "I'm sorry, Jake. You'll have to win without an alibi."

I pushed my chair away from the table and got to my feet. "Enjoy your stay, Amy. It's gonna be a long one."

1   A Brew and Burger Guy

Eight days earlier . . .

When the hot brunette in the tight black skirt waltzed into the courtroom, I was cross-examining a stubborn cop who wouldn't agree to "good morning."

"Isn't it true my client passed the field sobriety test?" I asked him.

"No, sir. He couldn't walk a straight line."

"Just how wide is that line, Officer?"

The cop shrugged, bunching the muscles of his neck. "Never measured it."

"Why not?"

He smirked at me. "It's imaginary."

"Really?" Pretending to be surprised. "And how long's that imaginary line of yours? Six feet? A mile? What?"

"I guess you could say it's infinite."

The brunette shimmied into a front-row seat, tugged the hem of her skirt, then fixed me with a look as friendly as an indictment.

"So, my client stepped off an imaginary line, which has an infinite length and an indefinite width. An invisible line. Is that your testimony?"

"Not at all. I can see it."

"You can see imaginary lines." I paused. "So you're delusional?"

The cop's eyes flicked toward the prosecutor. *Help.* But he didn't get any.

"Officer . . . ?" I prompted him.

"I'm trained and experienced. I've arrested hundreds of drunk drivers in the last—"

"I'm sure you have," I interrupted. "Now, what other imaginary objects do you see?"

"None I can think of."

"No unicorns?"

"No, sir," he said, through gritted teeth.

"Leprechauns, then?"

"No."

"Not even a chupacabra crawling out of the Everglades?"

"Objection!" Harold Flagler III, the young pup of a prosecutor, belatedly hopped to his feet.

"Grounds?" Judge Wallace Philbrick asked.

"Mr. Lassiter is badgering the witness."

"It's my *job* to badger the witness," I fired back.

"Judge Philbrick," Flagler whined.

"I get *paid* to badger the witness."

"Your Honor, please admonish—"

"C'mon, Flagler. Didn't they teach you trial tactics at Yale?"

"Mr. Lassiter!" Judge Philbrick wagged a bony finger at me. "Address your remarks to the court, not opposing counsel."

"I apologize, Your Honor." Sounding so sincere I nearly believed myself.

I swung around, as if pondering my next question. In truth, I wanted a good look at the woman in the gallery. Slender with military school posture, an angular jawline, and a somber expression. Tucked into her pencil skirt was a silk blouse, red as blood, with those big, puffy sleeves, as if she might be hiding an Ace of Hearts, or maybe a derringer. Chin tilted up, she stared me down.

I gave her a quick, crinkly grin and looked for any hint of interest. No inviting eyes or playful smile. *Nada.* Maybe if I wowed her in closing argument, she'd lighten up and slip me her phone number.

Occasionally, I get a groupie or two. Women attracted to a big lug with a craggy profile, a broken nose, and hair the color of sawgrass after a drought. Two hundred thirty-five pounds of ex-linebacker crammed into an off-the-rack, wrinkled brown suit. A brew-and-burger guy in a Chardonnay-and-paté world. I wrapped up my cross-exam, while sneaking peeks at our visitor. She pulled something out of her purse. I walked toward the rail and saw it was a photo, but I couldn't make out any details.

Flagler stood, fondled his Phi Beta Kappa key, and announced the great State of Florida rested its case.

My turn. No way would I let the presumably innocent Pepito Domin-guez testify. He was a twenty-year-old smart-ass with a diamond earring and a barbed-wire tattoo circling his neck. With no witnesses, I rested, too.

The bailiff tucked the jurors into their windowless room where they could surf for porn on their PDAs, and the judge turned to me. "Mr. Las-siter, Ah assume you got some legal mumbo jumbo for the record." His Honor came from a family of gentleman farmers in Homestead by way of Kentucky, and his voice rippled with bourbon and branch water.

"Motion to exclude the breathalyzer test," I began, going through the motions of making my motions.

"Grounds?"

"No evidence the operator was properly trained, the equipment prop-erly maintained, and the test properly administered."

Boilerplate stuff. No chance.

"Denied." *De-nahd.*

"Motion to exclude my client's statements to the arresting officer."

"Denied."

I checked the gallery. Mystery Woman was still there, eyes drilling me. *Who the hell are you?*

I'd had multiple concussions on the football field. Still, I thought I re-membered all my disgruntled ex-clients and infuriated ex-girlfriends. Maybe she was a Florida Bar investigator, building a case against me for yet another insult to the dignity of the court. Or maybe just one of those women with bloodlust. You see them at boxing matches and bullfights and murder trials. Not usually a rinky-dink DUI.

At the next break, I intended to plop down beside her. If she didn't serve me with a subpoena, I might ask her out for a drink.

"Motion for directed verdict. Do you want to hear argument, Judge?"

"About as much as Ah want to hit Dixie Highway during rush hour."

"For the record, I'd like to state my grounds."

"You can pour syrup on a turd, but that don't make it a pancake. Got any more motions you want denied, Mr. Lassiter?"

"I'm plumb out." Adopting a Southern accent of my own. Judge Philbrick peered at me over his spectacles, wondering if I was mocking him.

At the prosecution table, Flagler gave me his Ivy League snicker. If I wanted, I could dangle him out the window by his ankles. But then, I'd been picking up penalties for late hits while he was singing tenor with the Whiffenpoofs. Okay, so I'm not Yale Law Review, but I'm proud of my diploma. University of Miami. Night division. Top half of the bottom third of my class.

"You two want to talk a minute before Ah bring the jury in for closing?" Judge Philbrick picked up a cell phone and wheeled around in his chair to give us some privacy.

Flagler sidled up to me and said, "Perhaps it is a propitious time to discuss a deal."

"If my client wanted to plead guilty, he wouldn't need me."

"We could recess, have a latte downstairs, and work it out."

"I don't drink latte, with or without a hint of nutmeg."

"If I win, I'm asking for jail time."

"Ooh, scary."

Shaking his head, Flagler returned to the prosecution table and picked up his neatly printed note cards. The jurors filed back in, and Judge Philbrick ordered them to listen carefully to closing arguments, but to rely on their own memories, not those of the lying shysters. Actually, he said "learned counsel," but everybody knew what he meant.

I glanced toward the gallery. Yep, the woman was still there in the front row. I gave her a neighborly nod. She took it and gave nothing back.

Flagler bowed obsequiously to the judge and thanked the jury for leaving their fascinating jobs and coming to the courthouse in the service of justice.

Or a reasonable facsimile thereof.

After twenty minutes, he sat down and I stood up. "How did my client blow a point-six when stopped by the police officer but only a point-zero-nine at the station?"

Judging from their blank looks, math was not the jurors' favorite sub-ject.

"I'll tell you how," I continued. "There's *no* way! At point-six, my client's breath could have ignited charcoal in a hibachi."

Fearing he'd belch beer into the cop's face, my too-damn-clever client had squirted enough Listerine into his mouth to disinfect a knife wound. The mouthwash vaulted the kid's *mouth* alcohol off the charts, while the *blood* alcohol test accurately pinned the number at a notch above the law-ful limit.

Oftentimes, complete dickwads are undeservedly lucky, while the good get crapped on by life's endless shit storm. So it was with Pepito Domin-guez, who inadvertently, but fortuitously, screwed up the alcohol tests.

"If the tests don't fit, you must acquit!" I boomed.

Rest in peace, Johnnie Cochran.

After some more double talk and sleight of hand, I thanked the good citizens for not falling asleep and sat down. The judge recited his instruc-tions, and the bailiff returned the jurors to their little dungeon to delib-erate.

I spun through the swinging gate and plopped down next to Mystery Woman. Up close, she had full lips and a flawless complexion, without the hint of foundation, blush, or war paint. Her eyes were green with a touch of a golden sunset, her dark hair pulled straight back and held by a squig-gly elastic band. Late twenties or early thirties.

"Hey there." I gave her a lopsided grin that has been known to charm a number of barmaids.

"Hello, Mr. Lassiter." No smile. No warmth. No nothing.

"Have we met before?"

"My name is Amy Larkin."

She waited a moment, as if the name might provoke a reaction. It didn't.

"So what brings you to the courthouse, Amy Larkin?"

"You do, Mr. Lassiter. I need to ask you some questions."

Something in the way she said "questions" convinced me we weren't going to be chatting over Happy Hour.

"Fire away," I said.

She handed me the photo she had been holding. A small cocktail table in front of a stage. Pole dancer in the background. Front and center, two young women in string bikinis were draped over a thick-necked guy with shaggy hair and a bushy mustache the color of beach sand. The Sundance Kid with a shit-eating grin. Young. Cocky. Stupid.

I should know. The guy was me.

Embarrassing to look at now. I was a glassy-eyed drunk in a Dolphins jersey. Number 58. Not even traveling incognito. A red scab ran horizontally across the bridge of my nose. If you make enough helmet-first tackles, your face mask will take divots out of your flesh.

"Long time ago. Birthday party my teammates threw for me," I said. "Where'd you get the picture?"

She ignored my question and shot back her own. "Do you know the girls?"

One of them, a big-boned blonde, had her arms locked around my neck, her enhanced breasts squashed against my chest. The other one was younger. Slender. Auburn hair. Girl-next-door looks. She was kissing my cheek.

"The one with coconut boobs was a stripper. Sonia Something-or-other. She hung around with one of my teammates. I don't know the younger one's name."

"Krista."

I flipped the photo over. On the back, someone had scrawled, *The Whore of Babylon.*

"Okay. The girl's name is Krista. We're in a picture together. So what?"

She gave me a look hard enough to leave bruises. "She was my sister."

"Was?"

"She's gone."

"Gone meaning dead?"

"Disappeared and presumed dead."

Except for the two of us, the courtroom was empty now and silent as a mausoleum.

"I'm sorry. I'm very sorry to hear that." She studied me through hard, cold eyes. "But what's all this have to do with me?"

"I think you know, Mr. Lassiter."

"No, I don't. So why not stop dancing around and just tell me?"

"You seem agitated, Mr. Lassiter. Why is that?"

"Because you're playing me and you're not very good at it. Where'd you learn your interrogation technique, *Law & Order?*"

"Why would I need to interrogate you? Have you committed a crime?"

I stood up. "Cut the crap. If you're not going to tell me what's going on—"

"It's quite simple, Mr. Lassiter." Her eyes locked on mine, daring me to leave. "You're the last person who saw Krista alive."

2 Jake the Fixer

I long-legged it down the corridor, Amy Larkin in pursuit. The Justice Building was emptying now, just a few straggling girlfriends and wives of defendants who show up at hearings, some blowing kisses, others hurling insults about unpaid child support and broken promises.

"So you're not going to talk to me, is that it?" Amy raised her voice to my back.

"I don't know anything about your sister's disappearance. Got nothing more to say."

"What happened that night? You can tell me that."

"It was my birthday party. There were some girls. There always were."

"That's it?"

I stepped onto the down escalator, Amy right behind.

"It was a long time ago. I don't remember one night from another, one girl from another, okay?"

I hopped off the escalator and turned the corner, coming alongside Joseph Gillespie, proprietor of Let'em Go Joe Bail Bonds. He tipped his Florida Marlins cap and let me pass, so I could hit the next escalator in full stride. Amy Larkin was a step behind. Three more floors, then the lobby, then the parking lot. She was going to be on my tail for a while.

"So you're not interested in clearing your name?" she called after me.

"I don't know what happened to your sister. Hell, I don't even remember her."

"I don't believe you."

"I don't care!"

"Was she just another easy fuck for you?"

"Jesus!"

Three steps ahead, on the escalator, a young female probation officer turned around and glared at me.

"Did you hurt her?" Amy demanded.

I kept quiet.

"Did you kill her?"

Most people would say, "Hell, no!" But having spent fifteen years asking questions under oath and having read thousands of transcripts, I knew the questions wouldn't end with my simple denial.

Who else was there?

What happened in the strip club that night?

Did you ever see my sister again?

It would be endless, and there would be questions I wouldn't want to answer. Not truthfully, anyway. It was all so long ago. That guy in the picture. It was me, but a *different* me. Today, I would behave differently. I would be a better man. Or would I?

"Did you know how old Krista was?" Amy pressed me.

Again, I forced myself to keep quiet. It's the same advice I give my clients. Even the innocent ones? Yeah. Because no one is a hundred percent innocent. I wasn't. Not that night.

Amy was still jabbering when we hit the deserted ground floor. The lobby lawyers, guys who scrounge for clients near the elevator bank, had given up for the day.

She grabbed me by the sleeve of my suit coat. "If you had a shred of decency, you'd tell me everything you know." Her voice tight, her pain palpable.

She had that right. A shred of decency was about my ration.

"Walk with me," I said, figuring she wouldn't let up. "But stop pecking at me."

We exited the building on the 12th Street side and crossed into the parking lot. My old Biarritz Eldo was resting under a skinny palm tree at the far end of the lot, by the Miami River. A rust bucket freighter, its top deck covered with used bicycles, was steaming east, toward the ocean, and a distant port in the islands.

"I'm truly sorry about your sister," I said. "And for your pain."

She waited. I wasn't about to tell her *everything* I knew. But, ignoring my own counsel, I planned to tell her enough to get her off my ass.

"I *do* remember her." Hell, yes, I thought. Krista would be hard to forget.

Still, Amy waited.

I took a deep breath. I looked Amy Larkin in the eyes. Then I told her the story.

It had been Rusty's idea. Throw his pal a birthday party at Bozo's, a strip club on LeJeune Road near the airport. Not that I objected. I was a free agent, one year out of Penn State, busting my ass to hang on to the Dolphins' roster. Rusty MacLean was a flashy wide receiver with deceptive speed, best known for slanting hard across the middle, his long red hair flapping out of his helmet like flames trailing an engine. He was a bad boy and, of course, women loved him.

Rusty knew the guy who owned Bozo's. Hell, he knew all the guys who owned strip clubs, massage parlors, and peep shows. Rusty paid for the booze and half a dozen strippers. Lap dances included. Anything in the Champagne Room in back was between the stripper and the partygoer. Tips *not* included.

Rusty had been seeing Sonia What's-her-name for a couple months. He called her his favorite, but that's like Tiger Woods calling a seven-iron his favorite club or his wife his favorite woman. There were plenty more in the bag, when the need arose.

On that night long ago, I remember Rusty swooping down on the table where I sat with Sonia and the new girl. Sonia was all plastic boobs and hair extensions. The kid, Krista, had a sprinkling of freckles and a wide, innocent toothpaste commercial smile. Even toasted, I realized she didn't belong here with a bunch of degenerates like Rusty, my teammates . . . and me.

The offensive line sat at the bar, looking like giant beer kegs on a loading dock. Models of teamwork, the guys maintained their usual positions, the center in the middle of the group, flanked by both guards, and then the tackles. The tight end must have been taking a piss. One of our defensive backs—a showboater, but aren't they all?—was demonstrating his karaoke prowess, with a soulful rendition of "Midnight Train to Georgia." Half a dozen strippers were offering companionship in exchange for tips.

I had just won a drinking game called "Who Shit?" Yeah, I know, very mature. In those days, fueled by testosterone and tequila, I often engaged in clever activities, such as pounding holes in plasterboard with my forehead.

Rusty staggered over, grabbed Krista by the shoulders, and hoisted her out of her chair. "Wanna ride the wild stallion?"

Her body stiffened.

"How old are you, kid?" I asked, realizing she wanted no part of Rusty's rodeo.

"Twenty-one."

"Right. And I'm gonna make All-Pro. Rusty, why not pick on someone old enough to vote. Or at least old enough to drive?"

"Stay out of this, benchwarmer." Rusty slung her onto his back and gave her a horsey ride to the Champagne Room, a dark place separated from the VIP Room by a beaded curtain.

I gave Sonia a look, but she just shrugged.

Rusty will be Rusty.

We left it at that. Rusty was a star, and I was a free agent linebacker, specializing in kamikaze tackles on the kickoff team. My deepest concerns involved running faster and hitting harder. I read the sports pages and the Dolphins' playbook and little else. I was not given to profound thoughts.

A few moments later, I heard a scream from the back.

A man's scream. Rusty yelping, then cursing. The words starting with "motherfucking" and ending with a word that rhymes with "punt." I tore through the beaded curtain and flicked on the lights.

"Bitch stabbed me, Jake!"

Rusty was sprawled naked on the floor. A knife handle protruded from his right buttock, blood seeping around the blade.

"She had a fucking knife in her boot!" Rusty was gasping for air, and I was afraid he was going into shock.

"Calm down, cowboy. We'll get you to Jackson."

"No hospitals, Jake. No police. That doc in Hialeah. Get me there."

The girl was curled in the fetal position in a corner of the sofa. Sobbing. Nude except for one white patent leather boot. She had a bloody lip and her neck was ringed with red marks. Four fingers and a thumb had pressed into her flesh. I could even make out the imprint of Rusty's Super Bowl ring.

"Jesus, Rusty, what the hell did you do to her?"

"I paid for it rough." He hacked up a wet cough. "She knew what she was getting into."

By now, three of our larger teammates had crowded through the doorway. They debated who would take Rusty to Dr. Toraño in Hialeah, finally deciding all of them would go. Offensive linemen believe in teamwork. My job was to take care of the girl, or more accurately, make sure the girl caused no problems for Rusty or the team.

I stripped off my jersey and handed it to her. She put it on, sniffled, and wiped her nose with her arm. "You're not gonna call the cops on me, are you?"

"Why the hell would I do that?"

"I stabbed your friend."

"Knowing Rusty, he deserved it."

She gave me a look, somewhere between relief and disbelief.

"Some women I know would give you a medal," I said. "And trust me, the cops would be worse for Rusty than for you." I opened my wallet and pulled out several twenties.

Jake the Fixer.

I jammed the bills into her hand. Years before I became a night-school lawyer, I was already massaging the justice system. "Everything's gonna be okay."

She touched her neck with one hand, feeling where she had been choked.

"Let's get you cleaned up." I dabbed the blood from her lip with a napkin. Our faces were just inches apart, her green-gold eyes staring into mine.

"I need to get out of here," she said.

"Good idea. Do you have a car?"

"Out of Miami. Out of this . . ." Her gesture took in the stained vinyl sofa, the cheesy nude prints, the entire mildewed, sleaziness of the place. "Can you help me?"

"I'm not a social worker. Come on."

"You're kind of cute. Do you have a girlfriend?"

"Dozens. Now, where do you live? I'm gonna get you a cab."

"Let's go to your place."

"Nope. Too many sharp objects in the kitchen."

"Just for the night."

"And then tomorrow, what?"

"I never worry about tomorrow."

"Poetic. Where do you live?"

"Please. I'll do anything you want." In case I didn't get the point, her tongue darted between painted lips. When I didn't respond, she grabbed my hand and slipped it under the jersey and onto a warm, natural, silken breast. She took my other hand, raised it to her face, and stuck my thumb into her mouth. She sucked it. Hard and with plenty of tongue and slurping sound effects. Subtlety was not the girl's strong suit.

I was tempted. Who the hell wouldn't have been? But I was still thinking about Rusty and cops and curfews and Coach Shula. A human cold shower.

"Not gonna happen, kid," I said.

She pushed my hand out from under the jersey and spit my thumb out of her mouth. "Asshole!"

"Right. Okay, where do you live?"

"Miami Springs, but I don't want to go back there. There's this guy. . . ."

"There usually is," I said. Figuring she lived with some punk. A drug dealer or a pimp.

"An old guy," she continued. "Like almost forty. He pays my rent and wants me to do these gross movies, and—"

"No time for life stories. I'm paying for a cab. You decide where to go."

She looked at me then, her eyes empty and defeated. Another man letting her down. I imagined a father or a stepfather, a creep who did things that pushed her out the door and into a seedy place like this.

But I can't save the world. I can't even save one lost girl.

We didn't exchange another word, and after I tucked her into the cab, I never saw her again.

3 The Road to Hell

That was the story I told Amy Larkin.

Most of it was true. Rusty. The knife. The busted lip. The cash.

But I had left things out and cut the story short. I hadn't sent Krista home. No way would I tell Amy Larkin what really happened. The unedited version would feed her suspicion that I had a motive for wanting Krista to disappear.

"I don't believe you," Amy said, flatly.

"Why the hell not? If I was gonna lie, I'd have a better story."

"It's a smart story. Better than if you claimed to be a hero."

"Right. Who would believe that?"

"You come out looking like a shit, but not a rapist or a killer."

We were standing next to my Eldo convertible in the Justice Building parking lot, nearly empty now, the afternoon sun beating down on the pavement. A snowy white egret had migrated across the street from the river and was scratching at the asphalt where someone had spilled a bag of potato chips.

"Problem is, you're lying," she said.

"So you're a human polygraph, that it?"

She pulled out a leather case and handed me a business card. Amy G. Larkin. Fraud Investigator. Auto Division of some insurance company in Toledo, Ohio.

"I interview liars every day," she said.

"Lot of fender-bender cheats in Toledo, I'll bet."

"Do you have any witnesses? Anyone see Krista get into that cab? Who'll back up your story?"

That's the problem with lies, I thought. To keep them going, you have to fertilize and water them. Then they grow like strangler weeds.

"I told you the truth. Take it or leave it."

"So even by your own account, you had a chance to be a Good Samaritan, and you turned away."

"That's one way of looking at it. Another is that I'm not the last person to see your sister alive."

"The cabdriver you can't name?"

"And the guy she didn't want to go home to."

"And his name is . . . ?"

"No idea."

Three toots of a horn came from the direction of the river, a freighter asking for the drawbridge to open, pissing off motorists who'd be stuck for the next five minutes.

"You might want to track down where Krista was living in Miami Springs," I said. "Maybe there's some record of who paid her rent."

"I know how to investigate, Lassiter. It's what I do."

"Great. Then if there's nothing more you need from me . . ."

"Why so anxious to get rid of me?"

I imagined her asking the same question to a guy with an inflated bill to repair his rocker panel.

"Let me ask you something," I said. "Why's it taken you so long to find me? Your sister disappeared what, eighteen years ago?"

"That's not your concern."

"Fine." I pocketed her card. "I'll call you if I think of anything else."

"No, you won't."

She turned and headed toward her rental at the other end of the lot, forgetting to say what a pleasure it had been to meet me. I stood there a moment in the tropical heat, watching her go. Only when she had ducked into a red Taurus did I bring up the remaining memories of that long ago night.

The whole truth? I did not put Krista Larkin in a cab and send her home. Oh, I tried. But she refused to get in. Instead, standing in the street in front of Bozo's, she thrust out a thumb and tried hitchhiking up LeJeune Road. It took about thirty seconds for a car to stop. Four guys were inside, windows down, hooting and hollering, and bragging about the size of their equipment. I grabbed her and dragged her to my car.

She was laughing as soon as her butt hit the seat. She'd gotten what she'd wanted. I drove to my apartment, telling myself it was with good intentions. Yeah, yeah. I know what paves the road to hell.

I gallantly gave Krista my bedroom. I'd sleep on the sofa, and in the morning, we'd figure out what to do.

Deep inside, I knew it was bullshit, and so did she. Teenage girl, beautiful and willing. Horny jock—or is that redundant? It was a sure thing, and no guy I knew would have turned it down.

The mating dance was a simple two-step. I asked if she wanted to shower. *Yes.* She asked if I wanted to join her. *Yes.* I took her standing up under the steaming water, her legs locked around my hips. Then on the chaise on the balcony, Krista wanting to feel the breeze from the bay. Finally in the bed, where we conked out until close to noon.

When I awoke, I had no regrets. No pangs of conscience. My only worry was making my one o'clock practice. Being late would cost me $500 and enhance the possibility of finishing my career with the Saskatchewan Roughriders.

Krista found a white dress shirt in my closet. She wore that and nothing else and padded off to the kitchen, where she tried making French toast, creating a lake of egg yolks on the counter. Getting all domestic after one night of play.

My head ached from the booze. She was already talking about how we might spend the weekend.

"How old are you?" I asked. "Really."

"Twenty."

"Bullshit."

It took some persuading, but she finally admitted the truth. "Almost eighteen."

Shit. Jailbait.

"You gotta go now, kid."

"Whadaya mean?"

"I'll drive you to your place."

"I wanna stay with you."

"Not gonna happen."

"The stuff I did last night. I can do even better."

Her eyes brimmed. I felt sorry for her, just as she supposed I would. Still . . .

"Get dressed Krista. We gotta go."

"Asshole!" She tore off my shirt, popping all the buttons. She stamped into the bedroom. Fifteen minutes later, I was driving west on 36th Street through a frog-strangler of a storm, thunder rattling the windows of my old Camaro. When I pulled up to the curb, I saw a man standing under the awning of Krista's apartment building, smoking a cigar. Blocky build. Blue jeans and a brown suede jacket, an urban cowboy look. Thinning hair with a bad comb-over. He tossed the cigar into the bushes as we pulled up.

"Shit, it's Charlie," Krista said.

The guy's hands were balled into fists at his sides.

I did the semi-chivalrous thing. Double-parked next to a puddle and said, "see ya," as she got out of the car. The guy she called "Charlie" stayed under the awning, the rain drilling the canvas like gunshots.

"In the car, babe." He gestured toward a lobster red Porsche, the water beading on its waxy finish.

"I gotta get cleaned up, Charlie."

"Now! You're late and you're costing me money."

"You gonna be okay, kid?" I called through the window.

"Fuck you, asshole." She shot me the bird and headed for the Porsche.

Charlie stepped off the curb and splashed toward my door. He sized me up and didn't seem impressed. "Have fun, stud?"

"What's it to you?"

"Lemme guess. Best you ever had."

"Fuck off."

"Hell, she's the best I ever had, and I've had a helluva lot more than you."

"I don't keep score," I said.

"We all keep score. Even Boy Scouts like you."

From the Porsche, Krista yelled, "You coming, Charlie? Thought we were late."

He ignored her and looked at me with a mirthless smile. "Did you play rough? That's the way she likes it, you know."

"This how you get off? Talking to guys about fucking."

"You didn't leave any bruises, did you, stud?"

"Fuck you."

"If you did, it'll cost you."

"Who are you, her pimp?"

The guy laughed. "Pimp. Manager. Fuck buddy. Man for all seasons. But you, stud? You're just a john."

4 People Change

I have no excuses, other than being 23, with more sex drive than brain power. I seem to remember rationalizing my conduct: *Hey, she was a stripper. It's not like I deflowered her after catechism class.*

But the truth is that I didn't care about her. I simply took what was offered and gave nothing in return, except some crumpled twenty-dollar bills.

That was then. And now?

I didn't want to get involved in Amy's life, either. All I needed was to convince her that I wasn't the last person to see her sister alive. There was "Charlie." Problem was, my story of a rainy day and a mystery guy with a comb-over would sound like bullshit. The truth often does. If I could find Charlie's last name, I'd have something solid to give Amy. Then I would bid her good-bye, good luck, and have a nice life.

Jake Lassiter, still the escape artist.

Fifteen minutes after leaving the Justice Building with my DUI jury out, I was cruising across the MacArthur Causeway, headed toward my office on South Beach. It was a crystalline clear, breezy afternoon, the sun bursting into diamonds on the bay. To my right, one of the big cruise ships was steaming out Government Cut, headed to the islands.

I tried calling my old teammate Rusty MacLean. Back in the day, he'd known a lot of sleazebags. Maybe he could pin a last name on "Charlie." Rusty's voicemail promised he'd ring me right back, if he wasn't fishing, riding his horse, or coaching his daughters' field hockey team.

With the top down, my car attracts whistles, horn toots, and tail-fin envy. It's a 1984 Caddy convertible that's gone to the moon, according to the odometer.

The Biarritz Eldorado was my fee from Stan (Strings) Hendricks, a Key West piano tuner, who was picked up on the Overseas Highway with three hundred pounds of Acapulco Gold in the trunk. If I didn't win the case, Strings would do a dime for trafficking, and I'd get squat.

The sheriff's deputy testified that he had kept pace with the Caddy, which was supposedly speeding. After the stop, the cop said he smelled marijuana, giving him probable cause to search the car. But I subpoenaed the cruiser's videotape, and by counting the seconds between a clearly visible bridge and a gas station, I proved that Strings was going only 43 mph. Search quashed, marijuana excluded. My client went free, and I got his cream-colored Biarritz Eldorado with red velour pillowed uphol-stery. The car looked like a Bourbon Street brothel on wheels, and natu-rally, I loved it.

My cell rang just as I passed the Fisher Island ferry port.

"Jake, you worthless SOB," Rusty greeted me. "Where you been hiding out?"

"Unlike some people, I have to work for a living."

"Screw that. C'mon down to the Keys and let's chase some bonefish."

When he wasn't at his house-on-stilts in Islamorada, Rusty lived on thirty acres of what used to be mango orchards in the Redlands. He'd mar-ried a lovely woman and fathered twin girls. In his spare time, of which he had plenty, Rusty ran a foundation that kept at-risk kids in school and out of trouble. After Rusty the Reprobate retired from the game, he had changed. I respected him for that.

We swapped insults, and then I asked Rusty what he remembered about the night at Bozo's.

"I don't wanna revisit that shit," Rusty said. "I was a total dog back then."

"One hundred percent pussy hound," I agreed. "But it's important, okay?"

"I've pretty much erased the nineties from my memory bank. Except for '91 when I made the Pro Bowl."

I could have said, *"As an injury replacement,"* but that would have been unkind.

"Let me refresh your recollection, Rusty," I said, as if cross-examining a hostile witness. "You got rough with the girl, she stabbed you, and a friendly doc in Hialeah stitched you up under a tequila anesthetic."

"Yeah, still got the scar. All right, what do you want to know?"

"The girl ever mention a guy named Charlie?"

"Who the hell can remember?"

"Try, okay?"

"You got a last name?"

"That's what I'm looking for."

"Can't help you. Sorry."

"Ever see the girl again?"

"Why would I? What's this about, anyway?"

I told him about my meeting with Amy Larkin.

"Bummer," Rusty said, reaching back decades for the word. "But don't blame yourself, Jake. Jeez, compared to me, you were a gentleman."

"Compared to you, the Marquis de Sade was a gentleman."

"You want my advice, let it go."

"I intend to. But I'd like to give the sister a lead, some nudge in the right direction. Then I'm done."

"Wish I could help you, Jake."

"What about the other stripper?" I asked. "Sonia something."

"Sonia Majeski. You need her number?"

"You're still in touch?" I couldn't believe it.

"She called me a couple years ago after reading about Rusty's Scholars."

One of the New Rusty's good deeds. He selected several of the best—and poorest—students at Miami Central High School and took them on Caribbean cruises, along with volunteer guidance counselors and SAT tutors.

He told me that Sonia had gotten out of the life. Studied accounting at Miami-Dade, married a Customs agent, and snagged a job with Royal Caribbean. Now she was a purser on a cruise ship and got Rusty hefty discounts for his scholarship cruises.

He promised to text me Sonia's number as soon as we hung up. I told him I'd chase the wily bonefish with him soon. He called me a liar. I told him to fuck off. Translation: We're still asshole buddies.

In ten minutes, I would be sitting at my desk, punching the phone. With a little luck, Sonia Majeski would know what happened to Krista Larkin. With a lot of luck, maybe Krista wasn't dead. Maybe she'd changed her name and married a dentist and was living in Lauderdale-by-the-Sea in a four-bedroom house with two kids, a swimming pool, and a hybrid SUV parked out front.

Yeah, and maybe I'll be the first ambulance chaser appointed to the Supreme Court. Chances were, Krista was long gone. I just didn't want her sister running around town shouting that I had something to do with it.

5 A Man Named "Charlie"

My office is on the second floor of a building that's too old, too boxy, and too gray to be called art deco. My "suite," as the advertisement on craigslist called it, consists of a waiting room I share with a marriage counselor, a narrow book-lined corridor that ends at my assistant's cubicle, and my twelve-by-twelve slice of heaven with a window overlooking a municipal parking garage.

It was not always this way. I started in the Public Defender's Office, where I learned how to try homicide cases without pissing my pants. I moved into private practice with a deep-carpet firm of paper pushers who settled all their civil cases and pled out all their criminal clients. I was an oddity there, a guy who'd hit more blocking sleds than law books. They discarded me after one-too-many contempt citations. So now I fly solo and follow my own rules. It's the only way I can live.

The building is owned by Jorge Martinez, who runs Havana Banana, a Cuban restaurant on the first floor. A few years ago, I saved Jorge's *huevos con bacon* by keeping the Health Department from shutting the joint down. That's more than I could do for his earlier restaurant, Escargot-to-Go, which landed in bankruptcy. Turned out there wasn't much of a market for fast-food snails in paper cups. These days I defend food poisoning lawsuits involving cockroaches in the *caldo gallego.*

I do a few divorces, too. Mostly, they're referrals from the marriage counselor next door. His failures become my paychecks. I kick back one-third of the fee to him, which is dicey under the ethical rules, if you pay attention to that sort of thing.

I found Cindy, my assistant, in her cubicle, grooming her cuticles. She's Gothic pale with purple hair exploding in different directions like the twigs of an osprey nest. Today she wore a black sleeveless leather vest with dangling silver chains. Two chrome studs poked out of the flesh above her left eyebrow, and werewolf tattoos covered her toned upper arms.

"Hold my calls, Cindy," I ordered, moving past her.

"What calls?"

"And clear my calendar."

She waved a hand like a genie. "Poof! Done."

Sonia Majeski answered on the first ring. I told her who it was and she hollered into the phone, "No way! Lord, how long's it been?"

We did the pleasantries. She was aboard ship in St. Thomas. The passengers were sightseeing and buying duty-free liquor. American tourists will happily skip historic sites and forgo exotic meals for a chance to save a few bucks on their booze.

"I need to ask you about a girl from the old days," I said.

"I don't remember her."

"Whoa. I haven't given you a name."

"I've spent a long time forgetting the 'old days.' Not gonna start remembering now."

"This is important. I think the two of you might have worked together in a strip club."

"Not going there, Jake."

"Help me out, Sonia. This girl was underage."

"Lots were back then. So what?"

"Her name was Krista. Krista Larkin."

The pause on the line told me I had hit paydirt.

"Sonia?"

"Did they find her body?" she asked, softly.

I told Sonia about my meeting with Amy. Told her that Krista was missing but no body had been found, and I asked her to tell me everything she remembered.

Sonia said she'd been living in an apartment in Miami Springs, near the airport. The place was filled with stewardesses, as they were still called. Eastern Air Lines had recently gone under, and the building was only half full. Sonia was stripping in a club owned by Russian gangsters.

"One day, I get a new neighbor," she said. "Krista. She looked like a high school girl. Hell, she *was* a high school girl. But when she got dolled up, Jesus, Jake, bar the door."

"Did you know a guy named Charlie she hung around with?"

"That sleazebag. Charlie's the one who got her into porn."

I remembered what Krista told me that night at Bozo's. *"There's this guy. . . . An old guy. Like almost forty. He pays my rent and wants me to do these gross movies. . . ."*

And I was the dumb bastard who delivered her to the dirtbag.

"Any chance you remember his last name?" I asked Sonia.

"You don't want to be messing with this guy."

"So you know. Tell me."

"He's connected, Jake."

"Organized crime?"

"Political connections that are even scarier."

"Just tell me, Sonia. What's his name?"

"Ziegler. Charlie Ziegler."

It hit me then. "Charles Ziegler" was a bold-face name on the society page. There was a Ziegler wing of the hospital in South Miami. A Ziegler charity golf tournament in Coral Gables. But why fear that guy? He seemed more like Daddy Warbucks than John Gotti.

"You talking about the Ziegler who gives all that money away?" I asked.

"That's him. Went legit and made a bundle in cable TV. Back in the day, he was the prince of porn and Krista's sugar daddy. Rented a mansion on Sunset Island he called the 'Fuck Palace.'"

Change, I thought, was in the air. Rusty. Sonia. Even the prince of porn had become respectable. Which made me think again about the lunkhead in that photo at Bozo's. Just how much had I changed?

"His videos were called 'Charlie's Girlz,'" Sonia continued. "With a 'z,' as in 'Ziegler.'"

That was all I needed. I had a name to give Amy Larkin, crack insurance investigator from Podunk, Ohio. Now I could get the hell out. But something kept me on the phone with Sonia, asking questions. Maybe it was just curiosity. Or maybe, subconsciously, I was trying to make amends for having been such a shit all those years ago.

"Was Krista involved with anyone else?" I asked.

"Depends what you mean by 'involved.' Ziegler passed her around to his friends."

"Know any of their names?"

"Not really. Rich, older guys. Sick fucks, from what she told me. Into drugs and kinky sex."

The list of possible suspects just multiplied, I thought. Nothing is ever as simple as it seems.

"I tried to warn her, Jake. The men, the drugs, the violence. But she was a kid and you couldn't tell her anything. She started shooting four or five videos a week. Ziegler just cranked them out, using up girls and finding new ones."

"She get involved with any of the actors or crew?"

"Not that I know of. But she was doing her drug dealer off and on. A guy who called himself 'Snake.' Rode a Harley. Smelled like motor oil, but handsome as sin in that bad-boy way."

"A biker named 'Snake'?" I couldn't hide my rolling eyes from my voice.

"It's true. Tattoos, leather, the big ass Harley. He wanted Krista to go to California with him."

"You sure she didn't go?"

"Doubt she would have left Ziegler. He was paying the bills, giving her a sense of security."

"And the last time you saw her . . . ?"

"The parking lot of our apartment building. Said she was going to Ziegler's house for some wild party with the high mucky-mucks."

Whoa. That was big. If Krista was last seen heading to Ziegler's, he just stepped to the front of the line called "persons of interest."

"Any idea who might have been at the party?"

"All I know is Krista said there were always cops and politicians. Even judges, if you can believe that."

I could. Easily.

"Her car wasn't in its space the next morning," Sonia said, "but that wasn't unusual. A couple days later, she still hadn't shown up. All her clothes were still in the apartment. I didn't know what to do, so I drove over to Ziegler's office. They said they hadn't seen Krista, and Ziegler was out of town."

"Anyone file a missing persons report?"

"Me. But you know how it is. Stripper and porn actress. Not the cops' highest priority."

Over the line, I heard two quick whistle blasts and the exhalation of steam in the background.

"I found Krista's home number in her things," Sonia said, "and called her father. He flew down the next day."

That solved one small mystery. "You gave him the photo from Bozo's."

"Yeah. And I told him the truth about what Krista was doing. You could see the light in him just die. Maybe I did the wrong thing, Jake."

"The truth is always best."

A policy I didn't really believe and clearly didn't adhere to.

"I could tell from her dad's face," Sonia said, "he wasn't going to look for her. He just wrote her off."

We were both silent a moment. I heard two more whistle blasts. Then I asked the same question I leave with every friendly witness. "Can you think of anything else that might be useful, Sonia?"

After a moment, she said, "There's one thing, but I almost hate to say it."

"What?"

"I knew a couple girls who worked in one of Ziegler's clubs. They were always stoned, so you can't believe half of what they said. But one of them told me something really scary."

"Yeah?"

"That Ziegler was making snuff films in Mexico. Whenever one of the girls gave him a problem, he'd say, 'How'd you like your next movie to be your last?' Or 'You're worth more to me dead.' Creepy stuff like that."

"Did she see any of the films herself?"

"No, she was just repeating what she'd heard."

"Hearsay on hearsay."

"I know, Jake. But that day I went to Ziegler's office, looking for Krista, they told me he was out of the country."

"So?"

"They said he was in Mexico."

6 She Likes It Rough

"Sure, I remember Charlie's Girlz," Coleman said. "Thin story lines but decent production values. All hard core. A lot of S and M."

"I don't suppose you have any of their videos."

"'Videos?' No. Everything's been transferred to DVD." Coleman sucked on a Lucky Strike and gestured toward a back aisle. "Check between Hustler and Vivid in the last row."

A former client, Elmore Coleman was manning the cash register at a XXX-video store on South Dixie Highway. He was a small-time grifter in his fifties with grayish skin, a snow-white ponytail, and nicotine-stained fingernails. A couple years ago, he'd been caught at the airport soliciting cash for tsunami relief, but the only tidal wave was the whiskey he'd consumed with the money he'd collected. I walked him out of the courtroom with a nice fat Not Guilty. Then, a few weeks later, he was busted for selling counterfeit Girl Scout cookies. I lost that case, and Coleman served eight months before getting early release, courtesy of jail overcrowding. That's when he landed the job at the video store, thanks to his only lawful skill, an encyclopedic knowledge of pornography.

"The Charlie's Girlz brand had its run in the early nineties," Coleman told me. "Won a couple AVNs for its Bound and Gagged series. They're the Oscars of porn."

I thanked him and moseyed toward the aisle he'd pointed out. It was just after six P.M., and there were three or four guys in the place. All well groomed and normal-looking, deeply engrossed in examining DVD covers.

I scanned the covers of the Charlie's Girlz videos, searching for Krista Larkin. The photos were a succession of boobs and butts and a few bald crotches. The head shots started to look alike. Young blondes with fake eyelashes, phony smiles, and invented names. Cherry Cola. Lolita Lick. Jenny Talia. Many titles were highly descriptive: *Three Guys and a Girl*. Some sounded like instruction manuals: *How to Fuck on a Jungle Gym*. And others were just lousy puns: *Remembrance of Times Gone Bi*.

I found the "Bound and Gagged" series and thumbed through the stack of DVDs. It only took a minute before I found Krista—all auburn hair and freckles—on the cover of *She Likes It Rough*. Bent over a wooden stool, she wore a black leather bustier that propped up her small breasts, and her bare butt was being paddled by an unseen man.

Coleman inserted the DVD into a master player behind his counter, and I settled into a booth in the back. The plot, such as it was, combined incest with sadomasochism. Krista was a schoolgirl in a plaid mini-skirt, bunny barrettes in her hair. She'd been cutting class, a handy excuse for her father—potbellied and balding—to paddle her. The plot turned to irony here. Krista was supposed to like the paddling. The pinker her butt shone, the more she licked her lips and begged for another whack. But her eyes were dead, her mind elsewhere. "Harder, Daddy!" sounded hollow and false.

The air was bad in the enclosed booth, and I felt hot and itchy, as if spiders were crawling up my pants legs. When Krista straddled the lard butt and rode him, cowgirl style, a memory came back to me. That night long ago, I'd seen the same shimmy of her hips. Were there sparks in her eyes then, or the same cold flatness I saw now?

My stomach was starting to feel queasy, and I wanted to get the hell out of there. I had what I needed. "Charlie Ziegler" was the guy's name. Krista had been one of "Charlie's Girlz." I could turn this over to Amy Larkin and weasel my way off her Most Wanted list. Go back to my life of work and play and play some more. Focus on the present, not the past. Isn't that what we're supposed to do?

But something kept my ass glued to the chair, my eyes on the screen.

The camera cut to a close-up, revealing Krista's smile to be all artifice, her moans halfhearted. Girl at work. Her job was to make the pig grunt and to feign pleasure herself. This was a transaction. She was paying her rent.

On the screen, Krista was pleading, "Fuck me, Daddy!"

My stomach heaved, and I tasted bile. Was I any better than the bastard screwing her on the screen? Any better than Charlie Ziegler? For one night, at least, I was as sleazy as the pimp and porn king. Only difference, he made a career of it.

I couldn't take any more. I banged through the door of the booth and stomped to the register where Coleman was ringing up a customer with a stack of DVDs and a plastic tube of lubricant.

"You done already, Jake?"

"Pop it out. Give me the disc."

Coleman hit the EJECT button on the master player and handed me the disc. I slammed it against the counter, breaking it in two.

"What the hell!" Coleman's cigarette flew from his mouth. "That's fifteen bucks."

I tossed a twenty on the counter and crashed out the front door and into the humid night.

7 The Do-Over

I got into my car, pulled out Amy Larkin's business card, and punched her cell number into my keypad.

I paused without hitting the CALL button. Elmore stood in the window of his store, watching me. If I dived into the search for Krista Larkin, where would it lead? If Charlie Ziegler was guilty of some terrible crime, just what would my culpability be? Maybe Ziegler pushed her off a cliff, but I'm the guy who drove her up the mountain.

Damn, a mirror can be a lethal weapon, and self-knowledge a poisoned pill. I had been a self-centered and egotistical jock with all the trappings of stunted male adolescence. Back then, I had yet to develop the empathy for others that marks the passage into manhood.

The defense lawyer inside of me said I wasn't the proximate cause of Krista's descent. But why the hell hadn't I sized up the situation, grabbed Ziegler by the lapels of his suede jacket, and tossed him halfway across the street? I could have taken Krista to Social Services or a girlfriend's place or put her on a plane back home. Instead, I gift-wrapped her and delivered her to Charlie Ziegler.

There's a difference between criminal guilt and moral culpability. Sure, I was off the hook in any court of law for whatever happened to Krista Larkin. But while I could not be criminally prosecuted, I could suffer self-imposed shame.

I should have helped her.

Could have. Would have. Should have.

But we don't get do-overs.

Or do we?

I hit the CALL button. "You were wrong," I told Amy, when she answered.

"About what?"

"You said I wouldn't call."

"What do you want, Lassiter?" Her no-nonsense, no-bullshit tone.

"I have a lead on a guy Krista was involved with."

"*Other* than you?"

"I told you about that night. Nothing happened." Trying hard to sound truthful.

"And I told you I didn't believe you."

"I'm hoping, in time, you'll start to trust me."

"In *time?* What do you think, we're going to be friends?"

"Just hear me out."

"Give me the name you supposedly came up with."

"I can do more than that. I can help you find out what happened to Krista."

"Jake Lassiter, *help?* When I look at you, all I see is that grinning ape in the strip club. A man without a serious thought beyond his next beer and his next lay."

"I made a mistake. I want to make it right."

"Get over it. This isn't about you and your redemption."

"You're playing an away game, Amy. This is my town."

"What's that supposed to mean?"

"I have street savvy. Experience. Contacts."

"*You?*"

The concept seemed ludicrous to her.

"The State Attorney is a friend of mine."

"So what?"

"I can get you official help."

"Why should I believe you?"

"Let's have dinner and talk about it," I suggested.

"I'm not hungry."

"One drink, then."

"Not thirsty, either."

"C'mon. Let me lay out a plan. If you don't like it, I'll back off. Deal?"

"Give me the name of the man Krista was mixed up with, and I'll think about it."

"Nope."

"You're a real bastard, Lassiter."

"Yeah, but I'm your bastard. You might not like me, Amy Larkin. Hell, you might even hate me. But the truth is, you need me."

She let out a long, whistling sigh and said, "Where do we meet?"

8   The Taste of Wet Steel

Amy Larkin had been sitting on the motel room bed, cleaning a pistol when Lassiter called. Now she hung up the phone and pushed the brush through the barrel of the gun, scrubbing out wet streaks of lead.

Her father's gun. A Sig Sauer .380 that fit her hand comfortably. She'd never known he owned a weapon until he ended his life just six weeks earlier. One shot to the temple, with this very gun.

It was the beginning of this whirlwind. When she found the photo with her father's angry scribble on the back. *The Whore of Babylon.*

How Amy hated the self-righteous bastard. He had been so much happier believing sin—not the dysfunctional Larkin family—destroyed Krista. God, how Amy missed her sister. There had been an emptiness inside her from the day Krista left.

Oh, the damage our parents can inflict. When she was still a teenager, Amy's father had berated her.

"Your sister is Satan's mistress, and you're her handmaiden!"

"All I did was kiss the boy, Dad."

"Why don't you run away the way Krista did?"

No, she wouldn't do that. There was a better way to put distance between herself and her screwed-up family. As a child, she kept her parents hidden from her friends. Mom praying in tongues, Dad withdrawn into his silent world. Amy threw herself into schoolwork. She studied hard, paid her own way through Ohio State, and became a solid citizen with a 9-to-5 job and a 401k.

Whatever neuroses had been implanted at home, she'd buried inside. The anxiety, the sense of dread, all sealed tight beneath her polished exterior.

Why, then, was she unable to shake her mother's teachings? Why, when all logic told her that her mother's faith stemmed from ancient superstitions—not the word of God—did she still pray for the divine healing promised by the Holy Ghost? The contradictions chiseled away at her.

She jammed the brush through the barrel of the Sig Sauer, her thoughts turning to Lassiter. In just a few hours, he claimed to have found a lead.

"A guy Krista was involved with," was the way he put it.

Was he telling the truth? Or was he just coming up with a sideshow, some distraction to protect himself or someone else? An old teammate, maybe.

At first, she had thought Lassiter was just another man-beast, like so many she had known. Hiding their fangs behind toothy grins, oiling their way into women's beds.

Losers.

Users.

Abusers.

She had no proof that he had harmed Krista. But her instincts told her he had lied about that night at the strip club. He knew more about Krista than he was telling. Could he have killed her?

She squeezed her eyes shut, imagined herself pistol-whipping Lassiter, demanding the truth, threatening to blow his brains out. Would he talk? Revenge fantasies, her shrink had told her, were unhealthy. Yeah, well so is losing your sister.

Amy placed a white patch on the end of the push rod, dipped it in solvent, and cleaned the barrel of powder residue. She imagined it was the very residue of the bullet that entered her father's brain. Next, she dripped oil on a clean cloth and wiped down the gun, inhaling the wet steel smell that somehow reminded her of the taste of gin.

She would meet with Lassiter. Could he really get the State Attorney to help? And if he did, would that be proof that Lassiter wasn't involved in Krista's disappearance?

"The State Attorney is a friend of mine."

A cover-up. A conspiracy. Not out of the question. A network of old pals who looked out for one another, covered one anothers' asses.

An official investigation was something she hadn't expected. She doubted, after all this time, that the authorities would be interested. She considered for a moment the implications if Lassiter was on the up-and-up. If the State Attorney opened an honest inquiry, could he discover what happened to Krista? Could he gather enough evidence for a prosecution?

A trial was not what she had been planning. That was a secret she would have to keep from Lassiter. She had not come to Miami to prosecute the man who murdered her sister. She had come here to kill him.

9 Never Lost, Just Hard to Find

Twenty minutes after leaving the video store, I parked in front of City Hall, a waterfront art deco building that in the 1930s had been the terminal for Pan Am's seaplanes. I took a shortcut through the adjacent boatyard, dodging several oily puddles at the entrance to Scotty's Landing, a ramshackle fish joint next to the marina. A few yards away, sailboats were docked, halyards pinging in the wind. A three-quarters moon hung over the bay.

I spotted Amy at a redwood picnic table, closest to the water.

"Thanks for meeting me." I slid onto the bench across from her.

"Who's the guy you found?" Small talk was not in the lady's repertoire.

I told her about Charles Ziegler and Charlie's Girlz and the porn video I watched. A shudder went through Amy's body, and I gave her a moment to compose herself.

Then I told her Krista was last seen heading to a party at Ziegler's house. I didn't mention that I'd met the guy for about a minute, because that would have meant coming clean about my one-nighter with Krista. Amy had no need for the information, and I had no desire to take any more crap from her.

"Let me tell you my plan," I said.

"Thanks, but I don't need your plan. I'll confront Ziegler myself."

"No, you won't. He's a big deal in this town. He'll have lawyers, layers of people to get through. Besides, we've got nothing on him. There were lots of men at his parties. We may have only one chance to talk to Ziegler, and we need to do our homework first."

She nailed me with a cold, hard, insurance investigator's look. "Just what homework do *we* need to do?"

"We should pay a visit to Alex Castiel, the State Attorney."

"The guy you claim is a friend."

"We play basketball in the lawyers' league."

"That's it? You dribble to each other?"

I didn't explain that "dribble to each other" made no sense, basketball-wise. "Castiel has a staff of investigators," I said. "He works with cops. He can subpoena witnesses."

"Just how good of friends are you?" Suspicion laced her voice, or maybe that was her normal tone.

"A long time ago, I did a big favor for him."

"What kind of favor?"

"The secret kind. What I'm saying, he owes me."

It was true. I'd been carrying the guy's IOU for a long time, never intending to use it. But then, I'd never been accused of making a teenage girl vanish before.

"So if you're ready to work together," I said, "I have a bunch of questions about Krista that will help me get started."

Amy studied me, her eyes seeming to search for deception. I looked past her to an older couple pushing a cart of groceries along the pier. Tanned the color of a richly brewed tea, the couple was headed toward a Kaufman, a deep-water cruiser with a striking name on its transom, *Never Lost, Just Hard to Find*. I imagined them sailing around the world, but maybe that was my dream, not theirs.

"So how about it?" I prodded her. "Are we a team?"

"Do you win most of your cases, Lassiter?"

"Not even half. But damn few of my customers are innocent."

"Customers . . . ?"

"All I ask is a check that doesn't bounce and a story that doesn't make the judge burst out laughing."

"Nice."

"Hey, they don't call us 'sharks' for our ability to swim."

I figured she'd never buy it if I pretended to be Atticus Finch.

"Do you have any siblings, Lassiter?"

"A sister. Half sister, really. My mom had her out of wedlock after my father was killed down in the Keys. Why do you ask?"

"Krista's my half sister, too. We have the same father."

We were both quiet a moment, absorbing that small bit of commonality.

"Do you love her?" Amy asked. "Do you love your sister."

Another weird question but I went along. "Janet's a crack whore and a worse mother than Octomom, but yeah, I guess I love her."

"If someone killed her, what would you do?"

"I'd go after him. Hard."

Her eyes warmed up just a bit. It was the answer she wanted to hear. Better yet, it was true. "What do you need to know about Krista?"

That seemed to be her way of welcoming me aboard.

"Everything. About her, about you. About the Larkins of Toledo, Ohio."

Amy looked off toward the bay, her sunset eyes seeming to reflect the moonlight. She told me about their father, Frank Larkin. After divorcing Krista's mother, he married again, and his new wife gave birth to Amy. The two girls were close, even with the six-year age difference. Amy idolized her older sister. Krista was popular, smart, pretty. A cheerleader, but a secret one.

"Krista hid her uniform in her locker at school. She told Mom she was at Bible study group when they practiced or had games."

Krista's double life, it seemed, had started early.

"Why'd she run away?" I asked.

"Do you believe Jesus is the son of God?"

The question came so far out of left field it was beyond the bleachers. A waiter came over, giving me time to formulate an answer while I ordered a beer, smoked fish dip, conch fritters, and jalapeño poppers. Amy opted for white wine.

"I believe if there's an all-seeing God, he must have his eyes closed. The universe is chaos. The Big Bang banged. Little molecules grew into big molecules, and after a thousand millennia, something slithered out of the swamp and turned into the bloodthirsty animal we call man."

She looked as if I'd dropped my pants at Sunday vespers.

"No disrespect intended," I added.

"How do you live your life with such feelings?"

"I try to do the least damage possible to people and God's green earth."

"*God's* green earth?"

"I'm hedging my bets."

Amy fiddled with her napkin. "Mom was a Higher Life Pentecostal. Dad sort of went along, but he drew the line at speaking in tongues. Krista refused to go to church. Her way of rebelling against my mom, her step-mom. Krista taunted her. Smoked and drank and ran around with boys. One night, I overheard Mom on the phone, talking to someone about an intervention. Kidnapping Krista, taking her someplace where the church would program her."

It wasn't hard to figure out what happened next. "You told Krista your mom was gonna snatch her."

She nodded. "The next morning Krista was gone. Never even said good-bye."

Headed to South Beach to be a supermodel, I guessed. Glamour and fame just a Greyhound ride away.

"If I'd kept my mouth shut, Krista never would have left." Amy choked on her words. It was the first emotion, other than anger, I'd seen cross her face.

"You did what any sister would do."

As she made an effort not to sob, I listened to the groan of hulls against pilings, giving her a moment to mourn all over again. It only took a moment, and she composed herself.

"If Krista didn't say good-bye, how'd you know she came down here?" I asked.

"She called me after a week, said she was sleeping on the beach. She'd met an older guy who said she could make some money modeling, maybe get into the movies."

"I don't suppose she mentioned a name."

Amy shook her head. "No, but now I guess it was Charlie Ziegler."

"What did you tell your parents?"

"Nothing. Krista made me promise not to. A few months went by, and someone called Dad. He wouldn't say who."

Sonia Majeski, I knew.

"Dad just went to the airport, and when he came home, he said Krista had died in a boating accident in Florida, and her body was never found. He said we needed to get on with our lives."

"When did you realize your father was lying?"

"Not until he died six weeks ago. I came across his journals and the photo from the strip club. Krista was dead to him, so he decided she had to be dead to me, too."

That explained why it took Amy all these years to begin looking for her sister. I processed that and tried to figure just what it must have been like for an eleven-year-old girl growing up in that house. Thinking maybe I should cut Amy a break, given what she'd been through.

"Tomorrow, we'll pay a visit to the State Attorney," I told her. "Things are gonna start rolling."

"You haven't mentioned a fee. How much will this cost me?"

"Nothing. Not a dime. This one's not about money."

10 We, the Jury

The next morning, I was late for our meeting with State Attorney Castiel. Unavoidably detained, as they say. The jury had reached a verdict in Pepito Dominguez's DUI trial. So now I stood in Judge Philbrick's courtroom, arms folded across my chest, waiting for the clerk to announce the verdict.

A shitty little misdemeanor, the equivalent of powder-puff football in a tackle league. Still, my heart pounded.

Yeah, I know I said I didn't care. But now, with seconds to go, I was the guy on trial. The jury was about to rule on *me*.

It's always like this. I want to win.

And fast. Amy was waiting for me upstairs in the lobby of the State Attorney's Office.

The gallery was empty, except for a couple of seniors who came in for the air-conditioning, and dozed off in the back row. CNN had chosen not to cover the trial, and legal scholars somehow never showed up.

Judge Philbrick asked the magic question: "Has the jury reached a verdict?"

The jury foreman gave the right answer: "We have, Your Honor."

The foreman handed a slip of paper to the bailiff, who carried it to the judge, who glanced at it and passed it on to the female clerk, sitting directly in front of the bench.

"The clerk shall publish the verdict," the judge said, in stentorian tones.

The clerk, a fifty-ish woman with eyeglasses slung around her neck on a chain of imitation pearls, squinted at the page, then read aloud: "We, the jury, find the defendant not guilty."

She notched an eyebrow on the word "not."

The judge nodded, the prosecutor scowled, and the jurors started gathering their things. Pepito Dominguez threw his arms around me. "Papa said you were the best! And you are. Thanks, man!"

I peeled Pepito's hands off my shoulders. "You're welcome. Tell your old man the bill is in the mail."

"How 'bout I buy you a drink?"

"You shitting me?"

"Let's hit Lario's. Couple pitchers of margaritas. Place is full of models."

I wanted to bitch-slap the kid. I also wanted to keep my Bar ticket, and the folks in Tallahassee have warned me, scolded me, and placed me on double-secret probation several times. "Didn't you just get out of New Horizons?"

"My old man put me in, but I didn't need no rehab."

Maybe I shouldn't have been upset. The little prick was grateful, and so many clients aren't. If you win, they think, Hey, I'm innocent, why'd I need you? If you lose, they blame you.

I jabbed a finger into the kid's bony chest. "I'm gonna be watching you. And if I see you within fifty yards of a bottle, I'm gonna kick your ass."

Looking confused, Pepito tried to work up a cool retort, but his brain cells wouldn't cooperate. Finally, he said, "I thought we could hang together, even though you're, like, an old dude."

"Did you hear me? I represented you because I like your father. But I don't like you. Why don't you get a job and stop sponging off your parents?"

"I wanted to talk to you about that, too."

"What?"

"Dad said maybe you could hire me."

"Doing what?"

"I've always thought it'd be cool to be a P.I."

"Forget it. Tell your dad nothing doing."

The kid's old man, Pepe Dominguez, owned Blue Sky Bail Bonds. Pepe sent me clients, and unlike most bail bondsmen, never demanded kick-backs.

Now I turned to his punk-ass son. "You *want* to be a P.I. So you figure someone will just hand it to you? Ever think there might be some training involved? Some schooling? Some work? Your problem is, you have a great father but you're a rotten kid."

"I'm gonna tell Dad you dissed me." A sissy little whine.

"Tell him there's a limit to my friendship."

It was not the last lie I was to tell that day.

11 Digging Up Buried Bones

State Attorney Alejandro Castiel was waiting in his office atop the Justice Building. Amy had dressed for the occasion, a white silk blouse with girly ruffles down the front and a form-fitting navy skirt that ended just above a pair of lovely knees. She looked both professional and demure.

I introduced her to Castiel, who flashed his politician's smile as he steered us to comfy chairs, then leaned against the edge of his desk like a helpful doctor in a TV commercial.

He wore a dark Italian suit and was so deeply tanned he wouldn't need makeup if Channel 4 wanted a quick quote on the latest battle for justice. His hair—flecks of gray at the temples—was swept straight back like a young Pat Riley of Miami Heat fame.

My goal was straightforward enough. Convince Castiel to open an investigation into the disappearance of Krista Larkin eighteen years ago. He could start by questioning Charles Ziegler, his party guests, and a biker named Snake if he could be found.

"You putting on weight, Jake?" It was Alex's shoulder punch, a guy's greeting.

"Don't start," I said.

"I'm gonna hang 30 on you this week."

I sucked in my gut and said, "I still own you in the paint."

He laughed and explained to Amy that we played against each other in

Lawyers' League basketball. She replied that I'd already told her, and isn't it nice that boys can still be boys as they crept toward middle age?

Alex Castiel—"Alejandro" too long for a campaign poster—was a born politician. Miami knew his story well. The Castiels were Sephardic Jews who had emigrated from Spain to Cuba two centuries before Fidel Castro was born. So, Alejandro was a Jewbano. A crossover candidate, he spoke Spanish fluently and knew enough Yiddish jokes to make the yentas laugh. He won the election in a landslide of *pastelitos* and matzoh balls. Some people mentioned Castiel as a possible candidate for governor. I thought the guy could go even higher.

I liked him. Sounds strange, I know, coming from a defense lawyer who's chop-blocked a few prosecutors and been sucker-punched by many others. But most are hardworking and underpaid and believe in what they're doing. Alex was one of them.

"Ms. Larkin, Jake called me this morning," Castiel said, "so I had the police report pulled out of storage and messengered over." He opened a folder and grabbed a skinny document. "Let's start with the witness who said Amy was headed to Charlie Ziegler's house the night she went missing."

Charlie. The use of the diminutive did not escape me.

"Sonia Majeski," I said.

"What's her credibility?"

"I believe her. Isn't that good enough?"

He riffled through the report. "Exotic dancer. Arrested a couple times doing rub-and-tugs in a massage parlor."

"What's the relevance of that?" I asked.

He put down the file. "Ziegler told the cops Krista Larkin never showed up that night."

"What about the other guests? How many people did the cops talk to?"

"Apparently, no one else."

"Let me guess why. The party animals were prominent around town. Bankers, lawyers, power brokers. Maybe a police captain or two."

"No way to tell from the report, but it's a good guess."

"So Ziegler offers a drink to a rookie cop, gives him a box of porn videos for the station, and the investigation is closed."

Castiel ignored my shot at Miami's semi-finest and turned to Amy. "I have to ask you some difficult questions, Ms. Larkin."

"I'm a big girl," she fired back.

"Your sister ran away from home several months earlier."

"Yes."

"What makes you so sure she didn't run away again?"

"All her belongings were still in her apartment. Isn't that evidence that something happened to her?"

"Not necessarily." He looked back at the report. "Her car wasn't at the apartment. Maybe she left town in a hurry. Your sister was living dangerously. Drugs. Porn. She could have ripped off a dealer. Or just decided to try another city and start all over."

"At some point, Krista would have called me."

"Maybe once she began a new life, she decided to put everything behind her."

"She wouldn't have let all these years go by." Amy's lower lip trembled. Maybe she wasn't made of marble after all. "We loved each other."

Castiel moved away from his desk and put a hand on her shoulder. "I understand your grief. But there's no proof your sister is dead, much less that someone killed her."

"I don't want your sympathy, Mr. Castiel." She shook his hand away. "Dammit, I want you to do something."

Castiel recoiled as if slapped. I'd failed to warn him that Amy wasn't the touchy-feely type. He turned to me. "Jake, you see the situation here. Just what would you have me do?"

"Ask Ziegler to give a voluntary statement under oath. No subpoena and he waives immunity."

"Did you actually pass the Bar exam?"

"Fourth try."

"Why would Ziegler ever do that?"

"If he's a solid citizen with nothing to hide, why not?"

"Testify about a missing underage girl and remind people of his past. Why would he want to dig up all those buried bones?"

"Interesting choice of words."

He gave me that straight-on, challenging look. I'd seen it when he had the ball at the top of the key. Was he going to shoot the step-back jumper or drive to the hoop? Instead of waiting to find out, I decided to swat the ball away.

"What if I told you that another woman last seen in Ziegler's company disappeared and was never seen again?" I said.

Liar, liar. Briefs on fire.

"What woman? When?"

"I'm not at liberty to say." Like a gorilla shaking a tree, I was curious what might fall from the branches.

"You can't leave that hanging, Jake. Do you have evidence that Charlie Ziegler committed a crime?"

"Let me put it this way. I have a confidential source who says Ziegler was making snuff films."

Amy stiffened in her chair. "Jake, is that true?"

I hadn't told her what Sonia had said. Maybe it was cruel to spring it on her, but I wanted tension in the room, and I got it. I'd combined my total lie about a second missing woman with the dubious hearsay about snuff films. Of such whispers are wicked rumors born. And maybe a state investigation.

"Ms. Larkin, I wonder if you'd like a cup of coffee in our break room," Castiel said. He was speaking to my client but was looking at me through narrowed eyes. "I need to have a few words with your lawyer."

Watching Castiel glare at me, I had a pretty good idea what some of those words would be.

12   The Solid Gold Lighter

"Snuff films are a myth," Castiel said. "Who fed you this line of crap, anyway?"

"I told you, Alex. My informant is confidential."

"For a lawyer, you're a lousy liar."

"Don't let that get out, or I'll lose all my clients."

Castiel returned to his desk, the power position. I sat humbly in the visitor's chair, admiring the paneled walls. Castiel didn't plaster his office with photos of himself shaking hands with every cheap politico in town. No ribbon cuttings. No plaques from the Kiwanis or bouquets from the PTA. For a politician, he was almost a regular guy.

"Face it," Castiel said. "All you have is suspicion with nothing to back it up."

"The sleazebag was passing the girl around to his friends and making her do porn. She disappears. I'm suspicious, yeah."

"Sleazebag? You put labels on people, Jake. You see things in black and white, good and evil."

"You're right. I see rapists as evil. I don't care that Polanski made good movies or that Ziegler made bad ones. I just get pissed when the strong abuse the weak."

"A word of advice, Jake. Don't go around town talking trash about Charlie Ziegler. The guy's got connections."

"Meaning?"

"He could cut off your court appointments with one phone call, and there's nothing I could do to help you."

I had one more card to play, the one I'd carried in my vest for years. "If not for me, Alex, you wouldn't even be sitting in that fancy chair."

That seemed to take him aback. "You saying I owe you because you once did a public service?"

"I wore a wire for you because I thought it was the right thing to do. You got elected State Attorney, and I got treated like a leper."

To this day, I didn't know if I regretted my actions. I was a newly minted lawyer, learning the ropes in the Public Defender's Office. One of my first clients had discovered the identity of the confidential informant who had fingered him for robbery and extortion. My guy thought I'd make a good bag man to deliver money to a gangbanger who would kill the informant *and* the prosecutor, a newbie named Alejandro Castiel.

I had a choice. I could withdraw from the case, but I figured my client would just find somebody else to set up the hit. So I wore a wire and arranged to meet the gangbanger in a Hialeah warehouse.

"Why you asking all these questions?" the guy demanded.

"To make sure we're on the same page."

"Just give me the money and get the fuck out."

"Not a problem." I handed over a gym bag stuffed with cash. Maybe I was sweating or maybe something in my eyes gave it away.

"You wearing a wire?" the guy said.

"Fuck no."

"Prove it." He pulled a 9mm from his waistband.

He was half a foot shorter than me, and standing so close, I could feel his breath. I head-butted him, a quick, vicious shot that broke his nose and spurted blood over me. I stomped on his instep, and he dropped the gun.

A second later, the door burst open. Half a dozen cops flew into the room, followed by Castiel.

Starting with the press conference, Castiel became the hero of the story. I turned out to be the subject of some suspicion. Why, a newspaper reporter wondered, would a career criminal solicit me for a murder scheme, unless I was dirty? I didn't get the key to the city or even a thank you. Defense lawyers treated me like a pariah, and even penniless jailbirds wouldn't hire me.

Now Castiel looked troubled. No one ever wants to be reminded of an unpaid debt. "How much is Amy Larkin paying you, Jake?"

"In round numbers, zero."

"Are you nailing her?"

"Does she look nailable? When you put your hand on her shoulder, I thought she was gonna bite it off."

"Your stake in this case is *bupkis*. So why now?"

"Why now, what?"

"All these years, you never mentioned wearing the wire for me. Why you calling in that chit now? What's so special about this case?"

I'm not one of those sinners who finds relief in confession, so I didn't go anywhere near the story of my one-night stand with Krista. "If I don't help Amy Larkin, who will?"

"Not buying it, Jake. You don't give a hoot about your clients."

"Bullshit! I sweat blood for every one."

"You sweat blood to *win*. It's about you, pal. Not them."

That stopped me. After a moment, I said, "Never too late to change."

"Save it for your next client, because you can't help Amy Larkin. You can only hurt yourself."

When people tell me I can't do something, I generally work harder to prove I can. Everyone told me I couldn't make the Dolphins as a free agent. But I did, even if I sat so far down Shula's bench, my ass was in Ocala.

Castiel opened a fancy humidor made of polished cherrywood and pulled out a long, tapered cigar. Then he grabbed a guillotine clipper from his pocket and snipped off the end. We were in a nonsmoking building and the cigar was a Cuban Torpedo, but I decided against making a citizen's arrest.

He leaned against the credenza and waved the unlit cigar at me. "I've known Charlie a long time, and he's no killer. Trust me on this one, Jake."

"Great. He can call you as a character witness."

"Years ago, Charlie dealt in sleaze. But he's a changed man. You, of all people, should respect that."

"Me?"

"You were a hell-raiser, and now you're a defense lawyer, which means you believe in redemption. You're the guys always begging for second chances."

Castiel pulled a cigarette lighter out of his pocket and flipped it open. It was gold in color and looked expensive. He lit the long, illegal cigar, sucked on it, and exhaled a fine cloud of tangy smoke.

"Life is not always black and white, Jake. Mostly, it's colored in shades of gray."

"That's deep, Alex."

"The duality of man. There's good and evil in all of us."

"Very deep, indeed." What is it about men and cigars? A guy lights up and starts spouting two-bit philosophy.

Castiel grabbed a weathered black-and-white photo in a gilt frame from his credenza. A faded, vintage look. Two men standing in front of a roulette wheel, lots of classy folk dressed to the nines, as they would have said back then. A beautiful red-haired woman stood between the men. She wore a slinky cocktail dress with a flower pinned behind one ear. "That's my father on the left and my mother in the middle."

"And Meyer Lansky on the right," I tossed in. "The Riviera Hotel in Havana in the fifties. I remember your stories, Alex."

Bernard Castiel, Alex's father, was a handsome man in an old-fashioned way. Thick through the chest in his double-breasted suit, dark hair brilliantined straight back. Rosa Castiel had wild, flashing eyes and looked ready to mambo. She was taller than the man on her left, Meyer Lansky, the mobster. Finely tailored gray suit, thin face, wary eyes.

For as long as I've known him, Castiel has had a curious level of pride about his family's less-than-savory past.

"Can you imagine those times, Jake?" Castiel once told me. "Meyer Lansky, Lucky Luciano, and Bugsy Siegel all in Cuba at the same time, three guys who grew up together on the Lower East Side. It'd be like Mays, Mantle, and Aaron all playing on the same team."

There was always a lilt of excitement in Castiel's voice talking about those days. Tales of high-stakes gambling, dangerous men, and exotic women. In the late 1950s, Bernard Castiel was security chief at Lansky's Riviera casino. His most important task was delivering bundles of cash to President Fulgencio Batista. More mundane chores involved chopping off the hands of casino employees caught skimming. Or so Alex once told me with notes of contentment.

Castiel held up his cigarette lighter. "This belonged to my father. Solid gold."

He tossed it to me. Heavy as a hand grenade. I ran a finger around a raised ridge of gold in the shape of a crocodile with a diamond for an eye. The ridge was the outline of the island of Cuba. The diamond was Havana.

"Lansky must have been paying well," I said, tossing the lighter back.

"Bernard didn't buy it. President Batista gave it to him as a fortieth birthday present. Can you imagine its value to me?"

As much as a John Dillinger's Tommy gun to his heirs, I thought. But what I said was, "A lot, Alex. I know your family lost everything to Castro. And I know how your father lost his life."

The story was part of the Castiel mythology, and it helped propel Alex into public office. In January 1959, Castro's ragtag army was running amok through Havana. Looting, burning, killing. Bernard Castiel came across three rebels dragging a woman from a home in the ritzy Miramar section, beating her and stripping off her clothes. Castiel knocked one man unconscious and was pulling a second rebel off the woman when he was bayoneted in the back. He bled to death in the gutter, an early victim of Castro's butchery. Rosa was pregnant with Alex. Within two years, she would die of breast cancer, and Alex became an orphan.

"So, tell me, Jake. How do the scales tip? Does *mi padre*'s work for Lansky make him evil? What was he, hero or gangster?"

"He died heroically. That's good enough for me."

"But a hero can't be all good," Castiel prodded me. "And a gangster can't be all bad."

"I get it. Ziegler is okay because he gives money to good causes, not the least of which is the re-election of Alejandro Castiel."

He ground his teeth and his jaw muscles danced. "We're done here, Jake. Just do your client a favor and tell her to go back home to Indiana."

"Ohio."

"Marry the clerk at the John Deere store. Have a couple kids. Overcook burgers in the backyard."

"Don't be a patronizing jerk."

He shook his head sadly and pointed his cigar toward the door. "I'll see you around."

"Yeah, see you."

I walked out without another word, feeling cruddy. Guys can argue, maybe even take a swing at each other, and get over it. But this felt different. Like I was losing a friend.

Outside the door was the desk of his executive assistant, an efficient, older woman who began stuffing envelopes in her boss's first campaign and now held the keys to the palace gate.

"Charlene, which way to the rest room?"

"You know very well where it is, Mr. Lassiter. Down the hall to the left."

"I'll be quick."

She gave me a look that said, *"Like I give a hoot?"*

"We're doing a conference call in a minute," I said, matter-of-factly. Lies are best told with no gestures, little expression, and few effects. "With Charlie Ziegler."

Charlene wrinkled her forehead, punched a button, and an LCD display lit up. "You might want to hurry up," she said. "Mr. Castiel is already on with Mr. Ziegler."

Which is just what I feared. The door had barely closed behind me, and my old buddy was giving aid and comfort—and information—to the enemy. Now my job was to figure out why.

13 The Prince of Porn No More

Charles W. Ziegler, proud owner of the third largest house on Casuarina Concourse in Gables Estates, was pissed off. Ten minutes ago, his wife, Lola, had told him he might think about cutting back on the cheesecake. Not in those words.

"Charlie, you're looking positively porcine."

Porcine? Where'd she get that? The woman barely had a GED.

Yeah, okay. He was blubbery and mostly bald, and at fifty-eight needed a little blue pill to get it up. But why rub it in? He didn't give Lola grief about her liposuctioned thighs and shortened schnozz. Why couldn't his wife be more like his mistress?

Ziegler had met Lola back in his days as a tycoon of tits and ass. She wasn't one of Charlie's Girlz, his posse of porn stars. Just a hot, downtown secretary, looking to marry well. In those days, when still in the hunt for big game, Lola busted her ass to please in the bedroom. And damn, if her rusty trombone didn't make Ziegler come so hard he felt his skull was exploding. Then, once wedding vows were exchanged, big surprise: no more ass-licking.

Today, Lola's tongue never left her mouth, except to taste caviar, and Charlie Ziegler was legit. Honored and respected. A big hitter and major donor around town. He still enjoyed putting on a show and ruffling society feathers. Not long ago, he took some heat for hiring a massage parlor girl to give a rub and tug to a critically ill fourteen-year-old boy. But they call it "Make-A-Wish," and that's what the kid wanted.

Ziegler owned Reelz TV, where his reality shows were sprinkled with nudity and profanity but no money shots. His biggest hit was *Cheeterz,* a boffo show that featured wives catching husbands with their pants down. Then there was the teen gross-out show *Zitz,* syndicated in thirty-seven countries, despite a *Variety* review that called it a "steaming pile of excrescence."

He put the first letter of his last name in the title of every show. He'd even asked Lola to change her name to "Zoey," but she told him to go fuck himself, along with the script girl on *Size Zero,* his modeling show, and the babe at Beach Motors who sold him a vintage Datsun 280Z after blowing him under the cargo hatch.

Back in his hard-core days, he'd won the People's Porn award for *Driving Miss Daizy Crazy.* This year, he won the Miami Humanitarian of the Year award, presented by Archbishop Gilchrist.

From porn to priests in twenty years.

Now, at sunset, he stood in his front yard, puffing a Cohiba. Whenever he lit up, Lola evicted him from the house, which had cost him a cool eight million, land not included. The place was designed by one of his wife's pals, a trendy architect known for stylistic flourishes and skylights that leaked. The house was a shiny, snake-shaped cylinder of steel and glass, described by the architect as "curvilinear lines reminiscent of Le Corbusier." Ziegler thought the place looked like a giant plumbing fixture.

The bayfront neighborhood was bathed in orange light from a ribbon of clouds, backlit by the setting sun. Ziegler glanced toward the lot next door where a big-ass mansion was under construction. His neighbor—a pretentious trust fund kid—had two hundred seventy feet of waterfront, a full twenty feet more than his own, goddammit.

Something caught Ziegler's eye, a flash of movement next to a pallet of rebar. The construction crew was gone for the day, and building inspectors never worked this late unless they were picking up bribes. He pulled his eyeglasses out of a pocket, put them on, and squinted.

A tall slender woman, staring his way.

Shit. Was it her?

Alex Castiel had called him earlier. A woman named Amy Larkin had hit town, looking for her long-lost sister. Her lawyer, some ex-jock, named Ziegler as a suspect in the disappearance. The news had been eating at him all day, and he wondered what the hell he should do. He thought about calling Max Perlow but was afraid what the old hood would say.

Ziegler was too far away to get a good look at the woman, but it had to be the girl's kid sister. Stalking him, after all this time.

Blast from the past. Krista Larkin.

How did so much trouble get off the bus with that runaway girl? It seemed like a thousand years ago. There'd been a big market for Lolitas in those days. Saudi sheiks salivating over blondes from the Midwest. Billionaire pervs willing to pay big bucks for new talent.

He recalled the day he met the girl. He'd walked over to the 10th Street beach from the little office he rented next to a kosher bakery. Two cameras dangled from his neck, that professional photographer look. Still had most of his hair and an almost flat stomach. Krista Larkin had been in town two days. Sleeping on the beach under an umbrella. Tall girl with a peachy complexion. Said she'd come to Miami to model, and when she had saved enough money, she planned to enroll in the fashion design college she'd read about in *Parade*. From the moment he first saw her, Ziegler had other ideas for her. To fuck her, sure. But to make money off her, even better.

He talked her into coming back to his studio, so she could pose. Telling her he was locked into the top modeling agencies, and she'd be on the cover of *Vogue,* no doubt about it. Maybe get her into the movies, too. Of course, she took the bait. Innocent as a spring day, fresh as milk from a cow. In his experience, some of these sweet Midwestern girls couldn't wait to take their clothes off.

He even remembered what she was wearing. Flip-flops, khaki shorts, a white cotton blouse. Carrying a backpack with everything she owned. He told her about all the money she could make. That, at least, was no lie. *Lolita in Lauderdale* made a ton of dough, and she shot a sequel every week for two months. But that first day, he planned to keep PG-rated. Or at least start that way.

In the studio, she squinted into the quartz light and fidgeted as he clicked off the first few shots. Awkward, embarrassed, amateurish.

"You're tense," he told her. "Self-conscious. Your body's locked. Let's try something."

As if the idea had just come to him.

"Leave your blouse on, but take off your bra."

A girlish giggle.

"Don't be a kid now. Think Cosmo."

He punched up a C.D., Wreckx-n-Effect hip-hopping to Rump Shaker.

The music thumped with hot and sweaty sex. "All I wanna do is zoom-a-zoom-zoom and a boom-boom."

"Loosen your hips, Krista. Let the music flow through you."

She came alive, all fluid movements and breathy sighs.

"Now, unleash your sexuality. Feel the fabric on your nipples."

She was a natural. The sexiest girls, he knew, were the ones who didn't try. He might get a year or two out of her before she got used up or beat up or knocked up.

"Let's go for another effect. Now, this is going to be cold."

He tossed a glass of water on her blouse.

She writhed with the music. Peeled herself out of the blouse without being asked.

He did her that night, bent over his cluttered desk. And the next day and the day after that.

Who knew, Ziegler wondered now, that the kid would end up holding the keys to his fortune and his life?

He glanced toward the construction site, shielding his eyes from the setting sun. Whoever had been there moments before had disappeared into the gloaming like a distant dream.

14 Pimpmobiles on Parade

It was suppertime, as my granny called it, when I headed home. Canvas top down, I aimed the Lassiter chariot south on I-95, passing the darkened skyscrapers, many as empty as a loan shark's heart. Bankruptcy and foreclosure had hit the downtown corridor hard.

The expressway ended at South Dixie Highway. On maps, that's U.S. 1, better described as Useless 1. In my rearview, I caught sight of a candy-apple red Cadillac Escalade two cars behind me and one lane over. I'm not sure why I noticed it. The spinning wheel covers and rumbling lake pipes, maybe? Or because I'd seen the same car earlier today.

The Escalade—or its twin brother—had been double-parked on 12th Street when I pulled out of the Justice Building parking lot after my meeting with Alex Castiel. I hadn't thought anything of it. Now I wondered if someone was tailing me. But what a strange choice of vehicles. As inconspicuous as a stone crab in your Wheaties.

Besides, who would it be? A plainclothes cop or a private eye? Not in that car. Maybe a carjacker lusting after my Biarritz Eldo ragtop with its red velour upholstery. Put the two cars together, you'd have Pimpmobiles on Parade.

To hell with it. I just kept driving. I was worried about Amy's reaction to our meeting with Castiel. I had promised to get his help, and he drop-kicked my butt out of his office. I expected Amy to be pissed. Instead, when we exited the Justice Building, she gave me a small smile and a big thank you. No hug, though. Not from a woman so damned uncomfortable with physical contact. If she owned a dog, it would be in need of some serious ear scratching.

She admitted she finally believed me. That I had nothing to do with Krista's disappearance and she'd been impressed by my taking on the State Attorney. Then she asked if I had a backup plan. I did. We'd find Ziegler's friends and his foes and learn everything we could before confronting him. Sonia Majeski promised to come up with the names of a few men who were regulars at Ziegler's parties all those years ago. If she did, I'd start knocking on doors.

I checked the rearview. The Escalade was holding its position. On the C.D. player, Waylon Jennings wailed about riding a bus to Shreveport, then on to New Orleans.

"It's been making me lonesome, on'ry, and mean."

I sped up, slid from the left lane to the middle to pass two cars, then back again. The Escalade bobbed and weaved its way into position three cars behind me.

My thoughts returned to Amy. An exterior as hard as oak, but there seemed to be a brittleness to her. Before we got into our separate cars at the Justice Building, I had asked her to have dinner and she said, *"Why? We did that last night."*

"Actually, I eat every night," I told her.

"Are you asking me out on a date?" Her tone implying the absurdity of such a thing.

"No, I meant dinner with my family. My granny and my nephew."

She declined, saying she had paperwork to do for her job. I guess insurance fraud in Toledo, Ohio, is pretty damn rampant.

I checked the mirror once again. The Escalade was still there. I hit the left-turn signal as I approached Douglas Road to go south into Coconut Grove. The green turn arrow was lit but I came to a stop. The Mini Cooper behind me blasted its horn. In the mirror, I saw the driver shoot me the bird. *No problema.* In Miami, you only worry about road rage when a driver waves a semi-automatic.

Just as the yellow turned to red, I hit the gas and burned rubber turning left. The guy in the Mini stayed put. The pimpmobile pursuer was trapped behind him.

I could have continued into the Grove and lost the Escalade, but that would have just kept me wondering all night. So I swerved into the alley behind Don Pan International Bakery, where I sometimes stop for ham bread and guava pastries. Tonight, I just wanted to hide out a moment.

Once the traffic light went through its cycle, the Mini Cooper turned, followed by the Escalade. I pulled out of the alley and onto Douglas. The prey was now the hunter. I crept up behind the Escalade, saw its Florida vanity plate.

U R NXT

The traffic light at Grand Avenue turned red. I stopped behind the Escalade, hopped out, and sprinted to the driver's door. The windows were tinted black, and at the dark intersection, I couldn't even make out a silhouette behind the wheel. Whoever it was hit the gas, yanked the wheel hard left, and peeled out. I jumped back, the rear left tire barely missing my big feet. The car screeched left onto Grand, and I was left standing there, adrenaline pumping.

"Next time, asshole!" I shouted. "Next time, I'll drag your ass through the window and wipe up the street with you."

The adrenaline ebbed. Other drivers were pulling around my Eldo, giving me wide berth.

"What are you looking at?" I yelled at everybody and nobody. A moment later, with no one to hit and no one to shout at, I got back into my car and drove home.

U R NXT

Next for what?

15 Adjudged Delinquent

I live in a two-story coral rock pillbox that could withstand an attack by tanks and mortar fire. It *did* withstand the Great Miami Hurricane of 1926, a storm that pretty much blew the city straight into the Everglades.

I parked under a chinaberry tree and pulled up the canvas top to save what was left of the upholstery. Red velour does not appreciate juicy yellow berries. I got out of the car and called Cindy, my loyal assistant, on the cell, catching her at an unlicensed beauty salon in a friend's house just off Calle Ocho. I gave her the Escalade's vanity plate and asked her to get me the name of the owner. She used to date a Miami cop who still did favors for her, either because he had a kind heart, or because she had dirt on him.

The front door to the house wasn't locked. Seldom is. The humidity has swollen the door shut, but a solid *thwack* from my shoulder opens it.

My dog, Csonka, greeted me inside with a slobbery hello. A couple years ago, he showed up, crapped on my front step, and challenged me to do something about it. He's a mix of bulldog and something else, maybe donkey, and has the personality of a New York cabdriver. If you don't get out of the way, he'll barge into you. And yeah, I named him after Larry Csonka, the Dolphins' fullback who used his forearm the way Paul Bunyan used an axe.

The tang of cinnamon floated from the kitchen. Granny's sweet potato pie.

"You in the mood for catfish, Jakey?" Granny said, as I joined her at the stove.

"As long as it's not deep fried."

"No other decent way to make it."

I watched her drag a fillet through a bowl of cornmeal. Having grown up on Granny's cooking, I thought everyone made chocolate chip cookies with bacon and considered giblet cream gravy a beverage.

Granny's skin was still smooth and her hair was still black, except for a white stripe down the middle. "Give that pot a stir." She gestured toward her simmering swamp cabbage.

I did as I was told, all the while eyeing the sweet potato pie, cooling on the counter.

"Keep your mitts off," Granny ordered.

Dorothea Jane Lassiter was not my grandmother. A great-aunt, maybe. We never straightened that out. She just took over raising me after my mom took off. When I was a kid, Granny filled a bushel basket with her do's and don'ts. She taught me never to start a fight but to know how to end one. To be wary of the rich and powerful. And to go through life doing the least damage possible. Thanks to her, I favor the underdog. I root *against* the Yankees, the Lakers, and the Patriots. If Germany invaded Poland—again—I'd take the points and go with the Poles.

Now Granny was helping me raise my nephew, and I try to pass on her lessons, though without the clops on the head she dealt out for random acts of disobedience.

My mom left town two weeks after my father was knifed to death at Poacher's, a shitkicker saloon outside Key Largo. Dad was a shrimper. Mom was a bottle blonde who hung out by the jukebox and wiggled her butt to Elvis and Johnny Cash. That's right. We're Florida Crackers.

I miss my old man. He used to lift me in one hand and swing me over his head. It was like flying. When he held me close, I inhaled the aroma of sea-crusted salt and diesel fuel and fish guts. Nothing ever smelled sweeter.

"Where's Kippers?" I asked Granny, as she dropped a breaded catfish fillet into the fryer.

"In his room, and he needs a talking to."

"Yo, Uncle Jake."

Kip shuffled barefoot into the kitchen from his bedroom, where he'd likely been playing a video game in which a gang of criminals obliterates a major city. He wore my old Dolphins' jersey, number 58, which hung to his knees. The boy was towheaded and fair-skinned with a faint blue vein showing on his forehead. He's gangly and shy with a quirky intelligence and a smile so sweet, it clutched at my heart.

I hugged him, which under the rules, I can only do in the house, so his buddies can't see us. He smelled of potato chips and bubble gum.

Then I saw it, a purple welt under his left eye. "What's with the shiner, kiddo?"

He shrugged—*no big deal*—and headed toward the sweet potato pie.

"No dessert till after supper!" Granny wagged a finger at him. "Now tell your uncle what happened."

"I got in a fight with Kountz."

"Carl Kountz? He's two years older than you."

Carl was big for his age. Hell, he was big for my age. He was already starting at fullback on the Tuttle-Biscayne J.V. team. A frame like a set of box springs. By his junior year, the 'Canes, 'Noles, and Gators would come calling.

"So, why'd Carl pick on you?" I asked.

"I hit him first."

"No way."

"Carl said my mom's a whore and I'm a bastard."

Oh.

Genealogy-wise, Carl was spot-on. My half sister, Janet, was the unintended byproduct of a match made in hell, my alcoholic mother and Chester Conklin, a roughneck from Oklahoma. Just as Conklin and the Widow Lassiter never married, neither did Janet and her beau, whoever he was. Janet could only guess which unemployed, shiftless loser had fathered Kip.

Every six months or so, Janet drifted into town to see her son, dropping off presents and apologies. Then it was back on the road with some petty thief or drug-dealing boyfriend. Then a spell of rehab paid by me. The Lassiter family tree is not exactly the House of Windsor. Closer to the House of Pancakes.

"I told the boy you'd teach him to fight," Granny said. "He's gotta defend the family name."

What name? I wondered. *"Trailer Trash"*? But what I said was, "Granny, you don't understand these fancy private schools."

"You'd fight back, Jake. Hell, you *did*."

"When?" Kip asked.

"Never mind, kiddo."

I'm not proud of the story, and Kip wasn't yet ready to hear even a sanitized version. I was sixteen, working part-time mopping up puke at a roadside bar in the Keys. A couple biker punks got drunk and razzed me. Time and again.

"Ain't you the Lassiter kid? I fucked your momma in the parking lot."

"Shit, Billy," the other one said. *"Who didn't?"*

Wiry and mean, filthy jeans, dusty boots, and greasy hair. Born stupid, reared stupid, and they'd doubtless die stupid.

"Your mom takes it up the ass, kid."

"Only when she's drunk, Billy."

I barreled into the first one, bounced him off the wall, shattering the neon Budweiser sign. Clinched him and broke his nose with a head butt. Same move I'd use years later the night I wore a wire for Alex Castiel.

The punk's friend snapped a pool cue across his knee and whipped it across my temple. I staggered sideways and when he swung again, I stepped inside the arc and splintered his jaw with a straight right. I could have left it there, but I didn't. When he fell to the floor, I stomped him. Kicked him in the head, the gut, the balls.

Stomped him, not because I loved my mother, but because I hated her. Stomped him for all the pain of my childhood, for losing my father to a blade, not ten feet from where I stood, kicking the piss out of the biker.

The two punks landed in the hospital, and I did three months in juvie detention. Granny framed a copy of the judge's order, as if it were an Ivy League diploma.

"Jacob Lassiter is hereby adjudged delinquent. . . ."

I didn't want Kip to follow in my footsteps. But déjà-fucking-vu, those dang Lassiter genes.

"We'll work the heavy bag tomorrow," I told Kip. "Teach you to jab, a couple combinations, maybe some kick-boxing, too."

"I can't fight Carl. He's too big."

"No one's too big."

"Maybe not for you, Uncle Jake."

"For all of us. No one's too big and no one's too strong."

"Carl will kill me!"

"Listen up, Kip. I'm gonna teach you to hit Carl in the gut so hard, his eyes will pop out of his head, he'll shit his pants, and he'll vomit all over his shoes."

"That's my boy," Granny said.

16   Naked Came the Night

Kip was asleep in his bedroom and Granny was snoring in the rocking chair on the back porch when the phone rang. Cindy. The red Escalade, license plate U R NXT, was registered to a Miguel Sanchez of Homestead.

"Never heard of him, Cindy."

"Doubt he was driving, anyway."

"Why?"

"He's at FCI, awaiting trial on cocaine charges."

That solved nothing. Who the hell was driving the con's car, and what did they want with me? I was thinking a Jack Daniel's on the rocks might help answer the question when there was a knock at the door. A knock so dainty I barely heard it over the *whompeta* of the ceiling fan.

It took three tugs to yank the door open. Standing on the front step was a six-foot-tall caramel-skinned young woman in a stretchy mini-skirt and high heeled, strappy sandals sloped like a ski jump. Her breasts, round as cantaloupes, threatened to tumble out of her fluorescent orange tube top. A bare tummy, tanned and taut. Hair bleached white-hot platinum. She gave me a small, knowing smile, as sinful as the devil's laugh.

"Jake Lassiter?" she asked.

I said "Yes" on the assumption that she was neither a process server nor a Jehovah's Witness.

"I'm Angel Roxx. Rhymes with 'cocks' but spelled with two 'x's.'"

"Yeah?"

"Would you like a blow job?"

"Is that a trick question?"

"I work for Charlie Ziegler."

"Let me guess. Spiritual adviser?"

"P.R. consultant. And I act." She cocked a hip. You could have put a saddle on it. "Did you ever see *A Tale of Two Titties*. Or *Lawrence of a Labia*?"

"Not unless they were on ESPN. Why don't you come inside? Fewer mosquitoes."

She sashayed inside, dropping her bag on the wine barrel filled with umbrellas, fly rods, and a tarpon gaff. Csonka waddled over, jammed his nose under her mini-skirt and sniffed. She didn't flinch.

Angel's eyes danced around the living room, which looked like a garage sale at a fraternity house. My coffee table, a sailboard propped on empty milk cartons, seemed to amuse her. Or maybe it was my tree stump end table topped by a lamp in the shape of a vintage Miami Dolphins helmet.

She made an exaggerated motion of fanning herself. "What's with this heat? A/C broken?"

"I'm saving the earth, all by my lonesome."

"So what's Charlie want with someone like you?"

"You tell me."

"All he told me was to make sure you were in his office at nine A.M."

"After blowing me tonight?"

"He didn't get specific. Just said to prep you."

"Great idea. Lately, I've been prepping myself."

"You're kinda cute in a beat-up sort of way. You look a little like Studley Do-Right."

"Studley . . . ?"

"Duh. Major porn star, like a thousand years ago." She settled herself onto my old, lumpy sofa. Made of Haitian cotton, it had looked fine until one of my teammates dropped a lit joint between the cushions, starting a small but sweet-smelling fire.

"I hope you're not on steroids. I hate when guys have shriveled balls."

I put the pieces together. Earlier today, Alex Castiel had refused to investigate Ziegler and warned me to back off. Ziegler could be bad for my career, though Castiel failed to mention the guy could be good for my sex life. Either way, the State Attorney had called Ziegler and told him about me.

"Help me out here, Angel. If Ziegler wants to see me..."

"Why not just call you?"

"Yeah."

"Charlie's gotta be different. Gotta do things big. The grand gesture, he calls it."

"I still don't get it."

She pursed her lips, which seemed to gorge cute little lines in her forehead. Deep thinking mode. "Charlie needs to impress people. And to be liked. So, when you see me at your door, you're supposed to think, A present for me? What a guy!"

Actually, I was thinking, Charlie Ziegler, what a jerk, but I followed the logic.

"Anyway, that's the sweet Charlie," she continued. "The good Charlie."

"But there's another one?"

"You kidding? Lots more. Mean Charlie. Potty-mouth Charlie. Smack-you-around Charlie. You ought to see him when his face turns all red. Jeez!"

"I'm gonna go see Ziegler," I told her, "but not tomorrow."

"Why not?"

"Other plans."

Actually, I had other people to see first. Sonia Majeski had called an hour ago. She'd talked to a couple of stripper friends from the old days. They'd put together a list of five men who used to drift in and out of Ziegler's party circuit. No way to tell if any had been there the night Krista disappeared, but I would sure as hell ask. I also had a ton of questions for them about Ziegler.

Sure, I wanted to talk to him personally, but I might only have one shot at him, and I wanted to be ready. Young lawyers make the mistake of rushing to depose the main witness on the opponent's side of a case. They should be talking to everyone else first. Build your dossier before you put your antagonist under oath. By the time you say, "State your name for the record," you'd better know more about the son-of-a-bitch than his own saintly mother.

"We could still have some fun tonight," Angel offered.

"Yeah?"

"I can do you while you watch one of my flicks. It's a parallel universe thing."

I was tempted. How could I not be? I was single and unattached, and here was Angel, hot and willing, and with no demands that I be attuned to her needs or go shopping at Pottery Barn during the NFL playoffs. In another time, I would have been incapable of saying no. These days, I require some semblance of an emotional connection.

"Thanks," I said. "But I gave up one-night stands a long time ago."

"I could come back tomorrow night, too."

"Sorry. Doesn't work for me."

She crunched up her forehead again, as if presented with an especially tough algebra question. "No one's ever turned down my b.j. before."

"If it's any consolation, it's my first time, too."

There was the sound of bare feet padding across the Mexican tile. Kip, all sleepy-eyed, appeared from the corridor wearing his Miami Marlins pajama bottoms.

"I thought I heard voices," he said, eyeing my guest, or rather the twin globes rising from her tube top.

"Kip, this is Angel Roxx," I said.

"I know! *A Tale of Two Titties.*"

17   The Road Goes on Forever

The air was soggy as a steam bath as I started my morning run. The violet morning glories in my neighbor's yard were yawning open for the day, just like me. The grass wet with morning dew, the sweet tang of jasmine in the air. No breeze, the palm fronds hanging as limp as laundry on the line.

It's not a fancy neighborhood of mini-manses and well-tended lawns. More like a tropical jungle, small houses on crowded lots overgrown with ragged ficus hedges and creeping bougainvillea.

I wore an old pair of Penn State shorts and a T-shirt with the slogan "A Friend Will Help You Move, but a Real Friend Will Help You Move a Body." I'd only recently started carrying an iPod and wearing headphones. Off-season training would have been a lot easier if we'd had them in the old days. Still, there was a tradeoff. I missed the slap of shoes on asphalt and the call of the wild parrots in the neighborhood.

I slogged along, sweat streaming down my chest. Loquat to Solana to Poinciana, then south on LeJeune toward the Gables Waterway. A black-and-white wood stork strutted across the street, apparently lost. I wanted to point it toward Biscayne Bay. In my earphones, I heard Joe Nichols worrying that his lady was going out for the evening, and "tequila makes her clothes fall off."

Traffic was already building, and car fumes had overwhelmed the jasmine. I hung a right on Barbarossa, planning to cut over to Riviera and then north toward Dixie Highway. A pair of land crabs the size of catchers' mitts scuttled across the pavement, headed toward the waterway.

A black Lincoln followed me through the turn, then slowed to keep pace. I tried to see through the tinted windows but could not, the morning sun shooting daggers into my eyes. I picked up my speed, and so did the Lincoln. I slowed, and the car edged closer, until it was directly alongside me.

I stopped short, and the car braked. The passenger door opened, and a man in khaki pants and blue blazer hopped out. Nimble for a big galoot. Gray-blond crew cut, Marine neck, maybe fifty or so.

Ray Decker. Jesus!

"Where you going, turd face?" Decker said. He came onto the sidewalk and stood in my path, just out of arm's reach.

Turd face? And they say our era lacks sophisticated wit.

"Nice to see you, Ray. When'd you get out of jail?"

"Never been in jail, shyster."

"Another failure of our justice system. When will it ever end?"

He glared at me. The look of a man who wanted to step on a cockroach but didn't want to soil his shoe.

Decker had been a detective in the Sheriff's Department. In a marijuana case—possession with intent to distribute—I'd sweated him for five hours on cross-exam to show he lied on his affidavit. A judge dismissed another of his cases when I proved Decker repeatedly smacked my client in the testicles with a phone book while interrogating him. I didn't personally get Decker tossed from the force, but I didn't help him win any commendations, either.

The driver's door opened and another man stepped out, staring at me over the roof of the car. African-American, early thirties, smaller but with the broad, sloping shoulders of a body builder. Identical blazer and pants. There is no good reason to wear a jacket in the Miami summer unless you're hiding a shoulder holster.

"You got a license for that thing, Decker?"

"CWP signed by the State Attorney himself." He patted his jacket over the bulge. "I'm head of security for Ziegler Enterprises, and my boss wants to see you."

"Last night a woman delivered the same message. Offered a blow job. Same deal, Decker?"

The driver chuckled and Decker's face heated up. "Get in the car, asshole."

"Answer one question first. When Shorty isn't chauffeuring your fat ass, do you drive a red Escalade with spinners and lake pipes?"

"You think I'm a Liberty City pimp?"

"Nah. They have to be good at math."

"That's enough, dickhead. Get in."

"Changed my mind. If Ziegler wants to see me, he can make an appointment."

I turned away as if to resume plodding down Barbarossa Avenue. Decker's gun was holstered on his left shoulder. Meaning he was right-handed. I figured he would take one step and reach for me with that right hand.

He did.

I spun around and locked onto his right wrist. First with my left hand, then with both hands. I whipped his right arm behind his back, kicked him on the side of his left knee, and pushed him face-first to the ground. I reached around him, grabbed the lapels of his jacket and ripped downward, tearing the fabric at the shoulders, pinning his arms in the sleeves.

I knew the Lincoln's engine was running. I knew the driver would race around the car. I wasn't sure whether he'd pull his gun, but it didn't matter. By the time his top-heavy body rounded the hood, I had dived into the car through the open passenger side. I scrambled into the driver's seat without closing either door. Threw the gearshift into drive. Floored the accelerator. Heard the shriek of tires and the *thwomp* of the open door smacking the driver and cartwheeling him to the ground.

I hung a right on San Vicente and headed north toward Ponce de Leon and downtown Coral Gables.

Charlie Ziegler, you want to talk to me?

I got some things to say to you, pal.

18 Humanitarian of the Year

The sign on top of the building read, *Ziegler Enterprises*. The sign on the parking garage read, *Exit Only*. So there I was, plowing ass-backward into trouble, right past the sign that read, *Danger! Tire Damage*.

I drove Ziegler's Lincoln straight onto the sharp end of the curved spikes. I hit the gas and the spikes harpooned the front tires, tearing the steel radials to shreds. Accelerated again and bounced forward. Spikes punctured the rear tires, too. I listened to all four tires farting, then hopped out, entered the building, and rode the elevator to the top floor.

The receptionist was a flame-haired, warhead-breasted young woman in a black silk blouse two sizes too small. For a second she didn't sense anything unusual about the thick-chested man in running shorts and a sweaty T-shirt.

"Are you here for the auditions?" she asked.

I came around the desk, grabbed one arm of her swivel chair, and spun her away. She shrieked. I felt under her desk, found the button, and buzzed myself inside. Two seconds later, I was through the interior door, and the receptionist was shouting at me to stop. A couple toadies sat at their computers, looking alarmed but doing nothing to stop me.

I found a corner office with a giant bronze "Z" sculpture outside a set of smoked glass doors. I burst in and found a stocky man at his desk yammering into the phone. Older and heavier than the guy in jeans and suede jacket I'd run into that rainy morning eighteen years ago. But still a prick.

"Don't waste your time on Bangladesh, you stupid motherfucker!" Ziegler was in his late fifties, bald on top, with rust-colored fringes of hair dusting his ears. He wore a black silk suit that screamed "Italian designer" and a bright blue shirt unbuttoned a couple slots lower than absolutely necessary.

He didn't seem to care about my intrusion, just kept yelling. "They're not gonna buy *Bimbos of Baltimore*. They're Muslim!"

Ziegler punctuated his words by jabbing the air with a cigar. A Cuban Torpedo, judging both from its shape and aroma. They seemed to be the rage in certain circles. So did humidors of polished cherry. Alex Castiel had one in his office; its twin brother sat on Ziegler's credenza.

"Get me Bulgaria and Romania!" he shouted into the phone. "If you can't sell to those horny fuckers, I'll find someone who can!"

Abusing an underling. Real class.

Ziegler's phone beeped. He shot a look at his computer monitor and said, "Hang on, Irv. I got the Archbishop on the other line." He punched a button and radically adjusted his tone and volume. "Your Eminence. How kind of you to call."

I tossed the Lincoln's keys on Ziegler's desk and said, "If you want to talk to me, scumbag, don't send hookers and don't send thugs. Call me yourself."

Unfazed, Ziegler gave me the once-over. No indication he recognized me from our brief encounter all those years ago. He motioned with his cigar that I should sit down. I wasn't there to follow orders, so I stood rock still, hands on hips.

Ziegler listened a moment, nodding and smiling. "Ice skating rink for the orphans. You've got my support. Have a wonderful day, Your Eminence."

He punched a button and yelled into the other line: "Irv, drop your cock and sell some product!"

As Ziegler caterwauled some more, I took inventory of the office. All chrome and glass with light fixtures like dripping icicles and spindly chairs designed to make visitors slip a disc. The floor was green marble tile with gold veins running through it. Paintings—Impressionist nudes—looked expensive, but what do I know about art?

There was a "me wall." Fancy certificates, and award statuettes. The Miami Archdiocese's Humanitarian of the Year award, the B'nai Brith's philanthropy medal, and an achievement badge from the Florida Synod of the Lutheran Church.

An ecumenical asshole.

He wasn't hard to figure out. The merit badges were his soft spot. Now that he'd screwed all those girls and made all that money, what mattered to him was his reputation. I knew where to hit him and how to make it hurt.

"Gotta go, Irv," he said. "There's a guy in my office who's a dead ringer for Studley Do-Right, you remember him? Yeah, *Horny in America* back in the Reagan Administration. Guy packed a flagpole in his Speedos."

Ziegler hung up, waved the Torpedo like a scepter, and said, "Sit, Studley."

I didn't sit down. I stared him down. "My name's Jake Lassiter."

He stared back, took a long drag on the cigar. "I got pull in this town, Studley. What do you got?"

"A telephone. I'm gonna call a press conference. Tell the *Herald* what I know about the old porn producer and the missing girl. Helluva headline: 'Humanitarian of the Year a Murder Suspect.'"

"I'll sue you for slander."

"I hope so. Then I can put you under oath. I'll videotape you taking the Fifth at your depo. Gonna put you on a spit and light the fire. Let your country club pals watch you sweat."

"You don't have the juice."

"Then what are you worried about? Why send that cooch to my house? Or that moron Decker to pick me up?"

"To warn you to watch your mouth. And one warning is all you get."

"You ask me, you're running scared."

"Not scared of you, pal. You're a nobody."

"Fine. Then tell me what happened to Krista Larkin. Where'd you bury her?"

"*Please* sit down, Mr. Lassiter." A soft voice from behind me. An old man sitting on a sofa. I hadn't seen him back in the corner.

The guy must be in his eighties. He had a gut like a bowl of pudding, tired eyes, and a thin, Errol Flynn mustache. He wore olive green polyester pants with an elastic waistband, a short-sleeve shirt, and Hush Puppies the color of root beer. His hands rested on the head of a polished black cane, which he held between his legs.

I sat down because the old guy had asked nicely, and Granny taught me to be respectful to my elders.

"My name is Max Perlow, Mr. Lassiter. Have you ever heard of me?"

I hadn't and told him so.

"I used to be in the papers a bit. Before your time. I'm Charlie's business partner. I've been fixing problems for a very long time, so perhaps I can be of assistance."

"Just how do you propose to do that?"

"Permanently, Mr. Lassiter." Max Perlow leaned forward in his chair and spoke in a whisper. "When I fix something, it stays fixed."

As threats go, it was pretty impressive, especially coming from a guy who looked like he should be playing shuffleboard at Century Village.

"Surely, Mr. Lassiter," he continued, his tone amiable, "you know Charlie had nothing to do with the disappearance of some runaway girl."

Great, I thought, Al Capone vouching for Baby Face Nelson.

"I don't know anything yet," I said, getting my voice back. "Except good old Charlie pushed an underage girl into porn, then she vanished the night she was supposed to be entertaining his scuzzball friends."

Ziegler made a sound like a pig snorting. "I can ruin you, Lassiter. Take every cent you have and punch your ticket with the Bar."

"Shut up, Charlie." Perlow spoke softly, but with the authority of a man who is accustomed to having his orders followed. Turning back to me, he said, "Alejandro tells me good things about you."

"For a public servant, Alex Castiel gives a lot of private advice."

"His father was like a brother to me."

"Bernard Castiel, the gangster? Or Bernard Castiel, the hero?"

Perlow leaned back. "Do you sum up a man's life so neatly, Mr. Lassiter?"

"Sometimes. You, I'm guessing pure gangster. But a polite one."

"I was in my teens when Bernard gave me a job at the Nacional casino.

Before long, I was going to *Shabbos* services with his family at Centro de Israelita."

Perlow paused a moment, and I could swear his eyes teared up.

"Such a tragedy," he continued, "Bernard dying so young. I stood in for him at Alejandro's bris."

A tidbit missing from Alex Castiel's campaign brochures: *"Circumcised in Cuba."*

"When Alejandro's mother died, who do you suppose got him a Pedro Pan flight to Miami?"

"Wild guess, you."

"I made sure he was placed with a good family, that he wanted for nothing. He calls me 'Uncle Max.' Do you take my point, Mr. Lassiter?"

Suddenly, the State Attorney's role had come into focus. Castiel might be my basketball buddy, but he'd had a relationship with Perlow far longer and deeper. The old hood was grandfathered in.

"You own Alex Castiel," I said. "If Uncle Max wants a favor, he can't say no."

"You are so hasty with accusations, Mr. Lassiter."

"Always honest, seldom kind. That's me."

"Back in Cuba—"

"Max, is this shit necessary?" Ziegler interrupted. "This prick lawyer accuses me of murder, and you're telling Bar Mitzvah stories?"

"*Sha!*"

Hush! I didn't know much Yiddish, but a Jewish stockbroker I once dated was always telling me to shut up.

Ziegler sank deeper into his chair, sulking.

"Once in a while, in the gaming business," Perlow said, in a grandfatherly tone, "someone was entitled to wet his beak, but he starts drinking the whole birdbath. I didn't send out a couple half-wits to throw the guy into the backseat of a car."

"Aw, Jesus." Ziegler wheeled around and stared out the window.

"I invited the man to my suite," Perlow continued. "I offered espresso, *pastelitos.* We talk like gentlemen. He sees the error of his ways and agrees it won't happen again."

"You must serve good pastry," I said. "What's on the menu today?"

"Hypothetically, let's say I have a grievance with a lawyer. To make a living, this lawyer needs cooperation from judges, from prosecutors, even from the clerk of the court. If suddenly no one offers him a plea, if his files go missing, if every client gets the max, the whole town knows he can't deliver the goods."

I was starting to feel sorry for this hypothetical lawyer.

"Maybe the poor schlemiel starts cutting corners in order to survive," Perlow went on. "Someone lets the Florida Bar know of the man's male-factions. Soon he's broke and without a law license."

First Alex Castiel, now Max Perlow. Double-teaming me like two line-men on a draw play. "Ruining me seems like a lot of trouble to go to if your sleazy pal had nothing to do with Krista Larkin's disappearance."

"Fuck you," Ziegler shot back, still looking out the window.

Perlow tapped the floor with his cane. *Rat-a-tat-tat.* I think he was telling both of us to settle down. "There's another solution, Mr. Lassiter. Maybe you need some work. A retainer from Ziegler Enterprises."

"What the hell!" Ziegler whirled around in his chair to face his partner.

"Calm down, Charlie."

"How much?" I asked, being a stickler for details.

Perlow allowed a small smile, thinking he had me. "Serious shekels, I assure you."

Things were moving way too fast, I thought. First they send Angel Roxx to seduce me, then Ray Decker to escort me. Then I encounter Mutt and Jeff. Good gangster, bad gangster. I'd hit a nerve, and these two were freaking out. I sure as hell wasn't going to take their money, but I'd like to know why it was being offered. What did they have to hide?

"This *retainer*," I said. "I get the money whether or not there's work to do?"

"Isn't that how a retainer works?"

"So does a bribe."

"If it makes you feel better, I'm sure Charlie can find something for you to do."

Ziegler drilled me with eyes cold as coins. "Wish I was still in hard core. You could mop up jism on the set."

"Keep your retainer," I said. "I'd rather come after you."

"Take your best shot, shyster."

"I'll start by asking questions of your bigshot friends. Maybe the Arch-bishop has something to say."

Ziegler emitted a sound very much like a dog growling.

"A suggestion, Mr. Lassiter," Perlow said. "You're here now. Ask Char-lie anything you want. Whatever you learn, feel free to take to Alejandro."

Surprising me. "Sure, why not?" I said.

With a hostile witness, many lawyers begin with soft violins before they start pounding the kettle drums. They try to lull the witness into a false sense of security. I think subtlety is overrated.

"Were you fucking Krista Larkin when she was seventeen?" I began.

Ziegler blinked and shot a look at Perlow, who said, "Tell him the truth, Charlie."

"Yeah, I was fucking her. So what? I wasn't the only one."

"Did she come to parties at your house?"

"Yeah, lots of them."

"What about the night she disappeared?"

"Never showed up."

"You invited her?"

"On the set that day. She said she'd come by, but she didn't."

"Any idea why?"

"Maybe she was worn out from sucking cock all day."

"Am I mistaken, or did you just get the Humanitarian of the Year award?"

"Cor-fucking-rect, and I'm a Grand Claw, too. You know how much you gotta give to charity to get a golden bib?"

"Who cares? Underneath your bib, you're still a sleazebag."

He turned to Perlow. "A fucking criminal defense lawyer lecturing me."

"One difference," I said, "I don't pretend to be anything I'm not."

"You hypocrite! Max, did you hear him?"

"Not now, Charlie."

But Ziegler barreled on. "Hey, Lassiter, you think I don't remember you? You think Krista didn't tell me about you? I know what happened that night, you two-faced fuck!" He smirked at me. "Did you tell your client you fucked her sister? Or do you want me to?"

I couldn't breathe. It felt as if someone had cinched leather straps around my chest and pulled tight.

"Charlie, that's not the way to resolve this," Perlow said. "Mr. Lassiter, do you have anything else?"

I was reeling from Ziegler's accusations. I'd tumbled from the moral high ground to the gutter.

Ziegler knew.

He even guessed that I hadn't been honest with Amy Larkin. I had to fix that and fast.

I had blundered coming here. I could see it in his triumphant grin. If a snake could smile, that would be its look.

Perlow stirred, bracing his cane to get to his feet. "If that's it, Mr. Lassiter, it would appear you have nothing placing the girl in Charlie's company the night she disappeared."

"Maybe today I don't. But this isn't over. Hell, it hasn't even started." Trying to salvage the moment by sounding tough, but really just spraying a garden hose on the *Hindenburg*.

I turned to leave, listening to Ziegler snicker like a horse. Just as I reached the door he said, "Hey, Lassiter, why do you think I sent Angel your way?"

I didn't answer, and he said, "Because I *know* you. You're just like me."

"Bullshit. I sent her home."

"My mistake. Next time, I'll send jail bait."

He was still cackling when the door closed behind me.

19 The Marvelous Jew

"Nestor, what's the problem?" Perlow asked his driver and bodyguard. The creamy white Bentley was stuck in the exit lane of the Ziegler Enterprises building.

"Car being towed."

Perlow saw it then. Ziegler's black Lincoln. The car Ray Decker used. Four flat tires.

Lassiter, he thought.

What the hell to do about him?

Ziegler had gloated after Lassiter left. Thought he'd won the round. But all he'd done was bloody the nose of a street fighter. Lassiter wasn't a weaker foe because Charlie shamed him, but a more determined one. The lawyer didn't have a booming practice or a 24-karat reputation. But again, that only made him more dangerous.

"A man who has nothing in his pockets has nothing to lose."

Meyer Lansky himself said that more than half a century ago. The man President Batista of Cuba called *"El Judio Maravilloso,"* the marvelous Jew. The man with nothing in his pockets turned out to be a bearded guerrilla fighting in the mountains of Cuba. His name was Fidel Castro. Lansky tried to warn Batista that the rebel leader had a ruthlessness of purpose that not even overwhelming forces and firepower of the army could stop.

Charlie Ziegler never understood such things. He had always been undisciplined. Those damn parties with the girls and the drugs. There were men around town who would remember. Witnesses. If Lassiter turned up the heat, how would Ziegler react? Charlie was not the strong and silent type. Perlow figured he could crack like a piñata, all his secrets—*their* secrets—spilling out.

Perlow sighed, looked at his aged hands. He wished Meyer were still around. Meyer kept emotion out of the equation and never acted rashly. When the boys suspected that Bugsy Siegel was skimming from the Flamingo, Meyer urged caution. Only when the proof was overwhelming did he authorize the hit. Quick and efficient.

What would Meyer do now?

"If a man is a moneymaker, you can forgive a lot of his faults."

El Judio Maravilloso was right. With all his failings, Ziegler still made Perlow money from the reality channel and international distribution of porn. Not only that, it was all legitimate. Jeez, they even paid taxes. You had to be careful these days. With that RICO crap, they could convict you for just thinking about committing a crime.

"Nestor, you remember Jake Lassiter? Used to play for the Dolphins."

Tejada laughed. "First time I saw him play I was doing sixty days in Youth Hall. I liked his style, his helmet flying off when he made a big hit on a kickoff."

Sounded right to Perlow. A guy who would sacrifice his body for the team.

"Reminded me of a pit bull," Tejada said. "You ever go to a dog fight, Mr. P?"

"Never."

"A pit bull latches on to another dog and don't let go. Beat 'em on the head with a shovel. Chop off a hind leg. Don't matter. He just fights to the death."

Perlow felt revulsion at the description of a maimed animal. He never considered himself a violent man. On the few occasions when he had to make someone disappear, it was always with regret and sadness. More than once, he dipped into his own pocket to send money, anonymously, to the widows and children.

"Fought like a dog," Tejada said, tying up his thoughts. "Right up to the whistle and a little after."

When the tow truck pulled the Lincoln out of the exit lane, Tejada eased the Bentley toward Coral Way, the engine purring. Perlow considered the tattoo on the back of Tejada's shaved head. A five-pointed crown. Symbol of the Latin Kings, which Perlow thought sounded like Desi Arnaz's mambo band, but was the largest Hispanic street gang in the country. A steroid-pumped hulk, Tejada had done time for armed robbery and aggravated assault, both pluses on his résumé.

"You hungry, Nestor?"

"You know me, Mr. P. I can always eat."

"How about the Forge? I'll treat you to crab cakes."

"Forge is closed, sir."

"Jeez, I forgot about the remodeling."

I'm getting old.

Perlow thought of Vincent Gigante, "The Oddfather," wandering around Manhattan in his bathrobe, showing up for court unbathed and unshaven. The press thought Gigante was faking it, but Perlow knew the man. Alzheimer's was a bitch.

"How about Pumpernik's for a pastrami sandwich?" Perlow said.

Tejada laughed. "You're messing with me, Mr. P."

"Yeah. How many years they been closed, I wonder?"

Perlow longed for the old days. When you could still make a buck shylocking and running numbers and shooting craps in a cabana at the Fontainebleau. Before they had slots at the racetracks and offshore gambling on the Internet.

Jesus, video poker!

How can you trust a card game where you don't see the deck?

His thoughts returned to Lassiter. If Lassiter tried to go public with accusations against Charlie, he would have to be stopped. Perlow would find it distasteful, but what else could he do?

"Nestor, I haven't asked you to get your hands dirty for a while. . . ."

"Anything you want, Mr. P, you just ask."

"Thank you, Nestor."

"When do you want it done, sir?"

"I have to think it through. These decisions are never easy."

"If you don't mind my saying so, Mr. P, if your interests are threatened, the sooner you act the better. '*Más vale matar a la primera rata antes de que la casa se llene de ellas.*'"

"Something about rats in the house." Perlow had once spoken decent Spanish, but that was half a century ago.

"Better to kill the first rat before the house gets full of them," Tejada translated.

Perlow smiled. Meyer himself would have warmed to the concept.

20 Just Like the Rest of Them

I had nearly turned around after leaving Ziegler's office. I wanted to crash back through the door, hoist him from his chair by his designer lapels, and toss him through a wall. Let all those certificates and plaques come raining down. But I knew my anger was with myself, not him. I'd given Ziegler the ammunition and the weapon, and he'd been happy to blow me away.

I took a cab home, showered, and changed into fresh shorts and T-shirt. I called Amy's cell and told her we needed to talk. I didn't tell her I had a confession to make. She said she was going jogging on the beach, trying to sweat out her frustrations and clear her mind.

I drove across the Rickenbacker Causeway, watching a line of thunderheads rumble across open water toward Key Biscayne. Summer in Miami, where it rains every afternoon at 3:17 P.M., give or take.

I caught up with Amy on the white sand near the old lighthouse at the southern tip of the island. She wore cutoffs and a red bikini top and was Ohio pale, but her carved abs and rounded delts revealed she was no stranger to the gym.

I needed to tell her the truth about my night with Krista. If she heard it from Ziegler instead of me, I'd lose whatever trust I'd struggled to build. Amy might even begin to suspect me again in her sister's disappearance.

That's the problem with lies and cover-ups. They make the underlying wrong seem even more grievous.

"I want you to take precautions," I told her, as wind gusts rustled the palm fronds and swirled loose sand across the dunes. I couldn't bring myself to confess. Instead, I stalled.

"Why?"

"Ziegler's rattled and he's called in reinforcements."

I told Amy about the two tough guys in a Lincoln and my confrontation with Perlow and Ziegler, the old gangster and the new humanitarian.

"Perlow's the one who concerns me," I said. "He looks soft as a nougat but he's got flint and steel in his eyes."

"So we must be on to something."

"Yeah, but I don't know what. Just promise you'll be careful, and if you feel threatened in any way, you'll call me, day or night."

"Okay, sure. And thanks for caring, Jake."

Saying it as if she wasn't used to anyone giving a shit about her.

"You might think about moving out of the motel," I added.

"Where to?"

"I have an extra bedroom."

She looked at me with suspicion. Of course, that was a main component of her character.

"Hey, c'mon. No strings attached. If I wanted more, I'd come to your motel."

"Really?"

"What I meant was, I have my nephew and Granny at home. It's not exactly a bachelor pad."

She was shaking her head.

"What's wrong?" I asked.

"I was just thinking that eighteen years ago, Krista asked if she could spend the night at your place. But you turned her down."

"Actually . . ."

"What?"

A dozen terns, which had been pecking away at the wet sand, took to the air. I wanted to fly with them. But I took a deep breath of sea air and told her the truth. That I had taken Krista home with me, knowing deep down that it wasn't to protect her from the night. That she offered herself, as I knew she would, and I wasn't man enough to turn her down. As I spoke, the squall hit us, the rain driven sideways, fat juicy drops, warm as spit. A jagged lightning bolt passed over the island and hit on the bay side with a thunderclap that hurt my ears.

When I got to the part where I dropped Krista off in the morning, delivering her to the man I now knew to be Charlie Ziegler, Amy's face froze. She turned away and looked out to sea.

"You're just like the rest of them," she said, staring at the whitecaps sloshing toward the beach.

"Them?"

"Men!"

Without warning, she whirled and hit me, her fist bouncing off my temple. It didn't hurt, but the surprise knocked me a step sideways. She swung again. And again. I did the rope-a-dope, just standing there with my arms up, as a barrage of blows ricocheted off my shoulders and elbows. I let her punch herself out until, exhausted, she dropped to one knee, sobbing. Lightning zinged across the sky, followed by a thunderclap.

I crouched next to Amy in the wet sand at the water's edge. "I'm sorry. But I'll work even harder for you. For Krista."

"Bastard."

She said it so softly I could barely hear her over the wind and the rain.

Amy turned and ran up the beach, the wind howling in her wake. I watched until she disappeared. She never looked back.

21 Partners for Life

Sipping a mojito and cursing the gods for the crud they were throwing his way, Charlie Ziegler stood on the seawall separating his property from the roiling water of the bay. He watched the storm plow across Key Biscayne, the sky darkening in its path. He felt the first raindrops, knew the deluge was just seconds away.

"Goddamn lawyer," he said aloud. That crazy bastard. Can't be bribed, won't be scared. Threatening to go public. All these years of building up a reputation. All those galas for diabetes, kidneys, and cancer, every disease north of hemorrhoids. Nibbling canapés with the culture vultures, then snoring through the opera. He wasn't going to let Lassiter smear the good name he'd built.

Then there was his wife Lola, off to France, probably gonna charge the Eiffel Tower to her Platinum card. God, how he longed to be in his mistress's arms. Melody was a woman who—against all odds—seemed to actually love him for himself.

And what about Max Perlow? Jesus. Treating him like shit in front of that prick lawyer.

"Shut up, Charlie. . . ."

What the fuck was that about? After all the money I've made for him.

The money.

The old man might be getting senile, but he could still count. Fifteen percent of gross profits. All because of that loan twenty years ago. At least Ziegler had *thought* it was a loan. Once the porn business took off—all cash, all the time—suddenly the terms changed.

"*C'mon Max. I've paid you off, already.*"

"*There's no paying off. I made an investment. We're partners, Charlie. Partners for life.*"

So die, already.

Instead, Perlow insisted on picking his pocket.

At the time they made the deal, Perlow still had juice. Not a man to fuck with. But these days? *Who's he got, other than that gangbanger Tejada?*

Why the hell does Max even have a bodyguard? All his enemies are either dead or drooling into their oatmeal.

Except for me.

Lightning flashed over the bay, and the thunder took its time rumbling toward him. The air smelled of dust and nitrogen. He began taking his own measure as the raindrops pelted him. Could he kill Perlow? Knowing even as he asked that he didn't have the stomach for it.

What about Tejada? How loyal was he? Would he take $25K to drive the Bentley into a swamp with Perlow strapped into the backseat? Maybe, Ziegler concluded, it was worth pondering over another drink.

22 Talking Trash

Our upbringing may not determine where we finish the race, but it surely draws the starting line. I was mulling this deep thought while huffing and puffing up and down the basketball court. The Miami Mouthpieces—my boys—were taking on the Avengers, Castiel's band of prosecutors, and I was guarding my opponent.

Until yesterday, I had considered Alex Castiel a friend. We had bonded years ago when I wore the wire for him. We'd shared many meals and many stories since. If he turned out to be dirty, I would feel betrayed.

He was dangerously close to "Uncle Max." Then there was Ziegler. How well did Castiel know him back in the day? What would he be willing to do for Perlow? And one even bigger question nagged at me.

Yo, Alex, were you at Ziegler's party the night Krista Larkin disappeared?

I planned to ask, just as soon as I elbowed him in the ribs a few times.

Back then, Castiel would have been a young hotshot a few years out of law school. He'd gotten his name in the papers for winning a few high-profile cases and had recently been promoted to the Major Crimes Division of the State Attorney's Office. Just the kind of up-and-comer Ziegler wanted as a pal.

Castiel once told me we were friends because of similarities in our past. Both our fathers were murdered. Both of us were raised by surrogates.

Castiel was the adopted child of a wealthy Coral Gables family. I was raised by Granny, a tough, honest woman who took no guff.

In high school, I was not King of the Prom. I was Most Likely to Do Time. At Coral Shores High in the Keys, I was a fist-in-the-dirt defensive tackle who enjoyed the combat, much of which consisted of clawing, spitting, and cursing. I wasn't recruited for major college ball because I was a tweener. Not big enough to play defensive line and not fast enough to be a great linebacker. I walked on at Penn State, made the team, and earned straight C's in the classroom.

No NFL team drafted me. I was the last free agent signed by the Dolphins, usually a guarantee to get cut before opening day. But I made the final roster spot and hung on a few years, flying ass-over-elbows on what used to be called the "suicide squad," the kickoff and punt teams.

Similar story after law school. No downtown firms wanted to interview me. I got the job in the P.D.'s Office because I wasn't afraid to park in the jail visitors' lot after midnight, and I didn't worry about my clients having cooties. Basically, I've never been sought after for anything, but if I get my cleats in the door, you'll find it's hard to keep me out.

Now I backpedaled down the court, intent on keeping Castiel from scoring, or knocking him on his ass if I couldn't.

"You're not fast enough to cover me, Jake," he taunted, dribbling high, as if daring me to steal the ball.

"We talking basketball here, Alex?"

Top of the key. Castiel faked the jumper. I left my feet, and he streaked around me. Ed Shohat, a white-collar defense lawyer, tried to plug the lane, but Castiel let fly a teardrop floater. *Swish.*

Loping back down the court, Castiel laughed and talked trash. "A step too slow, Jake. You're a step too slow."

I know, I know. Story of my life.

Castiel was captain of the Avengers, the highly disciplined prosecutors' team. I was the leading scorer of the Mouthpieces, a rowdy group of criminal defense lawyers.

I liked playing against Castiel's team. Sure, the prosecutors threw some elbows, but they never whined over lousy calls. The worst were the personal injury lawyers, the Contingency Cats, who always faked injuries and threatened to file lawsuits. The Downtown Defenders—insurance company lawyers—tampered with the clock, refused to stop play when an opponent was hurt, and handpicked friends as referees.

Intending to put Castiel on his duly elected ass, I set up in the low post and took a bounce pass from Shifty Sullivan—the nickname stemming from criminal court, not the basketball court. My back was to Castiel, and he kept a hip planted on my butt. I pivoted and faked left, but Castiel knew I seldom drove that way. A weakness in my game, the left-handed dribble.

I tossed an elbow into Castiel's gut, heard him *whoomph* as I went around him to the right and sank a baby hook from six feet away.

He doubled over, fought for a breath, and could barely get the words out. "Hey, ref. You swallow your whistle?" Pantomiming my elbow toss.

"Crybaby!" I whooped.

It went on that way for the entire game. I hit Castiel hard enough to draw a flagrant foul and barreled into him enough times to draw two charges. I fouled out but still led the scoring with 21 for the Mouthpieces. With greater finesse, the unflappable Castiel led the Avengers to a nine-point win.

He approached me in the locker room, pressing a cold can of Heineken to his forehead where a welt was flaring up. "Buy you dinner, Jake?"

"Why?"

"To find out why you're so pissed at me."

"More like disappointed in you."

"Let's talk about it, Jake. C'mon, I'll treat you to martinis and a porterhouse."

"I'll go if you answer one question for me, Alex. Were you—?"

"Yes."

"Why not wait for the question?"

"I know what you're gonna ask. It's about Ziegler's party. And the answer's yes. I was there the night Krista Larkin disappeared."

23 Young, Single, and Horny

I don't usually order shrimp cocktail when they charge by the piece—eight bucks!—but tonight Castiel was paying, and I didn't give a shit about the cost. We sat on the front patio of Prime One Twelve, a noisy, trendy hangout for NBA players and others with the Am Ex Centurion card. The restaurant is at the foot of Ocean Drive on South Beach, the epicenter of hedonism run amok. We started with the shrimp and martinis—as cold as liquid nitrogen—with steaks to follow.

When we sat down, Castiel had said he would tell me everything he knew about Ziegler and Krista Larkin. That he had nothing to hide. *"I should have told you straight off, Jake, but I'm embarrassed about some of the shit from my past."* Well, that made two of us.

"I was at Ziegler's house," Castiel said now, "but Krista wasn't. She never showed up."

"To be so sure, you must have known her by sight."

"She was around a lot that summer. Charlie's flavor of the month. Maybe three months."

"And this night, who was the lucky girl?"

"Girls, plural. Half a dozen playthings. Porn starlets. Strippers. Strays. All interchangeable, all forgettable."

"Not to their families."

"I'm just saying how it was with Ziegler. One second he's doing a couple actresses in the living room, then three more girls are hopping over the sofa like a hockey team changing lines. The Larkin girl wasn't one of them."

"What were you doing there?"

"What do you think? I was young. Single. Horny."

Castiel sipped his martini and told me his story, while flicking that gold cigarette lighter that had belonged to his father. In the early nineties, when he was a young prosecutor, Castiel met Charlie Ziegler, courtesy of Uncle Max.

Ziegler's porn business was just taking off. He was renting a waterfront manse on Sunset Island that belonged to a Saudi sheik who came to town to buy diamonds and frolic with young women. Jewelers on Flagler Street provided the gems, Ziegler the women.

"The house was tricked out like a disco," Castiel said. "A glitter ball, a D.J., a sound system you could hear in Bimini. The place decorated like a bordello. Gold fixtures in the bathrooms, an infinity pool, marble columns with eagles on top, like some Roman emperor lived there."

"The Fuck Palace." I'd heard Sonia Majeski use the term.

"Oh, man, The Fuck Palace." Alex smiled at the memory. "That was the cabana. Silk canopies. Mirrored ceilings and wide-screen porno."

"Sounds like you knew the place well."

"Like I said before, I was young and single."

"And horny," I reminded him.

"I forgot about your time in the seminary," he shot back.

I sipped at the second martini, sharp as a dagger in the throat. Next to us, a boisterous table of eight sang "Happy Birthday" in Spanish, then Portuguese, and finally Hebrew. They'd gone through four bottles of Cristal at $450 a whack.

"You know a bunch of the guys who were there that night, right?" I asked.

"Some of them, sure."

"So subpoena them. Put them under oath and see what they know."

"You're talking about important men in this town. They have families now. Hell, some had families then. All of them are gonna have faulty memories."

"If you don't want to mess with those guys, I will. I have some names from Sonia Majeski. You must have others. I'll jump-start your investigation."

"Fishing expedition is more like it."

The steaks arrived—porterhouse for me, T-bone for Castiel. Round three of the martinis could not be far behind.

"Jake, there's no probable cause that a crime has been committed. You've got a runaway girl who probably started a new life, that's all."

"A runaway girl who's probably dead is more like it. Last seen headed to your pal's house."

"Even if you could place the girl with Ziegler, so what? He liked her. He screwed her now and then. What's his motive for killing her?"

"Maybe she was going to scream 'statutory rape.' Maybe she witnessed something she shouldn't have. Maybe it was an accident. Booze and drugs and a loaded gun."

"And maybe you're gonna score for the wrong team again."

"Cheap shot, Alex."

"Maybe it's a metaphor for your life. Scoring a touchdown for the opposition."

"Scored a safety," I corrected him.

Castiel knew just where to insert the needle. A long-ago game against the Jets in the snow and fog. I made a big hit on the kickoff and knocked the ball loose. Bodies were flying. I got there first and scooped it up, but somehow got turned around. Hey, I was playing with a concussion. I ran to the wrong end zone and cleverly spiked the ball. Two points for the Jets, we lose by one, and the headline on Monday said: "Wrong-Way Lassiter Dooms Fins."

Castiel was getting frustrated with me, and it was mutual. I decided to shake, not stir, him. "Why are you protecting Ziegler?"

"What the hell does that mean?"

"Friendship or money?"

He pointed his steak knife at me. "Don't say anything you can't back up, friend."

"You're letting a pornographer and an old mobster call the shots. What turned you? The pussy in the old days or the campaign cash now?"

"Goddammit!" Castiel shoved his plate aside. "Any other lawyer in town talked to me like that, I'd . . ."

He let it hang there. Maybe he didn't know what he would do. He pulled the napkin off his lap and tossed it on the table. He must have lost his appetite.

"If you want to take me on," he said, "bring it. I'll unleash the dogs, and it won't be a fair fight. You ever have a witness who lies, you ever take a fee from the fruits of a crime, I'll have your ass. I've got two dozen investigators and a sitting Grand Jury. You want to fuck with me, Jake, you better bring an army."

Ray Decker sat at an outdoor table at Prime Italian, directly across the street from its sister restaurant, Prime One Twelve. He'd been munching a loaf of garlic bread, sopping in butter, and watching the State Attorney and the shyster put away steaks and martinis. He owed Lassiter big-time for messing him up and driving off in Ziegler's Lincoln. He pictured himself coming up behind Lassiter and slamming him face-first into his shrimp cocktail.

Decker had planned on only having a calamari appetizer, but he started salivating while eyeing those assholes across the street, so he ordered a bone-in rib eye, black and blue, for fifty-six bucks. Ziegler would yell about the expense report. Like a lot of rich pricks, Ziegler burned money on stupid shit for himself, while starving the people who worked for him. Decker had once seen his boss order a bottle of Screaming Eagle Cabernet for $4,500, all to impress some ambitious, tit-enhanced reality show hostess wannabe who would have blown him for a glass of Boone's and a seven-episode gig.

Decker studied the body language across the street. He considered himself an expert from his days as a detective. People say more with their bodies than with their mouths. There was an ease between Castiel and Lassiter. He expected that. Ziegler had told him the two guys were old friends. That's what had concerned the boss. Could he trust the State Attorney?

Decker wasn't so sure. He hated all politicians. His old boss, the county sheriff, had rolled over instead of standing up for him. Thanks to Lassiter and a couple ACLU lawyers, Decker had been bounced from the force. As if exaggerating under oath and some rough stuff while making arrests were cause for firing.

While chewing his calamari, Decker noticed the change in the body language across the street. Castiel's shoulders got all stiff. He raised his voice. If it hadn't been for the traffic on Ocean Drive, Decker probably could have heard him. Decker lifted a small pair of binoculars to his face. He could see the vein in Castiel's neck throbbing. It got even better when the State Attorney pointed a steak knife at Lassiter, as if he wanted to stab him in the heart. Then Castiel tossed his napkin on the table, like a foot-ball ref throwing a penalty flag. He had a few more words with Lassiter, then signaled for the check.

Ziegler would be pleased. Those two weren't conspiring against him. Hell, they couldn't make it through a meal together.

Decker sat there a few more minutes. He wanted to see what car Lassiter was driving. The valet brought around a cream-colored Eldorado convertible. Mid-eighties, like some pimp or pusher would drive. It would be an easy car to tail. Not that Ziegler had told him to. This was strictly personal. He owed Lassiter a world of pain and intended to deliver it.

That thought made Decker even hungrier. He wondered if he should order fried Oreo cookies with vanilla ice cream for dessert.

24 The Kid Makes a Discovery

The morning after Castiel picked up the dinner check—and, I hoped, indigestion—I gave two research assignments to my trusty nephew. When I first appointed him my unpaid law clerk, he asked just what lawyers did.

"We play poker with ideas," I said, a tad pompously.

"Cool. Granny said all you did was push paper and tell lies."

I had already talked the case through with the boy while teaching him the finer points of a left-right combination on the heavy bag.

"Find the biker who called himself 'Snake' and find Krista Larkin's missing car," I told Kip.

"That's it? A biker named 'Snake'? You don't want me to find Osama bin Laden's body while I'm at it?"

"C'mon, Kip. You're a whiz on the computer. A lot better than me."

I dropped him off at the Tuttle-Biscayne computer lab. He promised to work hard, and I promised to teach him how to kick Carl Kountz in the nuts.

I was stuck in the office the rest of the day. Interviewing new clients, paying bills, handling the routine paperwork that made me wish I'd chosen another career. Shrimping, maybe, like my old man. Or coaching football at a little college in New England.

I kept replaying my conversation with Alex Castiel. I'd insulted him, and he'd lost his cool and threatened me. Maybe he'd slipped over to the dark side. Or maybe he was just playing it safe like every politico who avoids butting heads with the rich and powerful. And maybe he was right that I was pulling a Vallandigham.

Clement Vallandigham was a lawyer who—like me—would go to great lengths for his clients. Defending a murder trial in the 1870s, Vallandigham tried to prove that the victim accidentally shot himself when drawing his gun. So the lawyer pulled the gun from his pocket, and *bang*. Shot himself. Vallandigham died, but on a brighter note, the jury acquitted his client.

I wasn't going to stop looking into Krista Larkin's disappearance, but I would try to avoid shooting myself. Around midday, I called Amy, doubting she would talk to me. We hadn't spoken since she scored a TKO against me on the beach with a flurry of girlie punches.

"I'm sorry I didn't tell you the whole truth when we first met," I said, as soon as she answered.

"No, my fault," Amy said. "I shouldn't have berated you for the way you *used* to be."

"I deserved it." Competing to see who could bake the biggest humble pie. "The 'grinning ape,' you called me."

"That was the guy in the picture. If you were still that guy, you wouldn't be trying to help me."

"So, a truce?"

"Truce." She chuckled. It was not a sound I was accustomed to hearing from her.

I invited her to come over for dinner. A *family* dinner. This time, she said yes.

In late afternoon, I signed up a new client. A guy charged with siphoning gas from a police cruiser. No, I don't know why he chose *that* car. Or why he used a cigarette lighter instead of a flashlight in the darkness. Or how he'll look once he gets his prosthetic nose.

After a full day of upholding the Constitution in the ceaseless pursuit of justice, I headed home, listening to Billy Bob Thornton's Boxmasters offer a deal to girlfriends everywhere: "I'll give you a ring when you give me my balls back."

When I pulled up to the house, Csonka was sitting in the shade of the chinaberry tree, licking the claw of a land crab. He didn't ask for melted butter or mustard sauce. I smacked the front door open with my shoulder, just like always, and entered the house. I heard feminine voices coming from my kitchen. Okay, one was feminine—Amy Larkin. The other was a whiskey and tobacco contralto.

"Look what the cat drug in," Granny greeted me.

Cat being on her mind, what with another mess of catfish frying in an iron skillet.

"Glad you could make it," I said to Amy, who gave me a shy smile. Maybe she was embarrassed by the boxing match on the beach.

She sat at the kitchen counter. No makeup I could detect, with that frosting of freckles across her nose. She wore a turquoise tank top and jeans, her hair tied back with a simple band.

I told her about last night's dinner with Castiel and his angry threats.

She wrinkled her forehead and thought about it. "If the State Attorney won't help, what about the U.S. Attorney?"

"No jurisdiction without a federal crime."

"The local police, then?"

"I can try. But the missing persons investigation was closed a long time ago."

"What about taking what we have to the Grand Jury."

"Great idea, but we're just private citizens. Only the State Attorney can do that."

"And he wants to protect Ziegler, not prosecute him."

I didn't debate the point.

"You won't give up, will you?" Amy asked, real concern in her voice.

"Jake never gives up," Granny volunteered, dropping balls of jalapeño-spiked cornmeal into a pot of oil. Deep-fried hush puppies. The required side dish to fried catfish, a meal she insisted on cooking at least three times a week. "Nobody scares him, neither."

Not true. A lot of people scare me. I just swallow the fear, and I don't back down. As a result, I break a lot of dishes in the china shop.

"I won't give up," I promised, "and we'll find the truth."

That brought a warm smile from Amy, a look I hadn't often seen.

Granny shooed us out of the kitchen, so I took Amy to the backyard, where the sticky sweet aroma of mango trees hung in the air. Just as we settled onto the porch swing, the screen door opened and Kip joined us.

Even though it was well past dark, he wore sunglasses, his hair spiked with gel. This week's look.

"Kip, this is Amy," I said.

He gave her a bashful look.

Amy smiled and said, "Your uncle is helping me."

"I'm helping, too," Kip said.

"How's that coming along?" I asked.

"I tried to find the biker guy, Snake, but there's like hundreds of guys with that nickname who've been in and out of prisons."

"Thank you for trying," Amy said.

"No problem." He stared at the tops of his bare feet.

"What else, Kip?" I knew that look.

"I found some other stuff, but I don't think it's good. In fact, I think it's really bad."

"What's that?" Amy asked, her body suddenly rigid.

"Your sister's car. I found it at the bottom of a canal."

25 Mood Swings

Kip was doing the talking; Amy and I, the listening. Granny stayed in the kitchen, sprinkling cinnamon on her famous sweet potato pie.

"Right after your sister went missing," Kip said, looking at Amy, "the cops checked other departments for abandoned cars. Didn't find anything."

Amy clutched her left wrist with her right hand, her body rigid.

"It's a lot easier to now," Kip continued. "Recovered-car databases are all on the Internet, and that's how I found it. Six years ago, during a drought, an airboat hit a chunk of metal in a canal. It was the roof of a car. Take a look, Uncle Jake."

He handed over a thick document with the logo of the Florida Department of Law Enforcement. "Consolidated Report: Abandoned Motor Vehicles, 2000–2005." I thumbed through the pages until I came to an item Kip had underlined. The canal was in the Everglades about fifty miles due west of Miami, just before Tamiami Trail angles north into the Big Cypress National Preserve. Miccosukee Reservation land.

The canal ran along a dirt road that dead-ended at a levee. Anyone driving along there was either seriously lost or didn't want to be found. The car was pulled from the water by Miccosukee police, who inventoried it. No bodies, no bones. No suitcases or personal effects. The license plate was missing, but the vehicle identification number was intact. It matched a 1988 Honda registered to Krista Larkin, which is how Kip had cross-referenced it.

It was one of a few thousand cars pulled from Florida waterways each year. Some people find it cheaper to dump a car than have it towed away. The Miccosukee police didn't make a big deal about the Honda, which ended its life in a landfill after being dragged from the water.

Amy wrapped her arms around the boy and squeezed hard. Her body trembled, or maybe both their bodies did. She turned to me. "Krista's car with no license plate. As if someone wanted to hide any trace of her."

"That would be my guess," I said, unable to muster anything positive. A young woman missing eighteen years, her car buried. The words "foul play" did not seem quite foul enough to describe what likely happened.

Now we had evidence of a possible homicide. I pulled out my cell phone and dialed a number. When Castiel answered, I said, "Alex, I think you're gonna want to open a Grand Jury investigation."

I told him what Kip had found and waited for his congratulations.

"So what do you want me to do?" he asked.

"Dredge the canal, for starters."

"If it's on Miccosukee land, I've got no jurisdiction."

"But you can ask the Mics to do it. Call their chief of police."

He paused a moment before speaking. "You have no skeleton, right?"

"That's why I want you to dredge!"

"Any forensic evidence found in the car?"

"No, but they didn't treat it as a crime scene. It was just another sunken car."

"How long after Krista's disappearance did the car go into the water?"

"No way to know."

"Maybe Krista sold the car and the new owner dumped it there. Or a thief did it. Or a tow truck driver. Whatever, you've got no more tonight than you did yesterday."

"Goddammit, Alex! Who you working for? The people or Charlie Ziegler?"

The phone clicked off. Amy must have read it in my face. Before I could say a word, her look changed. In a matter of moments, she had gone from mournful to hopeful to angry.

"Ziegler owns your friend." She made it sound like my fault.

"So it would appear." It had taken a lot for me to get to that point, but the evidence against Alex just kept piling up.

"And all your talk was just hot air."

"My talk?"

" 'I have street savvy. Experience. Contacts.' " Her voice became even more sarcastic. " 'The State Attorney is a friend of mine.' "

"Okay, Alex didn't pan out. But there's another possibility."

"I'll bet."

"If Castiel is corrupt, there's a statewide agency that can help us. Investigating him could be the key to opening an inquiry into Krista's disappearance."

"Sounds like a long shot."

"But I'd like to try. It's the Florida Department of Law Enforcement. I'll call tomorrow."

"I suppose you have contacts there, too."

As a practitioner of sarcasm, I hate when it's used on me. "No, Amy, I don't have contacts there."

"So basically, you're just throwing darts, hoping something will stick."

"There's also a statewide prosecutor in Tallahassee. He investigates public corruption."

"You know the guy?"

"I've met him. We've talked." Technically, that was true. I'd listened to him give a talk at a Miami Beach Bar luncheon, and afterward I'd said, "Nice job," and he said, "Thanks."

"You've got nothing. It's all bullshit."

Her tone turning cold again, just as it had been the day we met.

"C'mon, Amy. Hang with me on this."

"I'm wasting my time with you."

"Amy, I'm concerned about you," I said, gently. "Your mood seems to . . ."

"What!"

"Swing. Up, down, then falls off a cliff."

"Screw that! Are you my shrink?"

"You're under a lot of stress."

"Maybe you should have been a shrink. You're not much of a lawyer." Her voice as hard as a cinder block.

I decided to shut up and let her slug me with her words.

"As a matter of fact, you're a really lousy lawyer, and I'm firing you."

"You can't stop me from investigating your sister's disappearance. So let's chill tonight, and maybe tomorrow you'll see things differently. Maybe—"

"I can take care of Ziegler myself."

"What does that mean? 'Take care of.' "

"Just stay out of my way, okay, Lassiter?"

She hopped off the porch and circled the house to her car, never saying good-bye, good night, or sleep tight.

26 A Hard Night's Sleep

The metronomic *swoosh* of the bedroom ceiling fan usually puts me to sleep.

Not tonight.

I couldn't get comfortable. Not while on my back with a pillow tucked under a bum knee. Not on my side. Not on my stomach.

I listened to the wind rustle the palm fronds outside my bedroom window. I listened to a police siren wail away on Douglas Road. I listened to the creaks and moans of the old house.

I was thinking about Amy.

We should have been on the same side. Amy felt guilty about telling her sister that dear old stepmom planned a religious intervention, prompting Krista to run away. I felt guilty for delivering Krista into the lion's den. Being fired meant little. I needed to find Krista Larkin for myself, as much as for Amy.

I considered for the hundredth time the actions—or inactions—of Alex Castiel. Why was he protecting a scumbag like Charlie Ziegler? What did he get out of it? I'm not naive. I know how the game is played downtown where power and money form an unholy alliance. But I've been pals with Alex a long time and, until now, I'd never seen anything to make me think he was dishonest. Ambitious, yes. Corrupt, no.

I got out of bed and padded barefoot to the kitchen. I was wearing my nighttime fashion statement, ancient Miami Dolphins boxer shorts, with the logo of Flipper leaping through hoops. I pulled a liter bottle of Jack Daniel's from the cupboard. Poured three fingers in a glass. Lassiter-size fingers, including two broken knuckles. Skipped the ice.

Went back to the bedroom, tucked myself in. I heard more nighttime sounds. Crickets or some other clickety-clack insects outside. A car engine on my street. Then I must have dozed off.

An hour later, or maybe it was five seconds, Csonka started barking. Sometimes he howls at the possum who climbs into my garbage can. Sometimes at the green parrots who escaped from the zoo during a hurricane. And sometimes he turns guard dog. Once, he captured some sky-high tweaker who pried open the jalousie windows of a rear bathroom and foolishly crawled inside. I had to pull the beast off the guy's butt.

Now I heard Csonka's claws scratching at the terrazzo as he scrambled down the corridor to my bedroom. He slid around the corner, propped his forelegs on my bed, wailed, and slobbered on me.

I got out of bed and followed Csonka down the corridor. I checked Kip's bedroom first. Sound asleep. I could hear Granny's snoring from outside her door. After her bedtime coffee cup filled with what she called "rye likker," the woman could sleep through a squall on a dinghy.

Outside, a car engine was starting up. I headed for the foyer and found the front door open a foot or so. I grabbed a baseball bat from an umbrella stand and barreled outside. Moonless night. Lights off, the car was already moving toward the intersection of Douglas Road. I couldn't see the driver. I couldn't even tell the car's make or model. It screeched around the corner, heading north toward Dixie Highway, and I stood there in my boxers, holding my baseball bat, watching Csonka take a leak against the chinaberry tree. After a moment, I lowered my shorts and did the same.

27 No One Breaks *Into* the Grand Jury

The next morning, I drove north on Dixie Highway, headed to the office. On the radio, Leonard Cohen was complaining that there "ain't no cure for love."

I'd walked around the street, asking a couple neighbors if they'd seen anyone lurking in the hibiscus hedges during the night. But no one had. So who the hell had it been? A random intruder or someone with a connection to Krista's case?

As I pulled onto I-95, I noticed a gray Hummer H2 behind me. Big as a battleship, it would have been hard to miss. I'd already seen it on Sunset Drive earlier this morning when I stopped at a bakery for coffee and a *pastelito de guayaba*.

Was I getting paranoid? First the Escalade owned by a guy in prison. And now this behemoth? Made as much sense as tailing someone in a Rose Bowl float.

I stayed in the right-hand lane in order to take the exit for the flyover to the MacArthur Causeway. The Hummer was directly behind me.

I was looking in the rearview mirror, trying to make out the driver's face, when my cell phone rang.

"Jake, get your ass over to the Grand Jury chambers now!" Castiel's voice.

"You've changed your mind? You're bringing Amy's case up?"

"Your crazy client just chained herself to the door. If you don't get her out of here, I'm gonna have her arrested."

I swung left out of the exit lane, barely missing the sand-filled barricades. The Hummer braked but couldn't make the turn

Lost you, pal. Whoever the hell you are.

Twenty-three citizens, good and true, make up the Grand Jury. They hear evidence presented by the State Attorney and render an indictment if they determine there is probable cause that a suspect committed a crime. It takes fourteen votes to indict, and the jurors usually do whatever the prosecutor tells them to. It's an old expression, but still true: a Grand Jury will indict a ham sandwich. Not, however, if the State Attorney fails to bring the meat and bread to their chambers.

The jurors gather in the civil courthouse downtown, an eighty-year-old limestone tower shaped like a wedding cake topped by a pyramid. In the winter, turkey buzzards circle the parapet near the peak of the building, inspiring jokes about predators in feathers above and Armani below. A colorful mural of old Florida is painted on the ceiling of the lobby. Who knew that Native American tribes were overjoyed to find Spanish sailors with muskets landing on the beaches?

I hopped into a balky elevator, surrounded by a passel of lawyers. They were jabbering about prosecutors who cheated, judges who fell asleep, and clients who don't pay their bills. Lawyers are great whiners.

I heard the commotion as I stepped into the corridor near the door to the Grand Jury chambers. A woman shouting.

"The State Attorney is corrupt! Can you hear me in there?"

A man shouting back, "Quiet down, now!"

The woman was a frantic Amy Larkin.

The man was a pissed-off Miami cop.

Three other cops formed a bulwark between them and the passersby in the corridor. One more guy in uniform and they'd have enough for a basketball team. That's the thing about cops. They travel in flocks, like the buzzards. On the floor were a pair of busted handcuffs and a three-foot-long bolt cutter. Amy had cuffed herself to the door. The cops had snapped off the cuffs, but now Amy was staging a one woman sit-in.

"Investigate!" Amy chanted. "Investigate! Investigate!"

Castiel came up behind me. "You've got exactly thirty seconds to get her out of here or she's going to jail."

"Amy, c'mon, let's go," I said, shouldering my way through the phalanx of cops. She was sitting cross-legged, arms folded across her chest, her back against the wall. A Gandhi pose, daring the constabulary to pick her up and carry her out.

"I want to testify. Testify!"

"I swear I'll have her Baker-acted," Castiel said. "Lock her in the loony bin."

"Amy, c'mon," I said. "No one breaks *into* the Grand Jury."

"Where is justice? Where is justice for my sister?"

"Amy, it's over," I said. "You made your point."

"Charlie Ziegler killed Krista! If you won't do something about it, I will."

"All right, enough," the first cop said, taking a step toward her.

I held up a hand, like a guard at an intersection. "Just a few seconds, okay?"

He swatted my hand away, and without my telling it to, my arm shot out, and I grabbed his wrist. He didn't pull away. He just looked at me. Hard. The look seemed to come naturally. He was three inches shorter than me but just as heavy, with a body builder's torso. A lot of cops are into steroids and HGH, and this guy made Barry Bonds look puny.

"You don't lay a hand on a peace officer," he said.

I let go of his wrist but stayed put between him and Amy.

"Peace officer? Who the fuck are you, John Wayne?"

"And you don't use profanity in a public building."

"Fine. Let's go outside. But let me get her out of here first."

"We're taking her in. She's refusing a lawful instruction by a peace officer."

Peace officer, again. Going all *True Grit* on me.

"I'm only going to ask you once, sir." His voice cranked up a notch. "Move!"

" 'Move' is not a question."

"Jake, you're crazier than your client. Do what he says." Castiel crashing our party.

"Amy, please come with me or we're both going to jail," I said.

"Miami cops are dirty!" she shouted.

"That's it," the beefy cop said. He pushed me aside, and I pushed him back. Which is when two of his pals slammed me, face-first, against the wall. Another grabbed my right arm and twisted it behind my back. A fourth cop, with nothing else to do, twisted my left arm to meet my right. That sent a lightning bolt through my shoulder. I'd had rotator cuff surgery back in my playing days, and the joint still bothers me when I do something foolish like hail a cab, shoot the bird, or get shackled.

The cops tried to get their handcuffs off their belts, which resulted in a jangling that resembled a bell choir. That gave me the chance to wrestle one arm free. Hercules unbound, I wheeled around, and the first cop zapped me in the chest with his Taser.

My knees turned to jelly, but I didn't fall. The second blast made me claw the air, searching for something to grab on to. I hit the floor, my legs splayed, my feet twitching. My ears were humming with static, so I barely heard Castiel. "Wrong way, Lassiter. Wrong way, again."

28 The Pork Barn

Charlie Ziegler did not want to be on a porn set. He'd made his movies, done his blow, banged his girls, and was smart enough to bail out when amateur video hit the market, and every kid with a Wal-Mart camera and an uninhibited girlfriend became a porn director. Doubly smart, because he sold the production end of the business for a bundle, while hanging on to the library and the low-overhead, high-profit distribution network.

Today, Ziegler drove to a dingy warehouse in the crotch of pavement where the turnpike met I-95. Once it had been his production office and soundstage. Today he came to see Leonard "Lens" Newsome, the finest porn cinematographer who ever lived. The man could make a pop shot—spouting beads of jism—look like the Trevi Fountain.

Lens had called last night.

"Some old shit's hit the fan, Charlie, and I don't wanna talk about it on the phone."

Which is what brought Ziegler to the pork barn on a stormy afternoon when he should have been casting *Texaz Hold 'Em & Strip 'Em*, a TV game show based on strip poker.

Much was still familiar. The crew dragging equipment carts, wheels clacking across concrete slabs. The smell of sawdust and fresh paint. Cables snaking along the floor, lights blazing, a makeshift dressing room with lighted mirrors, the girls pasting on their eyelashes. A metallic, air-conditioned chill in the air, goose bumps everywhere, nipples poking through flimsy lingerie.

Some things had changed, Ziegler knew. OSHA inspections, condoms, accounting departments with payroll deductions for taxes. Taxes! The party had become a business.

The crew looked younger, but maybe he had gotten older. Unshaven kids, earbuds plugged into their iPods, zoning out on the latest shit music.

Today's set was a bedroom—big surprise—propped up on a platform of two-by-fours. Klieg lights were just clicking off, a sizzle in the air. Leonard Newsome bent over awkwardly and struggled getting down from the platform. A touch of arthritis, maybe. His beard had gone silver, his thin hair tied back in a ponytail.

Time, Ziegler thought, is a ball-busting mistress who will bend your body and break your will.

"Lens, how they hanging?"

"Lemme buy you some coffee, Charlie." Newsome directed him to what passed for a craft service table. A sheet of plywood balanced on two sawhorses. A stained coffeemaker and a basket of pretzels. Two actresses in thongs and open bathrobes were sipping coffee and whining about an actor with a bent penis.

"Like it wants to sneak around the corner, but I don't have a corner."

"I know him," the other one said. "They call him 'Roto Rooter.'"

"Girls, why doncha go out for a smoke?" Leonard told them.

"Smoke? Do I look like I'd put a cigarette in my mouth?"

Lens rolled his eyes but kept quiet. The girls took off, shooting dirty looks at the men.

"What's up, Lens?" Ziegler poured himself some coffee that could flush a clogged drain.

"A woman showed up at my condo yesterday asking about a girl from the old days."

"Amy Larkin, looking for her sister?"

Lens nodded. "I was playing pinochle in the card room. I don't even know how she found me."

"The woman's an insurance investigator, Lens. She's not stupid."

"No shit. She asked what I remembered about Krista."

"What'd you say?"

"Told her, too many years. Too many girls."

"Thanks, Lens."

"Hell, it's damn near true. I hardly remember any of them unless they gave me a dose."

"What else she want to know?"

"That's where it got hairy. Wondered if you ever shot snuff films."

"Jesus."

"Told her, hell, no, not your style. Asked if I ever went to your house for parties, and I said sure. Asked who else was there, and I said I'm just a photographer. I don't see anything that's not in the lens."

"That end it?"

"She wanted to look at all the old films and videos, track down actors who worked with her sister. I told her there were a couple thousand titles and no one ever used their real names. It'd be like looking for a pubic hair in a haystack."

All Lassiter's fault, Ziegler thought. Giving the woman hope, stirring her up.

How the hell can I put a stop to it?

"I'd watch out for this woman, Charlie."

"Whadaya mean?"

"You remember Kandy Kane, Charlie?"

Ziegler cracked a smile, thinking about the day Kandy bit into Rex Hung's scrotum and spit out a testicle. It was Rex's fault, slipping it in her back door when Kandy's contract specifically forbade it. "Sure, I remember Kandy. So does One Nut Hung."

"I was looking through the lens at Kandy, just a second before she chomped old Rex. Same look on Amy Larkin's face when she mentioned your name."

Ziegler was processing that when he heard his name called, as if being paged in a hotel lobby. "Charles W. Ziegler!"

A short, trim man with a set of headphones draped around his neck approached.

"What the fuck are you doing on my set?" Rodney Gifford demanded.

The guy had directed most of the Charlie's Girlz videos and was as miserable a prick as ever told an actress to spread wider and moan louder. A dozen years ago, Gifford had bought Ziegler out, wildly overpaying for the studio. Instead of blaming his own stupid-ass self, he carried a grudge against Ziegler.

"Relax, Gifford. I come in peace."

The director waltzed over to confront him. "Closed set, Ziegler!" Raising his voice to impress the crew.

"Why, you shooting *The Da Vinci Code*?"

Gifford seethed. "You never understood the craft."

"What's to understand? Suck, fuck, and pop." Charlie looked to the growing crowd for agreement. "Your problem is, you complicate everything."

Gifford was dressed as if Calvin Klein might pop in and ask him to pose for an ad. Even now, at fifty-something, he played the role of preppie with an artistic bent. Pleated khaki pants, loafers without socks, a black silk shirt, tinted glasses, and that exaggerated glide in his stride.

Gifford had gone to film school and thought he was Ingmar Bergman. His interiors always had odd angles, quick cuts, and shadowy lighting, when all the whackers wanted were brightly lit close-ups of winking twats. "Off my set, Ziegler." Gifford pointed to the door.

"I'm leaving, Gifford. Only came by to say hello to an old friend, and that ain't you."

"Bullshit. I know why you're here. It's that Larkin woman asking questions." Gifford smiled maliciously, his teeth bleached as white as a porcelain toilet. "You can't bury your past, Ziegler."

"What do you know about it?"

"I got a call yesterday from an Amy Larkin. Ever hear of her?"

"What's your point?"

"Enterprising woman. She got my unlisted home number. Asked me to lunch."

"So?"

"I had the salad nicoise. Want to know what we talked about?"

"Fuck you, Gifford." Ziegler wouldn't give the prick the satisfaction of asking.

"The woman thinks you're scum, Charlie. I applaud her good taste."

"Fuck you twice."

Most of the crew were paying attention now. A topless Lolita type in a plaid cheerleader's skirt put down her book—*Sudoku for Dummies*—and watched the two men.

"Maybe I should have told her what I know," Gifford said, in a teasing tone.

"You don't know shit."

Gifford moved closer and whispered, his breath smelling of coffee and peppermints. "I was at your house that night, Ziegler. I know exactly what happened to Krista Larkin."

29 Boy Meets Punching Bag

Granny was preparing chicken-fried steaks and yammering about the money I owed her for posting my bail. I was not hungry. Maybe because I'm not partial to beef dipped in milk and eggs and then fried. Maybe because I was worried about Amy.

"Exactly what did she say to you?" I asked.

"Told you three times. I bailed her out of the Women's Annex before I got you. Figured you're more used to jail than she is. She said she'd be over for dinner because she favored my cooking."

"That's it?"

"She said to thank you for everything."

"Jeez, Granny. You didn't tell me that before."

"So?"

"It sounds like good-bye."

I tried calling Amy, got her voicemail.

"You gonna mash those taters, or do I have to do everything around here?" Granny said.

I picked up the masher and went to work. I heard the front door open and called out Amy's name. But it was Kip, shuffling into the kitchen, sniffing around the stove. "Chicken-fried steak again. Jeez."

"Wash up," Granny said.

"I'd rather have meat loaf wrapped in bacon."

"And hush up." Granny never took backtalk from me and wasn't going to start with my nephew.

"You make a rhubarb pie, Granny?"

"Didn't have time, and if you want to know why, ask your jailbird uncle."

Kip turned to me, and I saw the shiner, a purple welt under his eye.

Shit. Not again.

"Carl Kountz?" I asked him.

"Baseball practice. He clocked me at second base on a force out."

"Clean play?"

"Not really. He didn't bother to slide."

"You have words with him?"

"I told him to lay off, and when the coach wasn't looking, he hit me again. Hard."

"Granny, don't put those beefsteaks in the frying pan just yet," I said. "Kip and I are gonna hit the bag for a bit."

It was the third time we'd worked on kickboxing. For a skinny kid, Kip had a snappy left, and his right cross was coming along. I gave him an up-from-under bolo punch because he thought it was fun. Then we worked on front and side kicks. He was a quick learner. Coordinating the punches and kicks into a smooth rhythm would take longer.

Csonka lay in the grass, licking his balls, then watching us a moment, then licking his balls again. Priorities.

I told Kip to speed up his combinations. Sweat dribbled down his face, and the *pop-pop* of leather against bag became louder, the timing more consistent. We were twenty minutes into it when my cell phone rang. It had to be Amy.

But it wasn't.

"Lassiter, you like sushi?" Charlie Ziegler said.

"More than chicken-fried steak. Why you asking?"

"I'm inviting you to dinner. The gentlemanly way. No Ray Decker, no armed escort. Just come on over for sake and sushi."

Thunder boomed to the west, and the first flashes of lightning crackled the night sky. The wind picked up. Kip kept on punching and kicking.

"Why?"

"Castiel told me what happened today outside the Grand Jury. If a reporter had been there, it would be bad publicity for both of us."

"For you, maybe. A lawyer who goes to jail for his clients is a hot commodity."

"Don't be a dick, Lassiter. I'm making peace here."

"Yeah?"

"I haven't been totally honest with you."

Fat, warm raindrops pelted me.

"I want to make this right," Ziegler said. "I want to tell you everything."

30 Plan One, the Gun

Wind gusts drove the rain sideways, stinging Amy's face. She retreated from the pallet of rebar into the unfinished house. From there, she could still keep watch on Charlie Ziegler's mansion next door. A modernistic three-story structure of interconnected tubes with a metallic skin, the mansion resembled a ship at sea. How many millions did he spend on the place, money grubbed from the oppression of young women? God, how she hated the man.

She had come here as soon as she'd been released from jail. Two nights ago, she had sneaked onto his patio and crept right up to the windows, checking out the security. No cameras, no dogs, no guards. She had peered through the floor-to-ceiling glass of the solarium and watched Ziegler watering his flowers.

Orchids!

Orchids and Ziegler. Like a diamond necklace on a hog.

She pressed her face to the window. She was so close to the man who murdered her sister she could hear him whistling to himself. His day of reckoning was near, she thought. She sneaked back through a row of shrubs, razor-sharp leaves piercing her unitard and drawing blood from her thigh.

Amy knew she had gone off the deep end today. Snapped. She hadn't planned the stunt at the Grand Jury chambers. The actions just exploded from her without premeditation or planning.

Out of control. So not me.

When Lassiter seemed to be making progress, she'd put away the pistol. She had let him try to work the system. But the State Attorney, supposedly his friend, was in Charlie Ziegler's pocket. Sure, Lassiter had fought for her and had been Tasered, cuffed, and arrested for his effort. He'd proved his valor but also his weakness. He was outmanned and outgunned. Ziegler was too well connected.

And he's guilty! Why else would he be going to these lengths to stop us?

Lassiter had been leaving messages all afternoon on her cell. A new strategy, something about a statewide police agency. She should give him one more chance. If he failed—finally and unequivocally—she could always go back to Plan One.

The gun.

The Sig Sauer lay waiting, deep in her suitcase, back at the motel. She had fantasized about walking straight up to Ziegler and jamming the barrel into his forehead. Turn his skull into splinters, his brain into mush. Then maybe—she wasn't sure yet—taking a second shot, into her own temple.

Yes, Dr. Blasingame, I do have suicidal ideations.

A lightning bolt crackled the sky and hit the bay, the *boom* echoing across the open water. She was soaked through to the skin, but not cold. The rain was warm as blood. She dug into her straw bag, found a pack of Winstons and lit up. Smoking again. What would her shrink say?

"You have an addictive personality, Amy."

Yeah, just like Krista. Addicted to drugs and danger.

"At some level, you blame your sister for your own troubles," Dr. Blasingame had told her. *"But you love her and that causes dissonance."*

The shrink said she suffered from post-traumatic embitterment disorder with paranoid tendencies. It was similar to a stress disorder, but instead of fears and anxiety, she burned with anger and hatred.

"You're seething with thoughts of revenge, Amy."

So? Someone kills your sister, embitterment and revenge sound pretty damn rational.

Another lightning bolt struck, this one over land. The thunderclap shook the unfinished walls. She heard car tires squishing on the street, saw the glow of headlights cutting through the rain. There had been no traffic for the last half hour, except a big gray Hummer. A mammoth gas-guzzler, but maybe perfect for a night like this. The Hummer had gone around the block twice, then disappeared. She squinted through the rain and saw this was a different car, slowing as it approached Ziegler's house. For a moment, it looked like Lassiter's ridiculous old Cadillac convertible.

The car pulled into Ziegler's driveway.

No, it can't be!

Amy crept up to the construction fence to get a better look, the rain soaking her. She watched the driver get out of the cream-colored Eldorado, his face lit by a street lamp.

Jake Lassiter.

She watched as he walked to the front door and rang the bell.

How can this be happening?

The door opened, and she saw the silhouette of Ziegler's blocky torso. Lassiter went inside and the door closed.

She felt sick to her stomach. Anger tightened every muscle.

Jake, you bastard! You lying bastard!

Ziegler and Perlow. Castiel and Lassiter. *All* of them against her!

She clawed at the chain-link fence with both hands, wishing she had not left her father's pistol in the motel room.

31 A Question of Redemption

The rain drilled the Eldo's canvas top with such ferocity I could barely hear "My Hometown," Springsteen's ode to a boarded-up burg. I was on my way to Gables Estates to eat sushi with Charlie Ziegler. Given a choice, I prefer chowing down with someone I like. But on this rainy night, I couldn't pass up Ziegler's invitation.

I would listen to Charlie Ziegler and maybe drink some sake, too. The windshield wipers on my old bucket of bolts could hardly keep up with the storm. Casuarina Concourse was deluged, the pavement and bay merging into one gray sheet of water. Next door to Ziegler's manse, a house was under construction, a river of mud flowing from the site into the street. Some older houses in the neighborhood were Southern plantation style, all white pillars, circular driveways, and large porticos. Ziegler's post-modern, silver-skinned monstrosity was too hip to have a portico, so I got soaked getting from the car to the front door.

"Thanks for coming." Ziegler guided me inside. "C'mon. Let's eat while we talk."

Ziegler appeared relaxed in soft leather loafers without socks, canary blue slacks, and a knit short-sleeve shirt that had an expensive, Italian look. He said his wife was in Paris, a suite at George V, spending all his money and screwing the concierge.

On a monitor set into the wall, a videotape was playing. Four old men in tattered clothes were beating the crap out of one another with broom handles and garbage can lids. The logo on the screen read: "Bumzfight Revenge." One of Reelz TV's classy hits.

He led me into the bar, located in the high-ceilinged living room. Not a *bar* bar. A sushi bar, complete with bamboo mats, lacquered sake cups, and silk paintings of lotus flowers. Behind the bar was an attractive Asian woman in a white smock and red apron.

"Miyoshi's the best *itamae* in Miami," he said.

She nodded at me while slicing tuna with a Masamoto knife sharp enough to shave a cat's whiskers without causing a meow. "I haven't killed anyone yet." She smiled.

"The night is young," I replied.

I heard the *clack* of high heels on marble. The six-footer who called herself Angel Roxx walked into the room, tousling her platinum hair, looking as if she just woke up. Black stilettos, a skin-tight mini-skirt, a peekaboo sheer blouse, and nothing else, unless you count the silicone in those cantaloupes.

"Hi, big guy," she said to me. "Still don't want to play?"

"I'm off the team," I said.

"Get dressed and go home," Ziegler ordered.

"Charlie, it's a fucking hurricane out there." Pouting.

"Scram!"

Angel shot him the bird and clacked off.

Ziegler turned to the sushi chef. "Miyoshi, how about offering my guest a special treat?"

The chef grabbed a short knife with a porcelain blade and, with three brisk strokes, sharpened a wooden chopstick to a fine point. She jabbed the chopstick into a small aquarium, aiming for a plug-ugly five-inch-long fish that was minding its own business. She speared the little monster, which glowed red, as if it had just escaped a nuclear power plant.

"Scorpion fish," Ziegler said, as the chef offered the little wriggler to me.

"No thanks," I said. Raw is one thing, alive is another.

Ziegler sucked the creature into his mouth, swallowing it in one gulp.

He cleared his throat and said, "I like to feel its heartbeat in my gullet on the way down."

Message received.

You're an alpha male who drives a Ferrari, fucks porn stars, and eats living creatures. You've got testosterone oozing out your pores.

Miyoshi cut slivers of tuna, then eel, then mackerel, before picking up the bamboo mat to make rolls with roe, natto, and the dreaded sea urchin. She had the hands of a concert pianist.

"Do you believe in redemption, Lassiter?" Ziegler asked.

"Depends on the sin."

Ziegler grunted his agreement and dropped a slice of eel into his maw. "I'm trying to make things right. I'm not proud of the shit I did when I was young."

Who is? I thought.

He poured sake for both of us, "This is a daiginjo from the Yamagata Prefecture, made from a pure breed of rice. It costs five hundred bucks a bottle."

As if I give a shit.

"She was really something, wasn't she, Lassiter?"

"What? Who?"

"Krista!"

"I knew her for about twelve hours."

"That's long enough." He gave me a shit-eating grin. Maybe he wanted to bond over our banging the same girl.

"What's your point, Ziegler?"

"Krista went straight to the top of the Lolita series, making serious bank. She was a natural in front of the camera. Totally comfortable from day one. Smart. Intuitive. If you showed her a position once, she could do it. Standing bridesmaid, dirty doggie, wheelbarrow, even triple penetrations. She could do them all. Even liked most of them."

"That's bullshit. I watched one of your videos. Krista looked lobotomized."

"Bad day, is all. Trust me on this. She was into it. She could have been bigger than Jenna Jameson."

I figured he was rationalizing. Reducing his own guilt by rewriting history. "I didn't come here to discuss Krista's acting skills. Just tell me what happened that night."

He sipped the sake and said, "Miyoshi, why don't you take a break?"

When she had left the room, Ziegler continued. "A couple months before she went missing, Krista started hanging out with a biker who called himself 'Snake.' "

I already knew that from Sonia Majeski, but I kept quiet to see where Ziegler was going.

"Bastard got her hooked on crystal meth. Her first bump, that was it. I tried to keep her away from the guy, but he must have seemed exciting to her, while I was . . ."

"Old?"

"Yeah, to a seventeen-year-old, I was."

"You're saying she was with Snake the night she disappeared."

"Like I told you before, she was on the set that day. While we were talking, Snake came by on his Harley. He'd been slamming crank. The cops had a warrant for him. Some probation violation. He said he had to leave town."

"Krista left with him? That's your story?"

"I told her not to go. Yelled at her, maybe even grabbed her a little too hard. Told her Snake would sell her for a handful of bennies or drive off a bridge somewhere. She wouldn't listen."

"She say where they were going?"

"California, like all the dreamers. When it was clear I couldn't stop her, I gave her some cash plus the names of a couple guys in the business in the San Fernando Valley."

I couldn't help but think of myself, giving Krista a few hundred bucks and sending her back to Ziegler. I didn't like the parallel.

"I told her to call when she got there," Ziegler said, draining his sake and looking at me with forlorn eyes. "I never saw Krista or heard from her again. She never contacted my guys out there, either. I checked."

I studied him a moment, using my bullshit detector. Figuring Ziegler lied so often, he was world class. "Why didn't you tell the cops that Krista rode into the sunset with the biker?"

He refilled my cup with what I calculated to be about $85 worth of sake. "Anytime she wanted, Krista could have caused trouble for me. You're gonna think I'm a dick for saying this . . ."

"Too late."

"Last thing I wanted was for the two of them to get picked up somewhere with thirty pounds of crank in Snake's saddlebags. They'd swing some deal, get immunity for nailing me. Statutory rape. Child porn. Racketeering. To be honest, Lassiter, it was in my interest for the two of them to disappear."

The story was plausible, but most good lies are. "This Snake have a real name?"

"Aldrin, like the astronaut. Can't remember his first name, but you can check with the Corrections Department. He's the kind of guy who's either in prison or in between prisons."

Or dead, I thought. Along with whoever is foolish enough to hop on a bike with him and head west.

"Looking back now, I've got a lot of remorse," Ziegler said, "and I've been thinking about how to make it right."

"Yeah?"

"How about if I set up a missing persons fund? I'll pay your client a hundred grand. She can do whatever she wants with it. Look for Aldrin. Take ads on craigslist. Or go back to Ohio and get on with her life."

Buying redemption, I thought, just like his charitable contributions. Or just paying Amy to go away. Either way, he'd be off the hook.

Ziegler drained the last of the sake from the Yamagata Prefecture. "I'll cover your legal fees, too. How does thirty grand sound?"

"Like a bribe, and not a very big one."

"C'mon, Lassiter. I'm trying to help you both out."

"You just want me off your ass."

"You want my honest opinion?"

"If it's not too much trouble."

"I don't know if Snake killed her or she O.D.'d or got hit by a truck outside Amarillo," Ziegler said. "But if she'd gotten back into the business, I'd have heard about it. If she was broke and in trouble, she would have called me for help. If she was doing okay, at some point, she would have called her sister."

"What you're saying, there's no use our searching for her."

Ziegler looked off into space, and I could swear I saw tears welling. "The more I've thought about it, Lassiter, the more certain I've become. Krista's dead. Has to be. But I swear to God I didn't have anything to do with it."

I studied him for a long moment. Maybe I'd lost my edge, but the son-of-a-bitch looked for all the world like a man telling the truth.

32 The Missing Client

I left Ziegler's house around midnight. I wanted to tell Amy we had a lead on Snake Aldrin, so I risked waking her, but no answer. We hadn't spoken since the cops hauled us away from the Grand Jury, and I was worried.

Where the hell is she?

The rain had stopped and the asphalt shimmered like polished obsidian in the glow of the streetlights. I banged the front door open and walked into my dark house. I heard snoring from Granny's bedroom. Csonka lay on the living room tile, under a ceiling fan. He was snoring, too, hind legs twitching. Probably dreaming of chasing a lady bulldog through Bayfront Park.

A *smack-smack-thud* was coming from the backyard. I sneaked a peek and saw Kip, hitting the heavy bag. Rapid-fire combinations. Punch-punch-kick. Harder and faster than earlier in the evening. One flurry after another, matchstick arms lathered in sweat. Furious in his intensity. Watching him, I felt waves of heat inside me. I guess that's what unbridled love feels like.

I wasn't about to order him to go to bed. Let him be tired and sore tomorrow. Let him carry some self-confidence to school along with his algebra book.

I tried Amy's cell early the next morning, but the call went directly to voicemail. I thought about Ziegler's offer. Would Amy ask my opinion? I didn't want her to take the money and run. I wanted a stab at finding Snake, now that we had his real name. But was I able to give solid advice? Years ago, I'd failed Krista. Maybe now I was trying too hard to make it up to her sister.

The spicy aroma of carne asada greeted me as I walked up the stairs to my office. Jorge was already preparing lunch at Havana Banana. I sneaked past Cindy while she was on the phone, arguing with the repairman who could not seem to find parts for my black-and-white Edsel of a photocopy machine.

Still no return call, so I rang the motel on South Dixie Highway where Amy was staying.

"Checked out early this morning." The male desk clerk spoke with a backwoods twang.

"You sure?" I sensed trouble the way seabirds sense an oncoming storm.

"Tall, pretty girl. One suitcase. Paid cash."

"Did she leave a message for Jake Lassiter?"

"No messages. No smiles. Bit of a hurry."

"No forwarding address?"

"Ain't the post office. She was driving a car with Ohio plates, if that helps."

"Yeah, I know."

" 'Birthplace of Aviation.' "

"What?"

"On the plates. The Ohio slogan."

"Right."

" 'Open for Business.' That's West Virginia." I heard him chuckle. "I see a lot of states passing through here."

The clerk rambled on about the Ocean State, the Elevated State, and the Garden State while I tried to process the information about Amy.

Where did she go? Why won't she return my calls?

"When she paid the bill, did she say anything at all?" I asked.

"Sure, she asked for directions."

"What! Why didn't you say so?"

"You didn't ask."

"Where? Where'd she want to go?"

"Shooting range. She asked where she could go for target practice."

33 Target Practice

With the top down on my old buggy, tiny black gnats were dying squishy deaths, plastered against my face and ears. I kept the needle at 75, roaring west on Tamiami Trail. I was headed to the Trail Glades Range to catch up with Amy. I considered just why she wanted to take target practice, and every possible scenario ended with Charlie Ziegler facedown in a pool of blood.

I floored the accelerator, and my old warhorse responded, albeit two seconds after spurs had been applied to horseflesh. I passed squat one-story strip malls, with their discount dentists, pedicurists, and dog kennels. Two egrets flying overhead were reminders that we were in the Everglades, or what *used to be* the 'Glades, before draining and filling. Now, ticky-tack housing developments moved farther from the city and deeper into the wetlands.

The air was heavy with moisture, the heat stifling. No hint of the beach breeze just twenty-five miles to the east. Traffic was light. Thanks to the desk clerk, I couldn't stop looking for out-of-state plates. "Home on the Range" from Kansas, "Live Free or Die" from New Hampshire, "Land of Enchantment" from New Mexico.

The C.D. player was turned up full blast, Tom Russell singing "Tonight We Ride" over the wail of the wind.

"We'll skin ole Pancho Villa, make chaps out of his hide."

A tale of good-natured violence, the song speaks longingly of scalping, whoring, rustling, and robbery. Needless to say, it's one of my favorites.

About a mile from the range, I caught sight of an old Chevy Impala with whitewall gangsta tires, Superfly headlights, and a purple, metalflake paint job. Hard to miss, especially since I'd seen it pull onto the MacArthur Causeway behind me back on South Beach.

I hit the brakes and slid into a gas station. The Impala sailed past me, and I tore out after it. Within moments, we were both doing 85 on the straight stretch of pavement that heads into the slough and all the way to Naples. I got close enough to make out the Florida plate—Sunshine State—picked up a pen, and scribbled the number on my arm.

That made three different cars tailing me. The Escalade was owned by a federal inmate. I never got the plate number of the Hummer, and now a souped-up Impala. It made no sense.

I slowed just before Krome Avenue, the old Eldo kicking up a plume of dust as I skidded into the parking lot of the gun range. The Impala kept going west.

I parked next to a black sedan and vaulted out of my car without opening the door, just the way Magnum, P.I., used to do. I could hear the *pop-pop* of small-arms fire, a dozen different calibers, loud enough to simulate combat.

Once inside the clubhouse, I scanned the outdoor range through a large window. There were only a handful of shooters.

Amy Larkin stood at a shooting station, staring at a target that had been set about twenty-five feet away. She held a small gun in a two-handed grip, knees slightly bent, ear protectors in place. She fired. Waited. Fired again. From this distance, I couldn't tell if she'd punched a bull's-eye or winged an egret flying over the slough. She was taking her time. Five or six seconds between shots.

"You the husband?"

I turned. The man had a graying brush cut and a big body. His polo shirt's logo said, *"Range Master."*

"Come again?"

"Calamity Jane out there." The man pointed at Amy, who reset her feet and fired another shot.

"No. Why?"

"Boyfriend, then?"

"What's it to you?"

The guy folded his arms across his chest. I figured him for an ex-cop who missed the work. "When a woman looks like she's been crying all night and starts taking target practice first thing in the morning, it usually means she caught her man cheating. If he shows up, well, that's when I intervene."

"I'm her lawyer."

He studied me a second, and I must have passed his cop's lie-detector test. "Tell her not to try and shoot anyone. She can't hit shit, anyway."

I looked up and saw Amy zipping her gun into a nylon pouch. In a moment, she was headed along the path to the parking lot. I headed out to meet her.

When I approached, she was standing behind my Eldo ragtop, staring at my personalized license plate: JUSTICE?

Yeah. With a question mark. I'm not nearly as sure of things as I used to be.

"Amy, what's going on?"

She turned to face me. "Are you asking as my lawyer or Ziegler's?"

"What's that supposed to mean?"

"Where were you last night?"

Sounding like the cheated-on spouse the range master imagined. "At Charlie Ziegler's, but I think you know that. Were you following me or spying on him?"

"How much did Ziegler pay you to sell me out?"

"He offered thirty thousand."

"Cheap," she said.

"That's what I thought." I told her the rest. One hundred thousand dollars if she wanted to close up shop and go home.

"What's he paying you under the table to get me to go along?" Her eyes had gone cold.

"Nothing. And you can have my thirty thousand, too."

"How can I believe you when you're working for Ziegler now?"

"I went there to learn whatever I could. For you. He denied killing Krista and made the offer."

"And now he's waiting for my answer?"

I nodded.

She whipped out the gun, a little Sig Sauer. "Tell him this." She steadied the pistol with both hands, then popped a shot into the meat of my car's left front tire. Maybe she was a shitty shot on the range, but from three feet, she was deadly. The tire wheezed in pain.

"I'll bet you have a spare," she said.

"I do."

Her arm jumping a bit, she put a shell into the right front tire, the gunshot lost in the echo of a hundred other rounds. My wounded Eldo now looking like Ben-Hur's chariot.

"Amy, please put the gun down."

She aimed at my gut, a wider target than those steel-belted radials.

"I don't know why I trusted you," she said. "I should have gone after Ziegler straight off."

"Don't do this. I've got half a dozen new ideas I haven't even discussed with you." In fact, I had one, but half a dozen seemed more promising.

"I'll bet."

"I've got Snake's real name. It's Aldrin. He could be the key to—"

"Too late, Jake. I'm done." She started backing up toward her car.

"The second you're out of sight, I'll call the cops."

"I'll bet you would. You wore a wire and ratted out a client once, didn't you?"

"What about your religious beliefs? 'Thou shalt not kill.'"

"Maybe I'm wrong and you're right. The universe is chaos. There's no all-seeing God to reward the just and punish the wicked."

Why'd she listen to me about that? *Nobody* listens to me.

"Let's go talk to someone, Amy. A counselor, maybe."

"A shrink, you mean. Isn't that what your friend Castiel threatened? Commit me to the loony bin. Are you all in this together?"

Her gun hand was trembling, her index finger still on the trigger. I measured the distance between us, figured two steps, then a leap to reach her.

"Try it, I'll shoot you in the face," she said, reading my mind.

With that, she fired a third shot, puncturing the right rear tire. The tire wheezed like a lung shot through-and-through, and I stayed frozen in place.

34 Ratting Out the Client

I watched Amy drive off in her Toyota with Ohio plates. Birthplace of Aviation, indeed.

I wanted to call 9-1-1.

But do I say she's armed and dangerous?

No way I could ask a cop to stop her without warning about her gun. But what then? A jittery cop, an unstable woman with a gun. Disaster.

The sun pounding me with waves of tropical heat, I took out my cell and dialed a number.

"You got an answer to my offer?" Ziegler said, when he came on the line.

"Yeah. Amy would rather empty a clip into your gut than take your money."

"What the fuck?"

"She's got a gun, Ziegler, and she might be headed your way. But I'm telling you right now, if you or Decker or anyone else harms her, I'm coming after you."

"Are you insane? She takes a pop at me, I got a right to take her out."

"Lots of things you can do short of that. Lock down your building. Block her car when she pulls into your garage. Or if she gets into the building, seal the elevator."

"This is what I get for trying to work with you? You fucked up big-time."

And here I thought I'd get a big thanks for warning him. There was a pause on the line before Ziegler said, "Where are you? What's all that noise?"

"The gun range on the Trail."

"Get your ass over here and keep your lunatic client away from me."

"I can't. I've got flat tires. Plural."

"That happens to you a lot, doesn't it, jerkoff?"

He hung up on me and I quickly dialed Castiel's private number.

The State Attorney calmly told me he would get Coral Gables P.D. to send a team to Ziegler's building. There'd be a hostage negotiator, someone to talk to Amy. No trigger-happy rookies. I thanked him, and he said he would also dispatch a county truck to tow my car. I thanked him again.

Then he told me off. "Dammit, Jake, I warned you. If anyone gets hurt, I'll hold you responsible."

This time, I didn't thank him. "You've got it ass-backwards, Alex. I handed you evidence, but you wouldn't do a thing. You wouldn't even ask the Miccosukee cops to dredge the canal. Amy smells cover-up, and so do I."

"Let it go, Jake. For fuck's sake, let it go."

"To hell with that. I'm calling Tallahassee. Let the A.G. investigate Ziegler and look up your butt while he's at it."

"Take your best shot, pal."

The phone clicked off and I stood there in the damp midday heat, cursing at my old friend. A mosquito buzzed around my neck, and I swatted the little bastard, squashing him, and leaving a speck of blood in the palm of my hand.

I slid back into my wounded car and pulled up the top to get out of the sun. The tow truck should be here soon. I keyed the ignition and turned on the A/C. Thank God for air-conditioning. If not for the know-how of Mr. Willis Carrier—a native of Buffalo!—South Florida would be unlivable. On the C.D. player, Bob Dylan delivered the problematic news that "beyond here lies nothin'," advising folks there's no reward in the Great Beyond.

After twenty minutes, I dozed off. I don't know how long I was out because the next thing I remember, the driver's door flew open.

I toppled half out of the Eldo. The other half was helped—none too gently—by Ray Decker.

"Hello, dickwad," he greeted me.

He hoisted me to my feet and I saw the blur of a fist a millisecond before it hit my jaw. I crumpled against the side of my car and slid to the ground. I could no longer hear the gunfire. Instead, the bells of Notre Dame Cathedral began peeling.

"Asshole!" Decker, standing over me.

I was neither brave enough nor stupid enough to try to stand while comets blazed across a night sky. Instead, I curled into the fetal position, sucked in air, and tried to clear my head.

Decker kicked me in the back. "That's for fucking up Charlie's car."

Another kick, near kidney land. "That one's for messing with me."

A third kick glanced off my tailbone. He didn't say what it was for.

The wallops were starting to lose their *whoompf.* Was Decker tired already? Big guys who seldom get outside don't do well in Miami.

I uncurled. Reached out, grabbed an ankle when Decker was in midkick with the other leg. I yanked hard and he toppled backwards, his head clunking off the trunk of my Eldo. A solid sound, courtesy of U.S. Steel and GM, when those names meant something.

Decker crumpled to the ground, as woozy as I was. We both got up slowly, intent on doing grievous damage to the other. I took a swing that he blocked. He swung and I ducked it. I was panting and Decker's face was as red as the three-ball in billiards. We circled each other, Decker with his fists like a boxer, me crouched like a linebacker.

"Where's your old Impala, Decker?" I asked, looking around the parking lot.

"The fuck you talking about?" He could barely get the words out.

"The purple Chevy. You were following me on the Trail."

"Not me, pal."

I saw the black Lincoln then, the car I'd hijacked from Decker that first day. So who the hell was in the Impala?

"You were at my house night before last. You took off when my dog started barking."

"You're hallucinating, Lassiter."

I didn't know if he was telling the truth. But if he was, who could it have been? Amy came to mind. She left angry at me. Did she come back and break in? But why?

Decker started toward me, tired of foreplay. I did the same, my hands ready to break bones.

"Freeze, both of you!"

On television, if someone shouts, "Freeze," he's always holding a gun. I looked up and saw the range master standing six feet away. Unarmed. But next to him were half a dozen men and one woman. All with guns, all holstered. This crew didn't need to brandish them. A couple of uniforms. Miami P.D. County sheriff. A man and a woman in plain clothes, guns shoulder-holstered. And a guy in a muffler shop T-shirt, a Western six-shooter strapped to his thigh, gunfighter style.

"I want you two jerks out of here!" the range master ordered. "No violence allowed at the shooting range."

35 The Fairy Godfather

Twenty-four hours after Amy shot out my tires and disappeared, I was sitting on the coral rock wall along Ocean Drive, near my office, wearing a bandage on my forehead.

Amy hadn't shown up at Ziegler's office. Or her old motel. Or my office. I tried calling her cell a dozen times. Nothing but voicemail.

An hour earlier, Alex Castiel had called with the non-news that police couldn't find Amy. He wanted to charge her with reckless display and discharge of a firearm. Would I cooperate? No, I would not. I wanted to get her into a therapist's office, not a jail cell.

I was eating my lunch. My jaw ached with each bite, and for once, I couldn't blame the stale bread Havana Banana used for its Cuban sandwiches. Ray Decker's boot prints were tattooed on my back. My ribs felt brittle as crystal stemware, and it hurt to swallow. A patch of skin from my forehead had been left on the pavement. I'd been blindsided by tight ends before, but this was more like a head-on with a sixteen-wheeler.

The beach was behind me, The Scene in front. The air smelled of coconut oil and car exhaust. Ocean Drive was wall-to-wall outdoor cafés where wannabe actors served tables with an air of boredom with their work and superiority to their clientele. The tourists arrived sunburned, the pasta arrived al dente, the margaritas arrived watery. Models zipped by on Rollerblades. Bodybuilders with shaved, lubed chests paraded shirtless. A flock of green parrots streaked overhead, squawking—or maybe laughing—at what they saw below.

"Ay, *bubee,* you should see a doctor. You look like *drek.*"

I swung stiffly toward the voice, feeling like Frankenstein. Max Perlow waddled toward me, his cane clicking the concrete. He wore a gray silk guayabera with twirled piping and fancy buttons that looked like ivory. A skinny-brimmed green fedora sat on his head. His pencil mustache looked freshly trimmed and waxed.

"Thanks, but I feel great," I lied.

He looked across Ocean Drive toward the bustling cafés and shops. "I love this neighborhood. Such life it's got! Wouldn't Meyer have loved to see the changes?" Perlow gestured with his cane toward the canyons along Collins Avenue. "Meyer lived just north of the Eden Roc. Modest little condo. I used to keep him company while he walked his dog." Perlow grinned at the memory. "Yappy little bastard he called 'Bruzzer.'"

I didn't invite him, but Perlow sat down next to me on the coral wall, doffing his fedora in a polite, outdated way. The hat had a jaunty orange feather, and I wondered if a nearsighted heron might try to mate with it.

"Alex tells me you're gonna ask the Attorney General to open an investigation."

"His relationship with Ziegler compromises his impartiality," I said. "So, yeah, I'm gonna rattle some cages in Tallahassee, see if I can get a team of FDLE agents down here. Turn over some rocks, maybe find some scorpions underneath."

"Innuendos about Alex would be damaging to his career."

"Not my concern."

He gave me a look through those drooping eyelids, but the eyes themselves burned hot.

"Walk with me, Mr. Lassiter. I need the exercise."

I followed him, tossing the rest of the sandwich into a trash can. In the street, a creamy white Bentley crept alongside us.

Perlow waved at the driver, a Hispanic man who filled a considerable portion of the front seat. "Go on, Nestor. Leave us." The car pulled away, quiet as diamonds dropping on velvet.

"Your bodyguard?"

"*Feh!* Why would I need protection? I'm an honest businessman." He gave me a little smile. "Of course, Nestor is excellent with a handgun. As good as Lucky Luciano's boys, and they could shoot."

A BMW convertible drove by, top down, C.D. player cranked up, as if the entire neighborhood was dying to listen to Bob Marley admit he'd shot the sheriff but spared the deputy.

"Where's your client?" Perlow asked.

"I don't know, and if I did, I wouldn't tell you."

"Are you not concerned, Mr. Lassiter? A neurotic woman threatened you with a gun."

"And you care because . . . ?"

"She also threatened my partner. That makes it my business."

"I'll find her, and I'll deal with her. I don't want you or your pistol-packing driver anywhere near her."

"If she comes after Charlie, you can't protect her. Do you take my meaning?"

"I take it as a threat."

"It's simple advice. I've spoken to Alejandro. He won't charge her for that incident at the gun range if you can get her to leave town."

I shook my head and laughed.

"What?" he said.

"From walking Meyer Lansky's dog to delivering messages for the State Attorney. I can't figure out if you've come up or down in the world."

"Such a smart mouth you have."

We'd walked less than a block when Perlow stopped and said, "I'm bushed. Let's sit."

I followed him through a gate in the coral rock wall, and we found a bench in the shade of a palm on the beach, the fronds swaying in the ocean breeze. Thirty yards away, a shirtless, leathery-skinned man of maybe ninety worked a metal detector across the sand.

"I have no wife, Mr. Lassiter," Perlow said, somberly. "No children or grandchildren or blood relatives I give a shit about. Alex means everything to me."

"I know. His old man gave you a job at the casino. You stood in for him the day they snipped Alex's foreskin."

"Alex is the son I never had," Perlow said. "I would do anything for him."

I believed him. The godfather was a *real* Godfather.

"Years ago, when Charlie Ziegler was *schtupping* that underage girl, I told Alex to stay away from him."

"But Alex didn't listen."

"He was young. He couldn't see Ziegler for what he was. A weak man. A man of the flesh."

I thought of one of Granny's old cracker expressions. If you lie down with dogs, you're gonna get fleas. Or at Ziegler's house, chlamydia.

"If the Attorney General investigates," Perlow said, "there'll be a flood of publicity. Even though he's done nothing wrong, Alex will be linked to a man who seduced underage girls."

"Like I said before, not my concern."

"You're an intelligent man, Mr. Lassiter. Surely it is not necessary for me to underscore how precarious your position is."

"I think I got the point when you mentioned how good a shot your *pistolero* is."

Perlow used a knuckle to scratch at his Errol Flynn mustache. "So, why so damned stubborn?"

"Because I don't like being pushed around. When I am, I push back. So, no, I'm not gonna abandon my plans. In fact, I'll expand them. If Castiel is involved in a cover-up, the feds ought to be interested, too. I'll ask the Justice Department to take a look at all three of you. I'll bet there are files on you going back so far, J. Edgar Hoover hadn't started wearing dresses."

The old man shook his head and sighed. On the beach, two copper-toned young women were playing Frisbee. They wore micro-thongs and nothing on top. I didn't pay attention to their Frisbee skills.

"How's your knowledge of history, Mr. Lassiter?"

"I know who bombed Pearl Harbor."

"Do you know about Meyer Lansky ordering the hit on Ben Siegel?"

"I saw the movie *Bugsy,* if that counts."

"They'd grown up together, and Meyer loved Ben like a brother. But Ben was stealing, and after a warning, Meyer felt he had no choice. Do you take my meaning, Mr. Lassiter?"

"Lansky had Bugsy killed, even though he didn't want to."

"Think how it pained Meyer. And consider that I have no feelings whatsoever toward you."

Perlow nudged the fedora back on his head, got to his feet, and waved his cane in the air. It must have been a magic cane, because the Bentley immediately appeared, easing up to the curb.

Nestor, the husky driver and crack shot, came out and held the door open. Tats up and down both arms, a five-pointed crown on the back of his shaved head. Latin Kings gangbanger.

"Will you answer a question, Perlow?" I said.

"What?"

"That party that Krista Larkin *didn't* go to . . ."

"What about it?" Perlow ducked into the car.

"Were you there?"

"Of course, Mr. Lassiter" came the voice from the darkened backseat. "Everyone was there."

36 Three Mysterious Cars

Hoofing it back to the office along Espanola Way, I was especially alert. Head swiveling this way and that, I was on the lookout for anything or anyone out of the ordinary.

Like one of Nestor's Latin King hermanos.

When I got upstairs, I told my assistant, Cindy, about Perlow's threat, trying to make it sound funny, an old guy shaking his cane at me. Pretending I wasn't even a teensy bit scared.

Cindy immediately expressed concern.

"How about two months' severance?"

"But you're still working."

"Talking about if they sever your head. How about writing a check now?"

"Relax, Cindy. Nothing's gonna happen."

"Maybe not if you bail. Forget about Krista Larkin."

"Can't do it. I'm getting close or Ziegler and Perlow wouldn't be going bat shit."

"Really? You're getting close?" Cindy cocked a pierced eyebrow. "First Alex Castiel says there's nothing his office can do, he thinks Charlie Ziegler is a great guy. Then Ziegler sends a little honey to your house. Against all odds, you turn her down, and Ziegler has two thugs grab you. This Perlow guy tells you to back off or he'll wreck your law practice.

Then Ziegler says Krista ran off with some biker. But to make everyone feel better, he offers Amy a hundred grand and thirty for you. When that doesn't work, an ex-cop who works for Ziegler beats you up."

"I think that was personal."

"Oh, I almost forgot. Your client flips out, shoots the car you love, which?—just guessing here—means she fired you. It doesn't sound like you're getting close to anything except erased. Which is why I'm asking for two months' pay in advance, plus medical."

"Forget it." Before shooing her out of my office, I asked what she'd found on the old purple Impala that followed me to the shooting range.

"Registered to a Terence Connor of Boca Raton."

"Never heard of him."

"Pension planner who owns about a dozen vintage cars."

"Get me a phone number."

"Doubt he's gonna answer. He looted his clients' accounts, got indicted, and skipped town. He's a fugitive."

It made no sense. The owner of the Escalade was in prison, and this guy was on the run. I failed to get the plate number of the Hummer, so no telling who might own that vehicle, but I wasn't ruling out Bernie Madoff.

Cindy returned to her cubicle and I looked over my calendar of appointments. It was New Customers day, and pickings were slim. A lawyer pal faced disciplinary action for dressing as a priest and rushing over to a downtown building that had just collapsed. While giving last rites, he whipped out contingency fee contracts. I made a note to look into getting a seminary degree online—backdated, if possible.

The phone rang, as it does once in a while. I was hoping it was Amy. Cindy answered and buzzed me. "There's trouble at Kip's school, boss. Get over there, ASAP."

37 The Old Instep Stomp

I drove across the MacArthur Causeway on new steel-belt radials and looped onto I-95, which dropped me off on Miami Avenue. The top was down, and Ramblin' Jack Elliott was going full throttle, singing "The Sky Above, the Mud Below," a tale of horse rustling and kangaroo court justice.

"Someone go and dig a ditch, there may well be a hanging."

The old Eldo rolled through the business section of Coconut Grove, then under a canopy of Japanese banyan trees, and into the gated entrance of Tuttle-Biscayne, the ritzy bayfront school where Motor Boating is an elective.

A moment later, I was in the reception room of Winston Perkins, Director of Student Affairs. His assistant said "The Commodore" would see me now.

Commodore Perkins was in his fifties and wore a blue blazer with gold buttons, a blinding white shirt, and a red silk ascot. Yeah, an ascot like the Duke of fucking Windsor, or Don Knotts on *Three's Company*. My nephew sat in a chair in his regulation khaki pants, long-sleeve shirt, and a mossy green tie. I was the only one without neckware. Today's T-shirt read: *"I Would Kill for a Nobel Peace Prize."*

"Tell me, Mr. Lassiter," the Commodore said, "does violence run in your family?"

I didn't get it. Then he made a small gesture toward my face. Aha. The bruises and scrapes.

"Oh, this? I got stomped by an ex-cop I'd kicked around a few days before."

He looked as if he'd just tasted curdled milk, so I added, "But I've always taught Kip that violence is wrong."

My nephew stifled a semi-snicker.

"Then how can you explain his assaulting Carl Kountz?"

"You kidding? Carl's a horse, your star fullback and first baseman and whatever you call it in lacrosse."

"Mid-fielder," the Commodore said.

They played a lot of fancy sports at Tuttle. Squash. Golf. Sailing. Four-oar shells. Plus some varsity teams that didn't seem like sports at all. Paintball. Chess. And my personal favorite, the Green Technology Team.

"Carl is an outstanding scholar-athlete, and your nephew sent him to the hospital."

"That sounds serious." I tried not to sound pleased but didn't quite succeed.

"I hit him with the combination you taught me, Uncle Jake," Kip said. "A left jab, then a right to the jaw. He didn't fall, so I stomped on his instep as hard as I could."

The Commodore made a *tsk-tsk* sound. "Broke three metatarsals in Carl's right foot."

"The prick pissed in my locker, and all his friends laughed," Kip said.

"Watch your language, lad," Commodore Perkins said. "Even if Carl did such a thing, there was no reason for violence. We have channels to air grievances."

In my experience, you air laundry. You handle grievances by yourself.

"I didn't hit back right away," Kip said. "But then, at baseball practice, Carl sucker punched me, really hard."

"Only a bully and a coward does that," I said.

I hate bullies. Big guys who are puny on the inside. Filled with self-hatred, they take it out on those they think can't fight back. I'd told Kip to clobber Carl the next time something happened. A fist to the nose is a good start. It will make a man's eyes tear, and a gusher of blood makes some guys pass out. The instep stomp is a little more creative. I'd bought a dozen bags of potato chips for practice. After a few tries, Kip was able to explode the bag and shoot crushed chips halfway across the backyard.

"Carl denies instigating the event, either physically or verbally," Perkins said.

"Fine. Bring him in, and I'll cross-examine."

The Commodore tilted his chin upward so that I could count his nose hairs, and gave me a tolerant little smile. I hate that look.

"We don't have trials here, Mr. Lassiter. I personally handle all disciplinary hearings, as outlined in the parent-student handbook, which I assume you have read."

"Cover to cover."

"In this case, I will take into account Carl's stellar record and your nephew's problematic status."

"Meaning?"

"On his application, you failed to disclose his juvenile record. Trespassing. Malicious mischief. Destruction of property."

"A little graffiti tagging." I felt my face heat up, the scrapes on my forehead burning. "Kip was living in an abusive situation with his mother— that's my sister—and he acted out."

"Your sister, I note, also has a criminal record."

"She's a tweaker and a crackhead. You gonna hold that against Kip?"

"Only insofar as it affects his actions."

"Kip finished a counseling program, and the record was expunged." Then it occurred to me. The juvenile file was sealed. "How the hell did you get Kip's file?"

The Commodore shifted in his chair and looked out the window. He had a fine view of the campus quadrangle. Overprivileged girls in tartan plaid skirts and knee socks sashayed to class alongside gangly boys in white shirts and loosened ties.

"I have certain connections." Measuring his words like yeast in a bread pan.

"Where? Only the clerk and the State Attorney's Office . . ." I felt a ball of molten lava rising in my gut. "That bastard! Alex Castiel told you."

The Commodore didn't answer, but he didn't have to. Castiel was a "distinguished alumnus" with his photo in a trophy case in the lobby. He'd helped get Kip into the school. Now he was using that against me.

"That motherfucker," I said.

"Mr. Lassiter, please. You're making things worse."

"Okay, Commodore. Or Admiral. Or swab jockey, second class. Kip's situation is not 'problematic.' You expel him or suspend him or put a pissy little note in his file, and I'll tie you up in lawsuits for the next ten years."

"I think not, Mr. Lassiter. We comply with all laws, state and federal."

"Was that weed I smelled walking across your quad? Let's get some police dogs in here and open some lockers."

"I assure you, Mr. Lassiter, we monitor the students quite closely."

"Do you monitor the teachers, too? I'll bet there's some real popular young guy who's banging a cheerleader. A coach who's juicing his players. Now that I think of it, Tuttle-Biscayne is probably a racketeering enterprise that ought to be shut down."

"That's absurd!" The Commodore's eyes were wide, his cheeks flushed, and his ascot seemed askew. "I run a tight ship, and I yield neither to headwinds nor threats." The Commodore began flipping through his date book. "I'll set a date for a disciplinary hearing and we'll conclude this matter."

My cell phone rang. Caller I.D. said "Private Number," which pissed me off. If you're calling someone, you're going to say your name in a second, anyway. Why not give a little preview?

"I'm busy," I answered.

"Jake, it's Amy. Thank God you're there." Her voice rushed and frantic.

"Where are you, Amy? Where've you been?"

"They found me, Jake."

"Who?"

"Ziegler's people. I moved into a new motel. They broke into my room while I was gone."

"Try to calm down. Tell me where you are, and I'll come get you."

"Can I come to your house?"

"Of course."

"They tore up my things, Jake. Ripped my clothes to shreds like wild animals."

"Important thing is, you're okay."

"My gun, Jake! They stole my gun."

38 The Rendezvous

Driving north on I-95 on Saturday morning, Charlie Ziegler thought he was being followed by a bright red Cadillac Escalade with spinning wheel covers and chugging lake pipes. A rolling Miami cliché.

Ziegler's own wheels were a modern classic. A brand-new Ferrari, the California model, practically the first one off the boat.

Ziegler checked the side mirror. The Escalade was two cars behind. He hit the gas, and his Ferrari leapt forward like a feral cat. He eased into the speed lane. Did the Escalade follow him? No, it was stuck in the middle lane.

Who the hell are you and what do you want?

Ziegler had first noticed the car when he took the flyover at Golden Glades Interchange. He'd been thinking about a recent dinner at Bourbon Steak, a fancy joint a couple miles east in Aventura. The Governor had been there, talking about saving the wetlands—boring!—and raising money for a run at the open U.S. Senate seat. Ziegler would not only feed the governor's face but also his coffers. He'd solicit some downtown friends and bundle the contributions. In return, well, you didn't just come out and say those things up front. No, the quid pro quo was always ex post facto.

Lola was at the dinner, putting on her usual show of eating three micrograms of the most expensive entrée on the menu. Which turned out to be the Japanese Wagyu strip steak. One-hundred forty-five bucks!

"Try a bite, Charlie. It melts in your mouth."

If she really wanted something to melt in her mouth, Charlie told her, she could put béarnaise on his nutsack.

Ordinarily on Saturdays, he'd lie to Lola and say he was off to play golf at Riviera. No need this morning. She was out of town, and he was happily on his way to Lighthouse Point to see Melody Sanders, as he'd been doing for several years now.

He'd bought Melody a two-bedroom condo near the marina and put her on the payroll at three grand a month. Talk about a frugal fuckmate, he'd once paid that for six hours with an escort in Buenos Aires. On the books, Melody was listed under "consulting services," which was basically true, as she'd taught him the reverse Amazon, a position that let her do all the work and eased his aching back.

He loved giving Melody gifts. Inexpensive artsy and craftsy stuff he picked out himself. She was always grateful, not like the whiny Lola. He'd given his wife a kumquat-size diamond for their anniversary and still didn't get a blow job. Her excuses for refusing sex ran from the old, reliable headache to the exotic yeast infection. Lately, she insisted that she couldn't get turned on because of anxiety over global warming.

Melody was uncomplicated and undemanding and had pubic muscles that could squeeze the buttercream out of a pastry bag. Not long ago, he realized that Saturday mornings in Melody's bed were the high point of the week. Only one downside. His golf game was going to shit.

The Ferrari was purring through North Lauderdale, a steady 75, only possible on weekend mornings. He checked the mirror. The Escalade was back again, three cars behind and one lane over.

His thoughts turned to Lassiter. Had Perlow scared him off? Lassiter didn't seem like the kind of guy whose asshole puckered up when threatened. Was he really going to bring in the state Attorney General? And what's this shit about the Justice Department? No way Ziegler wanted the feds pawing over his tax returns.

Won't be long, he thought, imagining Melody's naked body entwined with his. Wouldn't those *alter kockers* at the country club be jealous? He could see the old farts now, taking a dip in the Jacuzzi. Pale and flabby, bobbing like matzoh balls in chicken soup.

With all the crap raining down on him, he needed Melody today more than ever.

Lassiter breathing down my neck.

Perlow picking my pocket.

And that cinema verité phony Rodney Gifford. Could he really know what happened the night of the party?

Just how much pressure could a man take?

Another check of the mirror. No Escalade. It must have taken an earlier exit. The only vehicle keeping up with him was a big gray Hummer directly behind his Ferrari.

Shit! Ziegler realized he was still in the speed lane, and the Copans Road exit was just ahead. He floored it and cut across the expressway. Horns honked behind him, and he saw the Hummer tear across four lanes and take the exit behind him.

Ziegler drove into the town of Lighthouse Point, feeling better the closer he got to Melody's bed. He pulled up at the four-story, pink stucco building with balconies overlooking the harbor. Sweet anticipation, he was starting to feel better already. He emerged from the Ferrari tumescent, thanks to the Viagra he swallowed before leaving the house. He took the elevator to the fourth floor and hurried along the exterior walkway to her apartment.

As he rang the doorbell, he heard the rumble of an engine, looked down, and saw the gray Hummer pull into the parking lot, where it stopped next to a Dumpster and sat there, idling. But he didn't take the time to think about it, once Melody opened the door wearing a black silk teddy and saying she was so horny, would he mind terribly if they screwed right away and had brunch later?

"I can live with that," he said.

39 A Semi-Pro P.I.

Where the hell was Amy?

After her motel room had been broken into, she said she was coming over to the house, but she never showed. I tried calling a dozen times. Never called me back.

I was thinking all this while the Eldo rumbled across the 12th Avenue bridge over the Miami River. I was headed south toward Coconut Grove and home. I passed what used to be the Orange Bowl. For the last few years, it's been an empty lot, sad as a cemetery. Now it's a hole in the ground, workers building a new baseball stadium for the Marlins, but it won't be the same. With its view of the downtown skyline, the rickety and rusty O.B. was a classic of the game. Home to Joe Namath's heroic Super Bowl, Doug Flutie's impossible Hail Mary, and the Fins undefeated season, two decades before I suited up.

I played for the Dolphins in the cold and sterile Joe Robbie Stadium, carved out of the sawgrass near a turnpike exit. The stadium was renamed Pro Player Stadium in return for some loot from a now-defunct clothing line, then back to Joe Robbie, then Land Shark Stadium because a beer company paid for the privilege, and finally Sun Life, after an insurance company. Ah, Miami. So rich in tradition.

I had already hit South Dixie Highway when I saw a candy-apple red Escalade two cars ahead and one lane over. Correction, I *heard* the

Escalade, the lake pipes rumbling like thunder. Then I saw the spinning wheel covers and the shiny paint job. Last week, I'd seen an identical pimpmobile double-parked in front of the Justice Building. Then it had tailed me down Douglas Road, barely three miles from here.

I passed the pair of cars between us and swung behind the Escalade, getting close enough to see the vanity plate, U R NEXT.

Gotcha.

Same vehicle. Miguel Sanchez of Homestead.

But who the hell's driving your car, now that you're an inmate at FCI?

The Escalade stayed in the right-hand lane and passed the Red Road intersection in South Miami. I was two cars behind when it turned right onto Sunset Drive, and I followed.

We passed South Miami Hospital and headed west. The driver gave no indication he knew he was being tailed. I let another car get between us. Just past 97th Avenue, the Escalade turned into a strip mall. I continued for another two blocks, hung a U-turn, and doubled back.

When I pulled into the lot, I saw the Escalade parked next to Scully's Tavern, a neighborhood joint known for its fish sandwiches fried in a potato-chip batter. At least, that's what the sign in the window said.

I parked in front of a snake and iguana shop a few doors away and headed for the tavern. I didn't know who I was looking for, but figured if the guy saw me, he'd react.

The lunch crowd was gone, and the place was nearly empty. In a side room, two guys in University of Miami T-shirts shot pool. They paid no attention to me.

A couple of solitary drinkers at the bar. A young couple at a table. I circled the bar and saw the guy. Recognized him from behind, thanks to the diamond earring and barbed-wire tattoo around his neck. Pepito Dominguez, my DUI client. Sitting on a bar stool, drinking a Bud.

"You asshole." I lifted him off the bar stool by the scruff of his neck.

"Jake!" His eyes registered shock, about twenty thousand volts' worth. "I'm sorry, *jefe*! Just one beer."

"I don't care about the beer." I let him fall back onto the stool. "Why you following me? What the hell's going on?"

"Just practicing, man. That's all."

"Practicing for what?"

"To be your P.I."

"Bullshit."

The bartender, an older guy in a Dolphins polo, came over to see if there was a problem. We both said no, and I ordered a Jack Daniel's on the rocks.

"It's true, *jefe*," Pepito said. "I tailed you for three days, and you only made me that once, at the traffic light in the Grove. Unless you saw me on the Trail, too."

"The purple Impala? That was you?"

"Yeah."

Then it came to me. Sanchez, owner of the Escalade, had been captured after jumping bail. A fugitive named Terence Connor owned the Impala. Both must have put their cars up as security, which is how Dominguez Bail Bonds got them.

"You borrowed the cars from your dad, didn't you?"

"Switched them every day," Pepito said, proudly. "That was my cover."

"Might have worked better if the cars weren't so conspicuous."

He gave me a little sideways grin. "Worked fine yesterday when I followed Charlie Ziegler."

That stopped me. "How the hell do you know about Ziegler?"

"The other night when it rained like hell, I followed you to an ugly-ass house in Gables Estates. Looked up the property records, found the owner's name. Charles Ziegler. Stopped in your office the next morning, shot the shit with Cindy, and she filled me in."

"You little sneak," I said. Meaning it as a compliment.

Our drinks arrived. Pepito hoisted his beer and offered a toast. "*Muerte a Fidel!*"

"Death to all Philistines," I agreed. "Now tell me what the hell you've been up to."

"I tailed Ziegler up to Lighthouse Point. He spent three hours in a condo at the marina. Place is owned by a Melody Sanders."

My look shot him a question, and he answered, "I checked the mailbox. Looked up the property records on Lexis-Nexis. She's thirty-nine. Single. Born in Sarasota."

"Sounds like Saturday morning nooky."

"Exactly what I figure, *jefe*. She bought the condo seven years ago. Paid all cash."

"You're showing off, Pepito."

He grinned at me. Okay, I *had* misjudged him. He's got real ingenuity.

"So you want me to follow Ziegler some more?" he asked.

"Maybe later. But I've got another job for you."

I told Pepito to find my missing client. I gave him the make and model of her car and told him where she'd been staying before checking out. We tossed around a couple ideas, and then I said, "Just so you don't get too cocky; I caught you in the other car, too. The Hummer."

"Big-ass H2?"

"Yeah."

"Gray?"

"Yeah."

"Windows tinted black."

"That's the one."

"Wasn't me."

I laughed. "Of course it was you."

"No, man. But I saw the Hummer twice. That night you drove to Ziegler's house, it was cruising down Casuarina. Then yesterday, I saw it tailing Ziegler on Copans Road."

That rocked me. "Get a look at the driver?"

"Never had the chance."

"Shit."

"Why's someone following both Ziegler and you, *jefe?*"

"I don't know. But if I can figure out *who*, I'll know *why*."

40 The Hummer

Sweaty and thirsty, Kip dribbled the basketball along the sidewalk. He'd been shooting buckets at the outdoor court in Peacock Park along the bay in the Grove. One hundred jump shots and one hundred free throws. Just like Uncle Jake taught him.

A man was cleaning the windshield of a big-ass gray Hummer parked next to the bike rack where Kip had locked his Cannondale.

Kip wouldn't have paid much attention, but the car was so big and the chassis so high, the guy had to stand on the running board to reach the middle of the windshield. Big guy, too, in a muscle tee. Sloping shoulders, pumped delts, tats covering both arms and running up his neck.

Kip unlocked his bike chain and squeezed the basketball into his backpack.

"Nice bike," the guy said, stepping off the running board.

"Nice wheels," Kip said.

"Ever ride in one?"

"Nah."

The guy shot a look toward the street, and Kip noticed the five-pointed crown tattoo on the back of his skull. Latin Kings. A sheriff's deputy had lectured at school, taught them all about the local gangs. The Kings were badasses.

"You wanna take a ride?" The gangbanger circled around him. The Hummer's passenger door was open.

"You some kind of perv?"

The guy laughed. "Just being nice, kid. I'm a friend of the family."

"What family?"

"Jeez, you don't remember. Me and your uncle are tight."

"What's his name?" Suspicious as hell.

"Jake. Jake Lassiter. Used to play for the Dolphins."

"Uh-huh. What's your name?"

It took a second before the guy said, "Bill."

Kip sized up the situation. They were in a cul-de-sac just thirty feet from the bay at the end of the park. Only one way out, McFarlane Road, where cars were cruising by. But the perv was three feet away.

He'd knock me off the bike and throw me into the Hummer.

"Lock your bike back up, I'll take you for a spin over to Jungle Island."

"Okay, sure."

Kip fumbled with the lock, and the perv stepped closer.

"Carbon frame?" the guy asked, grabbing the handlebars.

"Yeah."

The perv's hands were occupied. This might be his only chance, Kip thought. His uncle had taught him the side-blade kick against the heavy bag. With his weight on his left leg, Kip quickly shot his right knee toward his chest, pivoted, and snapped a foot squarely into the guy's balls.

The air whoomphed out of the guy, and he sunk to his knees, gasping.

Kip hopped on the bike, bounced off the curb into the street, and pedaled like hell. He was too scared to look back.

41 A New Deal

Sitting in his study, Ziegler was waiting for Max Perlow to rob him deaf, dumb, and blind. Fifteen percent forever. Guys who sell their souls to the devil get better deals.

What could he do, Ziegler wondered, to end the nut-busting arrangement? He'd prayed for divine intervention.

Please God. Smite the old bastard. A heart attack, a stroke, some kreplach *stuck in his throat.*

He had fantasized about pressing a gun against the back of the old man's head and pulling the trigger. Splatter Perlow's brains all over the Romero Britto painting of an Absolut Vodka bottle. Lola had picked it out, with the help of some pop art consultant who was banging her sideways in his SoBe studio.

The more Ziegler thought about Perlow, the more aggravated he became. Then he hatched a plan. He would draw a line in the Gables Estates sand.

"Max, it's time for a new deal. I've repaid you ten times over. It's done. Finished. Fartik. *You wanna threaten me, go ahead. But we both know you got no juice."*

It sounded good to him. At least, in his mind. He'd have to deliver the lines without his hands shaking or a tremolo in his voice.

Ziegler heard a *squeak* from the corridor. Perlow's Hush Puppies padding toward the study. He'd let himself in. The bastard had demanded a key to the house years ago, shortly after an old gangster pal had been assassinated while ringing a doorbell.

"Hello, Charlie." Perlow toddled through the open doorway, his cane banging the marble tile, his pudgy cheeks squeezing his rodent eyes into slits. "Jeez, where's Ray Decker? You got a crazy woman running around threatening you, and no security at the house."

"I can take care myself, Max." Intending a double meaning. He wasn't scared of a crazy woman . . . or an old hoodlum.

Perlow sagged into a leather chair in front of Ziegler's desk. "So, did we have a good month, Charlie?"

I had a good month, you fucking leech.

That's what Ziegler wanted to say, but what he really said was, "Not so great, Max."

Jesus, what am I afraid of?

"So work harder next month," Perlow said. "You got a check for me?"

"Bookkeeping's running a little late, Max."

The old man hacked up a wet cough. "You *momzer!* You make me waste my time coming over here?"

"C'mon, Max. Couple days is all."

"Screw that." Perlow pulled out a handkerchief, spat into it, then folded the corners toward the center, as if covering the *afikoman* matzoh. "Write me a personal check, then reimburse yourself."

"You gotta understand, Max. Revenue's down but payroll keeps growing."

Perlow nodded and Ziegler relaxed for a moment, thinking the old mobster had agreed. Instead, Perlow came back with, "Payroll. I meant to talk to you about that. Your chippy. What's her name?"

"Who? Who you talking about, Max?"

Perlow reached into his pants pocket, drew out a crumpled piece of paper and read, "Melody Sanders."

"What the hell? You snooping on me?"

"Nestor Tejada followed you to your little love nest. This Melody. She's on the payroll."

"What's the big deal, Max? I've had women on the books before." Not liking the sound of his own voice. Whiny. Pleading. Weak.

"I didn't know about this *maidel.*"

"What, I need your permission to get laid?"

"You in love, Charlie?"

"What kind of question is that? I like the woman or I wouldn't be spending Saturday mornings with her instead of working on my short irons."

"When a guy falls for a dame, he starts opening up. Talking about his business and his friends. He lets his guard down, and says stuff he shouldn't."

"Only thing I say is, 'Close your mouth, you're letting air in.' "

"I know you, Charlie. You got this sentimental streak."

"You don't have to worry about me, Max."

"*Sha!* Ben said the same thing to Meyer."

Here we go again, Ziegler thought. Bugsy Siegel and Meyer Lansky. Maybe Scorsese thinks mobsters are entertaining, but if he'd ever met Max Perlow, he'd have made romantic comedies.

"Ben was *schtupping* every starlet in Hollywood. He changed girlfriends like he changed his boxer shorts. But he fell for Virginia Hill, and before long, they were opening Swiss bank accounts."

"I know, Max. I know."

"Then you also know someone out of Chicago aced Ben right in his living room. Cops found one of his eyeballs halfway across the room."

"This is bullshit, Max!" Raising his voice to the old man for the first time in twenty years. "I don't talk to Melody about business. I'm not stealing. She's not stealing. And I've had about as much of you as I can take."

Perlow sat there, hands resting on his watermelon belly, sausage fingers laced together. "What are you saying, Charlie? Spit it out."

"My debt to you has been paid ten times over."

"You haven't been listening, Charlie. We're partners for life."

"Fuck that. My wife's not even my partner for life." Proud to be showing some guts after all these years of groveling.

"Weren't for me, Charlie, you'd still be on the beach, hustling girls with your Nikon."

"Fine. You gave me seed money, like a hundred years ago."

"Seed money? You little *pisher!* You ungrateful shit."

Perlow's face reddened and his jowls quivered. With any luck, he'd stroke out.

"Fifteen percent for life! That's the deal. You don't want to pay me, Charlie?"

Ziegler didn't answer. The courage he'd felt just seconds ago was slipping away. He was starting to hate himself all over again. "Maybe slice your piece down to ten percent."

"Pay me, you miserable *gonif!*" Perlow exploded. "Every cent." Perlow's little ferret eyes were wide open now, dark and dangerous. "Or do you want to finish this conversation with Nestor?"

Ziegler put his hands in the air, as if surrendering. "Sorry, Max. My meds make me nuts. Depression. Anxiety. I say crazy things."

Perlow still glaring at him

"Won't happen again," Ziegler promised.

Just as he was wondering if he should offer Perlow a conciliatory drink, Ziegler heard a jarring noise. A crash from the pool deck on the far side of the solarium. Sounded like one of the hundred-pound clay planters toppling onto the hand-cut tile.

"You got somebody out there?" Perlow demanded.

"No, Max. 'Course not."

"Then what the hell was that?"

"Don't know."

"You been acting queer all night." Keeping his eyes on Ziegler, Perlow yanked up a polyester pant leg and drew a small handgun from an ankle holster. "Let's find out what the fuck's going on, *partner.*"

42 Orchids and Blood

The moment they walked into the solarium, Ziegler felt the warm air and smelled the moist earth. His favorite corner of the world, home to his beautiful and blessedly silent orchids. His refuge. From his wife, his work, his life.

But not from Max Perlow, whose Hush Puppies squeaked a step behind.

A toad with a gun.

Floor-to-ceiling glass looked directly onto the pool deck, the glare from the solarium lights turning the windows into mirrors. The two men could only see their own reflections.

Ziegler stopped, listened. Nothing.

Perlow shuffled past him, the lavender leaves of a hanging Mendelli orchid catching the old man's arm. Perlow seemed not to notice the Mendelli or the Sophronitis the color of a Cabernet Sauvignon or the vanilla orchid, its column a delicious snowy white, open like a wet and willing pussy.

"My fucking sinuses," Perlow said. "How do you live with all these weeds?"

The man is a barbarian, Ziegler thought.

Another sound. Softer. Something brushing up against the glass outside. Spanish bayonet shrubs were planted there. The leaves so thick and dense they barely moved in a windstorm.

Unless someone was out there.

"Turn off the lights," Perlow barked.

Ziegler flipped the switch, and the solarium went dark. Night lights illuminated the pool deck and cabanas, the Roman pillars casting shadows across the water.

The next few seconds went by in a blur.

Perlow pressed his face to the window.

Outside, a flash of movement in the bushes.

"Max!" Ziegler shouted.

"Sha!" He yelled through the closed window: "Who the hell's out there?"

An explosion of glass. Behind them, a hanging pot splintered and crashed to the floor.

Ziegler dived under a table.

Unfazed, Perlow stood rock still. Crisis calmed him. He'd once finished a side order of cioppino, moments after a tablemate had his throat slit in a Little Italy restaurant.

"You?" he said, looking into the eyes of the shooter outside. Perlow raised his gun. Maybe thirty years ago, before arthritis chewed at his joints, he would have been faster.

The second gunshot hit him squarely in the chest and knocked him on his ass.

Stunned, Ziegler crawled out from under the table and saw the silhouette of a person running away from the house. Trembling, he gazed at Perlow, flat on his back.

"He-lp," Perlow croaked, blood oozing from his chest.

Ziegler's mind careened, his thoughts shooting rapid-fire. Was the bullet meant for him? Would the shooter come back? Could there be another gunman?

"Who was it, Max? Who'd you see?"

"Nine-one-one," Perlow whispered.

More questions shot through Ziegler's brain. Did Tejada, around front in Max's Bentley, hear the shots? How long would an ambulance take? Could the old buzzard survive?

"Paramedics. Please, Charlie."

A memory flashed back to Ziegler. The worst night of his life. Eighteen years ago. "Paramedics!" he spat out the word.

"Charlie?"

Perlow's voice pleading, his eyes showing his fear.

Ziegler calmed, feeling a clarity of purpose. He caught sight of a vanilla orchid, its petals streaked obscenely with blood. Perlow was going to die, Ziegler thought.

There is a God, after all.

A God who looks after porn producers, lousy husbands, and tax cheats. Okay, so maybe it's not God with a capital "G." Maybe it's just a cloud of cosmic gases that floats across the Milky Way and settles over the earth, bringing joy to the wicked and Mammon to the greedy. But it's still a force that evens the score, though it might take decades.

"You want CPR, Max?"

"Huh? Huh?" Wheezing but hanging on. Harder to kill than a cockroach.

"Chrissakes, help me."

Perlow propped himself up on one elbow, fumbled for his cell phone. Ziegler kicked Perlow's arm out from under him and the phone skittered away. The old man toppled backwards. Ziegler slipped off a soft leather loafer.

"Hey, Max. Got something for you."

He stepped on Perlow's rib cage. Careful not to leave bruises. He heard a blast of air, like a farting balloon. Or . . . a punctured lung.

Perlow cried in pain. "Charlie. Whaaaa . . . ?"

"That's for Krista, Max. Remember her?"

"Char . . ."

"You didn't call the paramedics for Krista, did you, Max?"

Ziegler adjusted his foot and pressed harder. Blood exploded from Perlow's chest like a whale spouting.

Perlow didn't say another word.

"And that lifetime deal of ours, Max," Ziegler said. "It just expired."

43 Going Biblical

"Sorry, Uncle Jake. I should have gotten a license plate."

"No problem, Kip. Your description was great. I've seen the guy."

"Really?" The boy's spirits were picking up.

"The tattoos nailed it."

We sat at the kitchen table, Kip sipping a mango shake. His mood had roller-coastered ever since he had pedaled home in record time. Hyper-excitement, then a spiral downward, and now he was rallying. The boy didn't realize just how shell-shocked he was at nearly being kidnapped. For her part, Granny was baking maple bacon brittle, her salty-sweet anti-dote to any childhood ailment.

"I kicked the poop out of the guy," Kip said.

"He underestimated you. Happens to me in court sometimes." I tou-sled the boy's hair and said, "Proud of you, kiddo."

"I wasn't scared, Uncle Jake."

Right.

"It's okay to be scared, as long as you still do the right thing."

"Are you gonna whomp the guy?" Kip asked.

That had been my first inclination. But Nestor was Perlow's bodyguard and would have been following his boss's orders. Raising lots of questions. Did Perlow intend to snatch Kip or just show me he could get to someone

I loved? Did Ziegler know what was going on? What about Castiel? Was there a larger game plan?

Something else had just become apparent. It must have been Nestor in the Hummer, following Ziegler to Lighthouse Point. Meaning there was a rift between Perlow and Ziegler. But why? And, more important, how could I take advantage of it?

Too many questions needed answering before I punched anyone out.

Perlow didn't have a listed phone number, so I asked Kip to use his computer skills to find out where the old hood lived. Two minutes later, my nephew showed me an aerial shot of a 1930s Spanish-style house just off Andalusia in Coral Gables. A ficus hedge shielded an alley behind the place. It would be a good way to get onto the porch undetected.

"I'm gonna go talk to Nestor and the guy he works for," I told Kip.

"Talk, Uncle Jake?"

"Yeah. But if either of them gives me any shit, I'll go biblical on their asses."

Kip looked at me, waiting for an explanation.

"I'll bring the walls down on their heads like Samson at the Temple of Dagon."

44 Eyeball Witness

A circus, Ziegler thought, watching from the pool deck.

His house, the big tent.

Uniformed cops, plainclothes detectives, crime scene investigators, medical examiners, techs in plastic gloves with tweezers and flashlights. Cameras popping off photos in the solarium, on the deck, up against the windows, and deep in the bayonet bushes.

A moment before he was to give his statement to homicide detectives, Ziegler caught sight of a distraught Alex Castiel jogging toward him. Ziegler tried to arrange his features into a reasonable facsimile of grief. "Alex, it was awful. I know how much you loved the old guy."

Castiel pulled him aside, out of earshot of the cops. "Was it her, Charlie? Was it the Larkin woman?"

"Couldn't really tell. Too dark. And I was scared shitless."

"Who else could it be?"

"Shit, I don't know, Alex. Wish we could ask Max."

They were quiet a moment as a police helicopter flew overhead, its searchlight sweeping across the seawall.

"What do you mean?" Castiel asked.

"Max saw the shooter."

"How do you know?"

"Because he said something."

"What, exactly?"

"He said, 'You?'"

Castiel ran a hand through his dark hair. "That's all, Charlie? 'You?'"

"Like he recognized the shooter. But Max never saw Amy Larkin, so I'm thinking maybe it was someone else."

"You're reading a helluva lot into one word, Charlie."

"I don't know what you expect me to say."

Police radios squawked. A tech walked by carrying several plastic evidence bags.

Castiel lowered his voice. "Step up to the plate. I need an eyeball witness."

"C'mon, Alex. You asked if I saw her, and I'm saying I can't swear to it."

Eyes wild, Castiel jammed a finger into his chest. "Didn't you ever learn anything from Max? Do what's gotta be done!"

"What the hell does that mean?"

With a plainclothes cop approaching, Castiel hissed in his ear, "There are only two people who could have killed Max. Amy Larkin and you, Charlie. It's up to you who goes down for it."

45 No Alibi

Drained from his near-kidnapping and stuffed with maple bacon brittle, Kip had conked out on the sofa. I carried him into his bedroom and tucked him into bed. Then I went through his backpack and found a note from Commodore Perkins at Tuttle-Biscayne.

Would I please select which date was convenient for Kip's disciplinary hearing?

The Commodore thoughtfully provided nine different days. I decided to choose the last one, then, at the last moment, ask for a continuance. If I did this often enough, maybe Kip could graduate before he was expelled.

An hour later, I was lying in bed watching television. Csonka was sleeping in the corner of the room, snoring and farting. I flipped through the channels, found an old *L.A. Law* episode just starting. The opening credits rolled, soaring horns and banging drums inviting me to spend time with some lawyers who had a helluva lot more time for bed-hopping than I did.

My phone rang. Too late for good news. Caller I.D. told me it was our esteemed State Attorney.

"What's up, Alex? One of my clients steal your purse?"

"What are you doing right now, Jake?" Castiel said.

"Whatever I want. I'm in the privacy of my own bedroom."

"Let me speak to Amy Larkin."

"Why would she be in my bedroom?"

"I thought maybe you were nailing her. What time did she leave?"

"What are you talking about? She wasn't here tonight."

Castiel sounded brusque, but smug. "Thanks, Jake. You haven't been this much help since you wore the wire."

Damn. I'd let my guard down. It happens sometimes after three fingers of Jack Daniel's. "Wanna tell me what just happened?"

"You just ruled yourself out as an alibi."

Oh, shit.

"What is it you think Amy did?" I asked.

"She killed Max Perlow. One bullet to the chest."

I bolted up. "No way. Why would she?"

"Shot at Charlie Ziegler and missed. Charlie I.D.'d her."

I could hear my own heart sledge-hammering. Had she really done it?

"They pulled a .38 slug out of Perlow," Castiel continued. "If it matches the bullets she fired into your tires . . ."

"Wait a second. How'd you get those?"

"You forgetting I sent a county truck to tow your pimpmobile?"

"You had the slugs pulled from my tires?"

"I planned to prosecute your client for firearms violations. Who knew?"

"Someone stole Amy's gun two days ago."

If it's possible to hear a man shaking his head, I heard Castiel's spinning. "You make this shit up as you go along, Jake?"

"Amy told me. Someone ransacked her motel room and stole the gun. She was all freaked out about it." Even as I said it, I hated the story. How damn convenient.

"Just tell her to turn herself in, Jake. I don't want anything messy."

I told him I would if I could find her. It's one of the ethical rules I happen to believe in. You don't tell a client to run away. You bring her in to face the music and do your best to keep it from being a funeral march.

"I loved Max like my own father," Castiel said, somberly. "This is personal, Jake."

"Don't handle the case yourself, Alex."

"You're the one who better get out. I don't give a shit about collateral damage."

"I don't abandon clients, you know that."

"Up to you. But from here on out, our friendship is meaningless, Jake. I'm taking her down, and I don't give a shit if I take you down with her."

46 Innocence Is Irrelevant

The next morning, I was having my healthy breakfast of sugary Cuban coffee and guava flan at Versailles in Little Havana when Amy called.

From the jail.

She said she'd seen the story of the shooting on television in a restaurant bar. She'd been shocked—yes, shocked—to see her driver's license photo on the screen. She called the police and turned herself in.

"I didn't do it, Jake," she said.

"Not another word on the phone," I ordered. "I'll be there in twenty minutes."

I knew what was coming. An indictment for First Degree Murder. Meaning the state had evidence of premeditation. Boy, did they. Surveillance and stalking. Threats. Target practice. And shooting the wrong guy is no defense.

I carried my coffee to the car and headed east on Calle Ocho, passing Woodlawn Park Cemetery. It's filled with statues of angels, elaborate crypts, and mausoleums. Woodlawn is where Latin-American rulers go to their eternal rest in marble mausoleums and, this being Miami, it's a hot tourist attraction.

When I got to the Women's Annex, I presented my Bar card at the security window and sat in the visitors' room on a metal bench that seemed specially designed to put me into traction. I stood and studied the frescoes, which adorned the plaster walls. Mothers and children in splashy Caribbean colors. Shining suns and towering palms. Painted by the inmates, the frescoes seemed to reflect the repressed desires and unobtainable goals of these sorrowful, maladjusted women.

In a few minutes, a female guard brought Amy into a lawyer's room with a large glass window, a table, and two chairs. My first question to a jailed client is never *"Did you do it?"* It's always *"How much money do you have?"*

Amy gave me a number, a few thousand dollars in a savings account. I would run through that for expenses and expert witnesses, so she retained me for her usual fee. Zero.

"I didn't kill him, Jake," Amy blurted out. "Honest, I didn't."

I still hadn't asked.

"Hold that thought," I said.

"Why would I shoot that old man?"

"Castiel says you were trying to kill Ziegler and missed. Either way, it's First Degree Murder." I recited the murder statute from memory. "That's the 'unlawful killing of a human being perpetrated from a premeditated design to effect the death of the person killed or any human being.' It's the '*any* human being' part that does you in."

"But I didn't shoot anyone!"

"Just speaking hypothetically. If you aim at Peter and hit Paul, it's what the law calls 'transferred intent.'"

As they say, a good lawyer knows the law. But as they also say, a *great* lawyer knows the judge.

"You believe me, don't you, Jake?"

"When you lie in wait to kill someone, that's the premeditated part of the crime." I wasn't done with my Crim Law 101 lecture. "Your hatred of Charlie Ziegler for your sister's disappearance is the motive."

"It wasn't me! Jake, are you listening?"

"The penalty is life without parole."

I let that sink in a moment.

Life. Without. Parole.

It's forever and ever and ever, and the thought of it is nearly incomprehensible. Day after day of endless sameness. The same starchy, tasteless food. The thin, lumpy mattresses. Incompetent medical care. Lethal cellmates and pissed-off guards. The smells of sweat and disinfectant and the numbing noise, the clanging of steel doors, desperate voices echoing off concrete floors.

Amy's face had lost its color.

I wondered if I'd forgotten anything. Oh, yeah. "There'll be no bail pending trial, so try to get used to your surroundings. Don't make friends with any of the other inmates. By that, I mean don't talk to them about your case. If you do, you'll have someone claim you made a jailhouse confession."

I had one more item to bring up before talking about the evidence. "I need to ask you about that night when I called Castiel to ask him to dredge the canal."

"Yeah?"

"You got mad at me and left."

"I'm sorry about that."

"Question is, did you come back later? Like in the middle of the night."

"Why would I do that?"

"You tell me."

"Okay, yes. I was going to apologize to you for the way I'd acted. Blaming you because Castiel was being a jerk."

"So you pushed the front door open?" She'd seen me whack it with my shoulder and I recalled telling her that it was never locked.

"I'd had a couple drinks, and it seemed like a good idea at the time. But then your dog started barking. I panicked and left."

I wasn't sure about her story. Had she really been there to apologize? It was just as likely that she'd wanted to berate me some more. Or possibly even shoot me. With Amy, every turn in the road seemed to lead deeper into a maze.

"Two days ago, you told me someone broke into your motel room and stole your gun."

"What about it?"

"Did you file a police report?"

"No. Why?"

"C'mon, Amy. You're smarter than that."

"Someone took the gun."

"If the ballistics tie your Sig Sauer to the shooting, Castiel will send in a marching band and break out the champagne."

"If my gun was used, someone else fired it."

"Where were you last night?" I fired the question quickly, wanting to see if she blinked, reddened, or turned away.

"Nowhere near Ziegler's," she fired right back. A touch of anger, which was okay. "I was with a man."

That surprised me. "Who's the lucky guy?"

"Can't tell you."

"Why the hell not?"

"It's too dangerous."

"What's that mean?"

"If he testified, his life would be in danger."

"What about *your* life?"

She fingered the opening of her flimsy orange smock. "He wants to help, but I won't let him."

"That's my decision, not yours. Give me his name."

"I can't."

My lower back was throbbing again. "I'm thinking your alibi is bullshit."

"You just have to trust me, Jake."

"The hell I do. Lie to your priest or to your lover. But if you lie to me, I can't help you."

"I'm not! I wasn't at Ziegler's. I didn't shoot anyone."

I studied her, looking for the averted gaze, the tightened lips, the nervous twitch. Nothing.

"I'm innocent, Jake. Dammit, isn't that enough?"

"Innocence is irrelevant! All that matters is evidence. So give me your alibi, or the jury will give you life."

She took a moment to think it over before saying, "I'm sorry, Jake. You'll have to win without an alibi."

I pushed my chair away from the table and got to my feet. "Enjoy your stay, Amy. It's gonna be a long one."

47 So You Wanna Be a Gangbanger

The man was simply too large for the chair, Ziegler thought.

Nestor Tejada's rhino shoulders spilled over the backrest. He propped his feet on the asymmetrical glass table, playing the big *macher*. Just like his late and unlamented boss.

Tejada had barged into the Reelz TV headquarters without an appointment, and Ziegler didn't know what he wanted.

"So your bottom line is looking up," Tejada said.

"Meaning what?" Ziegler didn't like the way it was starting.

"You don't have to pay Mr. P that fifteen percent anymore."

Jesus. Perlow afraid of what I'd tell Melody and he's shooting his mouth off to this frigging gangbanger.

"So you've got extra capital to put into the business," Tejada continued. "Or extra cash to pull out, depending whether you're thinking short term or long."

"Who are you, Warren Buffet?"

"I studied Business Organization."

"Bullshit."

"At Okeechobee Correctional. But I learned more from Mr. P than any course."

Sure you did. Perlow had a PhD in extortion.

Ziegler telling himself to be careful. He'd learned a long time ago not to judge a person's intelligence based on appearances or upbringing. He'd known a couple of scary-smart porn stars in his time.

"I'm just wondering how you're planning to use that extra dough," Tejada said.

"Are you shaking me down?"

"I'm here to help you."

"Screw that. You're running a protection racket. Jesus, I thought you were out of the Latin Kings."

"Ain't like the Rotary Club, Ziegler. It's blood in, blood out. You cut a throat to get in the door, and you don't leave till you're six feet under."

"Lovely. Just lovely."

"But I don't need your money. Mr. P gave me a piece of his gaming business."

"A piece?"

"My guys service the slots in Indian casinos. I got the company in Mr. P's will."

Un-fucking-believable. Max Perlow feeling all fatherly to Alex Castiel was one thing, but adopting this jailbird?

"Now, you wanna hear my idea for a new show?" Tejada said.

Ziegler immediately felt better. He leaned back and exhaled. The guy wanted to pitch him, not strong-arm him.

"Ideas, my friend, are the trash of the business," he said. "Everyone has an *idea* for a show. The question is, who can take the little feathery notions that make up an idea and spin them into gold?" Repeating what he'd heard some legitimate producer say at a seminar. Stephen J. Cannell. Or Dick Wolf. Or Stephen Bochco. One of the big-timers.

"It's called, 'So You Wanna Be a Gangbanger,'" Tejada said, unperturbed.

He took a few minutes describing the show. Start with a dozen ghetto teens. They spray graffiti on expressway overpasses, then move on to shoplifting, purse snatching, car theft, maybe dealing some crank on street corners. Drive-by shootings with paintball guns, extra credit if you nail a cop. Real gang members decide who goes to the next level. In the season finale, there'd be an initiation ceremony, laced with sex and violence.

"Not a bad idea," Ziegler said, when the spiel was over.

Thinking, great fucking idea. The next generation of reality shows.

Edgy, urban, street-wise, it punched all the buttons. Ziegler imagined a franchise of inner-city spinoffs, starting with *Carjack!* which would reward the guy who stole the hottest wheels.

"Not bad?" Tejada said. "That's it?"

Ziegler felt in command. He loved being pitched because it gave him a chance to bust men's balls and break women's hearts. "It's okay. Like it, don't love it. Either way, it's really generic, not specific at all."

"You shitting me, *cabron?*" Tejada said.

"Problem is, I don't see where you fit in."

"I'd be the whadayacallit, the executive producer," Tejada said.

Ziegler wondered if the bastard read *Variety* at Okeechobee Correctional. "You gotta be kidding. You want to be the showrunner?"

"The top dude, yeah."

"You need experience. Credits in the biz."

"I got credits on the street."

"Thing is, I could hire any ex-con as a consultant for five hundred bucks a week and all the Colt 45 he can drink."

Tejada straightened in his chair, deltoids flexing. "You're a bigger asshole than Mr. P thought."

Ziegler placed his thumb on a red button below his desk. "I got a guy in the next office named Ray Decker. He's an ex-cop and he's licensed to carry a concealed firearm. If you try any shit, he'll come in here and put a bullet in your thick fucking skull."

Feeling unbeatable.

"Mr. P taught me that violence is only a last resort," Tejada said, placidly. "Instead of hitting a man, just find his weakest spot and press gently. If he doesn't respond, press a little harder."

Ziegler knew he was leaping at the bait, but he didn't care. Perlow was dead and he was in charge. "So, Nestor, what's my weakest spot?"

"I saw you kill Mr. P."

The words spoken softly, almost apologetically.

Ziegler tried not to blink, failed. Felt something thud inside his skull, hoped he wasn't having a stroke. "The fuck you talking about?"

"I was sitting in Mr. P's Bentley, windows down, when I heard the gunshot. I ran around the back of the house and saw you through the glass stomping on the old man's chest."

Ziegler remembered the moment, the blood pumping, Max wheezing. Now he felt as if his own aorta might burst. "Why didn't you stop me?"

"I thought about it. Almost did it. That old Jew was good to me."

"Screw that! You wanted the slots business! You wanted him to die!"

"Yeah, maybe. But I'm not the one who killed him. You are."

Ziegler swallowed hard. "About the show . . ."

"Yeah?"

"A man of your experience, I could see as co–exec producer. It's one notch from the top. Let someone else do the heavy lifting."

Tejada nodded. "As long as it pays, I don't give a shit about the title."

"Smart," Ziegler agreed.

"How does fifty grand an episode sound?"

Like highway robbery, Ziegler thought.

"Like a good deal, all around," he said.

48 The Maniacal Obsession

"My name is Jake Lassiter. Before we go on the record in *State v. Larkin*, let me say that if I ever catch you within a hundred yards of my nephew, I'll kick the living piss out of you."

Nestor Tejada kept his cool and turned to Castiel. "Can he talk that way to me?"

"Technically, no. But you'll get used to it."

"Do you want me to take this down?" the court stenographer asked, fingers curled over her keyboard.

"Not yet," I told her.

We were in a Justice Building conference room, and I was supposed to be taking Tejada's pre-trial deposition, not threatening him.

"Wasn't my idea, Lassiter," Tejada said. "Mr. P wanted me to scare the kid to get at you."

"Why don't you try to scare me, tough guy?"

"Jake, you made your point," Castiel said.

"It's okay," Tejada said. "I apologize to the man. We shouldn't mess with family." He turned to me. "We cool?"

"We're cool, dickwad. Now state your name for the record."

His testimony was less interesting than the preliminaries. He'd been sitting in front of Ziegler's house in Perlow's car. Heard a gunshot, ran to the back of the house, didn't see the shooter.

Discovery was moving along smoothly. I had waived preliminary hearing and accepted the state's discovery without whining about documents being withheld. I made no combative motions and quickly prepared for trial.

Most defense lawyers love delay. With enough time, the state's case can fall apart. Witnesses die or forget or change their minds. Evidence is lost or mishandled. The prosecutor gets a better job and dumps the case onto the desk of some overworked kid.

I am not like most defense lawyers. I like to move for a speedy trial. My theory is that the state has harder work to do. It must gather evidence, prepare its witnesses, do the lab tests, and prepare a logical case where A leads to B and B leads to C, and "C" stands for "conviction." The state needs boxes and files and color-coded notebooks. The state has the burden of proof, and I have the burden of staying awake. I can defend a case with a blank yellow pad and my slashing cross-examination.

In the legal world, the prosecutor is a carpenter, pounding his nails with a steady hand, building a house out of sturdy beams, while the defense lawyer is a vandal with a can of gasoline and a Zippo lighter. Sometimes you don't even need the pyromania. Just huff and puff and the state's shaky house will crumble.

Castiel's case, however, was built of sturdy stuff, starting with a truckload of physical evidence. Fingerprints on the window, a solid match with Amy. A speck of fabric in the bushes, positive link to Amy's unitard. We had answers for both pieces of evidence, though extremely risky ones. Amy would have to take the stand and admit she trespassed on Ziegler's property several days before the shooting. She'd crept up to the solarium window through those thorny bushes, and that's when the fabric and prints were left behind.

We'd be conceding that Amy had a maniacal obsession with Ziegler. She blamed him for her sister's disappearance. She stalked him from next door, sneaked onto his property, and peeped at him through the windows. How much more difficult is it to believe that she came back another time, gun in hand?

Our case had other problems, too. Even if I cast doubt on the forensic evidence, I had no answer for the ballistics. The bullet pulled from Perlow was fired from the same weapon that Amy used to mortally wound my tires. Her uncorroborated story that the gun had been stolen two nights before the shooting was so lame, it ought to be taken out, blindfolded, and shot.

Then the biggest problem of all. Charlie Ziegler. On deposition, he had testified that he saw the shooter through the window. Amy Larkin. He would repeat the story at trial. If I couldn't prove he was either lying or mistaken, we would lose. To destroy Ziegler's testimony, I needed evidence that Amy could not have been at his house that night. A rock solid alibi.

Whenever I visited Amy in the jail, she was clutching a Bible. She had retreated to her upbringing. Scriptures and prayers. She also clung to her story that she didn't shoot Perlow. Couldn't have. She was with a man somewhere else the night of the shooting.

Where?

Can't tell you.

Who?

Same thing.

Who do you suppose shot Perlow?

No idea.

How do you expect me to win?

Divine Providence.

I told her that, in my experience, God helps those who help themselves.

As the trial date approached, I considered the situation and came to a few, well-thought-out conclusions. It was pretty simple, really. I had a client I didn't trust and a case I couldn't win.

49 Jailhouse Rock

Lucinda Bailey loves fine wine. At Christmas, I buy Lucinda a case of Syrah from the Eberle Winery in California. All year long, she keeps me informed of the comings and goings at the county's penal institutions.

Lucinda runs Information Technology for the jail system, and she'd been calling me every morning for the last nine weeks. I had asked her to keep tabs on Amy. If my client really had been with a man the night Perlow was shot, I figured that guy might visit her in jail. But each day, Lucinda had the same news—no visitors the previous day. Until this morning.

I was in the office. I had no customers, so I was studying the pre-season college football betting lines. Alabama was the favorite to win its second straight national championship. But pre-season wagers are sucker bets. Too many variables. A twelve-game season, plus a conference championship game, plus the BCS title game, if the Crimson Tide got that far. I'd wait until September, place a sentimental bet on Penn State, and start studying the point spreads week to week.

Lucinda Bailey's call interrupted my dreams of greenbacks. "Your client had a male visitor at 8:05 A.M. yesterday. Stayed for thirty-seven minutes."

"Finally! What's his name?" I was prepared for a guy named John Doe with phony I.D. and a Groucho Marx nose and glasses.

"Charles Ziegler, Anglo male, lives on Casuarina Concourse in Gables Estates."

What the hell!

The man Amy supposedly intended to kill comes visiting. Bizarre. He couldn't be her alibi witness. He was two feet away when Perlow took a slug in the chest, and he claimed Amy was the shooter. So what was he doing there? What hadn't my client told me?

I headed for the jail. Driving across the causeway, I ran through what I knew and what I didn't know, the latter outweighing the former. I had stirred up the waters surrounding Krista Larkin's disappearance. Castiel, Ziegler, and Perlow all went to battle stations. Perlow threatened my life, but he's the one who ended up dead. What secret was I close to discovering? If I could figure that out, I would know who killed Perlow.

Or was it far less complicated? Had my client simply taken a shot at Ziegler and hit the wrong guy? Had she used me to find the guy who killed Krista, not for a trial, but for an execution? Which still didn't answer the question of why Ziegler came visiting.

Something else. My previously high-strung, nerves-rubbed-raw client was oddly at peace, just a week before she was to be tried for murder. On the other side, Alex Castiel was so cocky of a conviction he didn't even offer a plea.

Forty minutes after taking Lucinda's call, I was sitting across from Amy in the glass-walled lawyer's room at the women's jail. She seemed intent on making me an even less effective trial lawyer than I already was.

"I can't tell you why Ziegler was here."

"Sure you can. What did you talk about?"

"I'm sorry, Jake."

"Is it dangerous for Ziegler, too? Like your bullshit alibi witness? Mr. X?"

"I just can't."

"You want to know my theory? You and Ziegler killed Perlow together."

"Why would we do that?"

"Beats the hell out of me."

"I didn't shoot Perlow. I swear it."

"You know what? I don't care. I quit. I'm firing myself."

"You can't, Jake. I checked. No judge will let you out right before trial. Besides, you don't quit on people."

"Says who?"

"You."

Great. Just great. I was going to trial not believing my client, and that wasn't the worst of it. I knew land mines were buried in the sand, but the only way to find them was to run blindly ahead, awaiting the roar.

50 Where the Wind Was Born

Castiel was not happy with his star witness. "You look like shit, Charlie."

"Lemme alone, Alex."

"You having trouble sleeping?"

"Not bad enough to call Michael Jackson's doctor . . . yet."

They were on Ziegler's pool deck just after sunset. A warm breeze tickled the fronds of the tiki hut bar. Castiel had stopped by to check on his photographers and graphic artists. They were doing their last round of photos and illustrations for the state's trial exhibits. Castiel believed in entertaining the jurors. He knew that people retain information more readily when it's presented visually. His trials were renowned for their compelling slide shows, computer graphics, and animations. All to keep the jurors alert and involved.

Castiel wanted to do another session of trial prep, but the tequila snifter in Ziegler's hand and the two bottles of Clase Azul on the table ruled that out.

"With the trial coming up, you really ought to watch your drinking, Charlie."

"You do the watching, Alex. You were always good at that."

Uncle Max had been right all along, Castiel thought.

"Use Ziegler for your own purposes, but don't get too close to the man. His life is like Sodom and Gomorrah."

Castiel looked at the man now, sprawled on a chaise, hairy belly sticking out from under a Hawaiian shirt. His face was stubbled with gray whiskers and he smelled like dried sweat and booze. Trial was starting next week and Ziegler would have to pull his shit together before Lassiter cross-examined him.

Castiel knew better than to underestimate his old buddy. Lassiter ate prosecutors for lunch and crapped out cops before the afternoon recess. Cross-exam was his forte. He didn't adhere to any of the accepted styles taught in legal seminars. Lassiter once told him over drinks that he viewed the courtroom as a saloon in an old Western. He liked to burst through the swinging doors, knock over a poker table, pistol whip a gunfighter, toss a big lug through a window, and flip a chair into the mirror above the bar.

"And that, Alex, is just when I say 'good morning.'"

In the Larkin murder trial, Lassiter didn't have much to work with, but Castiel knew that's when he was at his best. Give Lassiter an easy case, and he gets bored. He becomes just another lawyer asking the witness, "What happened next?" Give him a sure loser and he'll latch onto an opposing witness like an alligator and take the guy's leg off at the knee.

All of which made Castiel nervous about Ziegler.

How will Charlie hold up?

Lassiter needed to raise reasonable doubt by suggesting there was an unknown assassin hiding in the bushes that night. To do that, Lassiter would try to prove that Ziegler was a sleaze and Perlow a mobster. He wanted to link the worlds of pornography and organized crime and suggest that there were lots of potential killers who might have fired that shot through the window at either man.

"Where were you this weekend, Charlie?"

"Bahamas. Want to see my passport?"

"You take Lola?"

"She's in L.A. getting work done. Bigger boobs or smaller thighs, can't remember which."

"Your girlfriend, then."

"She was knitting a quilt for the church."

Over by the solarium window, the techs were packing their metal boxes. Job done. Castiel waved to them, and the photographer responded with a thumbs-up sign. If he could just get through the trial without Ziegler cracking, the saga of Krista Larkin could be put to rest forever. Ziegler was always the weak link. A sieve when it came to keeping secrets. Max had said that eighteen years ago when all three of their lives became inextricably entwined.

Castiel turned toward the channel where some kids in a Boston Whaler were heading toward the bay, the boat's wake slapping the seawall. "I had lunch with Archbishop Gilchrist yesterday. He told me you're gonna fund a facility for teenage runaways."

"That's right."

"Thirty-six beds. Counselors, social workers, teachers. The Archbishop couldn't stop talking about it."

"Yeah, so what?"

Castiel turned back to Ziegler. "Jesus, Charlie. Why not just put a sign on it, 'Krista Larkin Memorial Foundation'? What's next, throwing roses in the ocean on the girl's birthday?"

"Got nothing to do with her. It's something I've been thinking about for a long time."

Castiel got in Ziegler's face, inhaled his sour breath. "Max told me you were acting squirrelly ever since the sister came to town."

Ziegler's eyes seemed to clear and he looked straight at Castiel. "What if the Larkin woman isn't the shooter?"

Castiel felt his breath slip out. "Of course she's the shooter. The forensics nailed her, and you I.D.'d her."

"C'mon, Alex. You know I didn't see who did it. I said what you wanted, what I had to say to get the woman out of our lives. It didn't seem so bad when I thought she was guilty."

"She *is* guilty!"

"What if she's not? What if I send away an innocent woman?"

"That's your fucked-up guilt over Krista talking. Don't start trying to do the right thing, Charlie. It's not in your nature."

Ziegler straightened in the chaise, pulled his shirt down over his bulging gut. "Breeze is kicking up."

"So what?"

"You ever wonder where the wind starts? That air you feel on your face right now, did it come out of the Caribbean or somewhere farther away? How old is it?"

"How old's the wind? That what you're asking?"

"Is it the same air Columbus felt when he crossed the Atlantic? Was it the hot, desert air Moses felt crossing the desert?"

"Moses? Columbus? What the fuck are you talking about, Charlie?"

"I've been thinking about the origins of things, Alex. You ever do that?"

"I'm thinking about the end of things, Charlie. Now, you better hold it together, or you'll lose everything."

51 The Right Reverend Snake

My nephew is a damn smart kid. Hey, someone in the family had to be. But he doesn't bat a thousand. For weeks, he'd been surfing the Net, armed with the last name "Aldrin," looking for a man they called "Snake." Coming up empty.

Still, the kid persisted. Each morning, he Googled and Lexis-Nexised and scoured the Web. He dug into arrest records and Corrections Department files. Nothing. Until yesterday, when he found the man.

In church.

Or rather, in a newspaper advertisement for services at All Angels Recovery Church in Lauderdale-by-the-Sea. The reverend's name was George Henry Aldrin. A self-described ex-addict, ex-biker, ex-con. Current lay minister at All Angels and, incidentally, owner of Foot Longs, a sub shop on Commercial Boulevard in West Broward.

The day before jury selection was to begin, I took the turnpike north and found Foot Longs in a strip mall just west of University Drive in Lauderhill. A U-shaped counter, four tables inside, another four outside. A high school kid was mopping the floor, smearing mayonnaise from one tile to another. A large, bearded man in an apron was at the cash register, counting one-dollar bills. He wore a small, gold cross around his neck, and his thin gray hair was pulled straight back and tied into a ponytail. A round helipad of a bald spot crowned his head. A worn copy of the New Testament poked out of a pocket of his apron and, true to his name, the tattoo of a cobra crawled up his arm.

Aldrin might have once been handsome and rugged. Now his eyes were rheumy, and his skin was as gray as a mullet's belly. I guessed his weight as just south of three hundred pounds.

"George Aldrin?" I said.

"Yeah?"

"I'm Jake Lassiter."

The name didn't cause him to either salute or reach for a shotgun. "It's good to meet you, Jake Lassiter," he said evenly. "What kind of sandwich can we fix you today?"

"I'm looking for Krista Larkin."

"Sweet Jesus," he said, looking skyward.

"Do you have any idea what happened to her?"

He shook his head, sadly. "She disappeared, when was it...?"

"Eighteen years ago."

"Another lifetime. Lassiter, you said?"

"Right."

Now a glint of recognition in those moist eyes. "The football player?"

I nodded.

"The night Krista stabbed that jerk. *You* were there."

"Yeah."

"Krista told me all about you."

Oh, shit.

I expected the worst, but then he said, "She liked you."

"I find that hard to believe."

"Why? 'Cause you tossed her out of your place the next morning?" He said it matter-of-factly, no note of judgment in his voice.

"Because I didn't help her. I ..."

"Soiled her."

I nodded. Not the word I would have used, but yeah.

"One of many, Lassiter. Yours truly included. Have you repented?"

"Not in the way you mean. But I'm trying to do the right thing now."

"Godspeed, then." He turned to the kid with the mop. "Yo, Javier. Take a break. But no smoking weed."

The kid shrugged and left. "Rehab," Aldrin said. "I'm his mentor."

He flipped the *Closed* sign around on the glass door, looked through the window at the parking lot, and motioned for me to sit at one of the small tables.

When we were seated, he said, "Who knows you found me?"

"Why do you ask?"

"There are a couple guys from my past who I'd just as soon never see again."

I hazarded a guess. "Charlie Ziegler and Max Perlow."

He nodded.

Obviously, Aldrin spent more time reading the Bible than the newspapers. I told him Perlow was dead. Gave him the shorthand version, including Amy going to trial for murder.

"I don't countenance the slaying of a fellow man," he said, "but I shed no tears for him."

After a respectful moment of silence—about two seconds, I said, "My gut tells me Ziegler is responsible for Krista's disappearance, but I can't prove it."

"Ziegler never wiped his butt without Perlow's okay."

"Meaning what?"

"I supplied Ziegler with coke and meth. Which made Perlow crazy. He thought Ziegler talked too much when he was fried."

"Was he right?"

"A hundred percent. Krista was always telling me shit those two were doing. The girl knew too much, and Perlow realized it."

"You saying Perlow might have had Krista killed?"

He shrugged. "The man was ruthless, I can tell you that."

All this time, I'd been thinking Perlow was only protecting his business partner Ziegler from prison and his beloved Alex from bad press.

"What's Ziegler say happened?" Aldrin asked.

I told him about my conversation that rainy night in Gables Estates. Ziegler claiming that the reverend, in his Snake days, had shown up on the set, scared about getting picked up on a probation violation. That he left town with Krista on the back of his Harley.

"Peckerwood's telling half the truth," Aldrin said. "I saw them both that day, but not at the set. At the party."

"Krista was there?"

"Just arrived. It was early."

I sat back in my chair and let out a breath. Aldrin was the first eyewitness to place Krista at Ziegler's house the night she disappeared. Meaning everyone else had lied. Castiel. Perlow. Ziegler. Whatever happened to Krista, they were all in it together.

"I was delivering some very fine Colombian blow to Ziegler," he said.

"Tell me everything you remember."

"Not much to tell. I was only there four or five minutes. Told Krista I was headed west. Asked her to go along, but she chose to stay with her sugar daddy."

"I thought she wanted out of that life."

"Maybe she did, but coast to coast on a Harley must not have sounded like a step up."

He was silent a moment, maybe considering the role he'd played in Krista Larkin's short life. "She woulda left Ziegler for you, Lassiter."

"I only knew her for about twelve hours."

"Yet look at the impact she made. All these years later, you're looking for her. Trying to make amends would be my guess."

"Maybe."

"Then take it from me, Lassiter. Fucking things up only takes a few minutes. Making things right, now, that's a lifetime job."

52 The Boy Under the Bench

The courtroom was quiet. I sat at the defense table, sifting through my files. Castiel was perched a few feet away at the prosecution table. Opponents awaiting kickoff, or in this case, waiting for the judge on the first day of jury selection.

"I used to be in the papers a bit."

That's what Max Perlow told me the day I met him in Charlie Ziegler's office. So I'd asked my trusty law clerk—Kip by name—to get me everything he could on Perlow. I was relying on the classic SODDI defense.

Some Other Dude Did It.

An unknown rival who waited for his chance to take out Max Perlow. One of a veritable army of assassins who had it in for the old gangster. As part of my due diligence, I figured it wouldn't be a bad idea to see if there might be a shred of truth to my theory. At the same time, I wondered if that enemy might be sitting next to me. Did Amy find something I'd missed? Evidence that Perlow killed Krista, as Aldrin suggested. In which case, Amy wasn't such a bad pistol shot, after all.

Kip is an industrious kid. He found lots of references to Perlow in the *Miami Herald* and *The Miami News* plus some in the *International Herald Tribune* and *The Havana Post,* an English language paper in pre-Castro Cuba. Many articles that mentioned Perlow also named his business associate Meyer Lansky. Grand Jury investigations of illegal gambling in

Broward County. The slaying of Albert Anastasia in New York. The Kefauver Committee hearings on organized crime. Castro's takeover of Lansky's Riviera Hotel. Fun and games from days gone by.

When Lansky sought Israeli citizenship in the 1970s, one of the affidavits attesting to his sterling character was signed by Max Perlow, described as a "consultant in the hotel and entertainment industry."

There was virtually nothing in the clippings that bolstered my theory of a man with enemies. At least not now. Except for a few real estate notices—buying and selling condos and vacant lots—Perlow hadn't been mentioned in the papers in the last twenty years. Most of his known associates were long dead.

One clipping, though, fell into the category of irony or coincidence, or whatever the hell it is when the world spins thousands of times and returns to the same exact place.

"Alex, take a look at this," I said, holding the *Herald* clipping.

Castiel glanced toward the gallery, where eighty potential jurors waited, most willing to commit perjury to avoid spending three weeks locked in a room with total strangers, some of whom fail to bathe regularly.

"What is it?" Castiel wore his expression of prosecutorial solemnity. He didn't want to walk to my table. That would send the impression to jurors that we were equals. And he wouldn't ever want me to saunter over to his table and drape my arm around his shoulder. That would convey the notion that this was just a game, that the lawyers would go through their paces, feigning anger at each other, then spend the evenings drinking and carousing. In truth, there's less of that these days, which I think is a pity.

"Take a look. It won't bite." I held the clipping at arm's length so he wouldn't be infected by defense lawyer cooties.

It was a news story from April 1970. Lansky, sixty-eight years old at the time, had been charged with illegal possession of barbiturates—ulcer medication—for which he had no prescription. If there's a drug charge that's the equivalent of jaywalking, this would be it. But what was really interesting was the photo. It was taken in the corridor outside this very courtroom. There was Lansky with his pal, Perlow, along for moral support.

Spine straight, Castiel extended his arm and grabbed the clipping as if it might be radioactive. A second later, he smiled and his body relaxed. "Jesus, forty years ago, Jake." He read the headline aloud: " 'Judge Dismisses Charge, Slams Prosecution.' "

"I'm going for the same result in this case," I said.

Castiel moved closer, leaning over me, letting go of his Inspector Javert persona. "I remember that trial," he whispered.

"How? You were, what, eight years old?"

"Just turned nine. Uncle Max brought me to court." He tapped an index finger on the photo. "Wanted me to meet Meyer Lansky."

I understood Perlow coming to support his pal. But yanking precocious little Alex out of classes at Tuttle-Biscayne? What sense did that make?

"Are you gonna make me beg or just tell me?" I said. "What was Lansky like?"

"A tiny man. Very polite, very soft-spoken. He wore a sport coat. Soft fabric. Black and white; herringbone, maybe."

"You have a helluva memory."

Castiel smiled, eyes far away. "Something memorable happened."

"Yeah?"

"It was the week of my birthday. Max had given me a Swiss Army knife, and I showed it to Lansky."

"Yeah?"

"Lansky said he'd give me a hundred bucks if I proved I was a brave little boy."

"He asked you to stab the prosecutor?"

"He told me to carve my name under the judge's bench."

"No way."

"The *emmis*, Jake."

"Most kids go to Chuck E. Cheese on their birthdays. You cut deals with the FBI's Most Wanted."

"I waited till the lunch recess, and as soon as the judge was out of the courtroom, I crawled under the bench and carved my name. At least I think I did. It was pretty dark."

A great story, I thought, picturing little Alex Castiel, crouched on his haunches, using all his strength to scratch at the wood with his shiny new knife. "Lansky pay off?"

"A hundred dollar bill. Only time I ever took a bribe."

I thought again about Castiel's theory of the duality of man, the thin line between good and evil. He believed you could step across the line, then step back again. Or maybe just straddle the line, one foot in heaven, one in hell. He had never explained precisely how he put that theory into practice.

"Helluva story, Alex," I said.

"When I crawled back out from under the bench, Lansky asked me, 'Were you scared, boychik?'"

"And you said . . . ?"

"'No way, José.' Lansky got a big laugh at that. Told Max to take me to Wolfie's for a hot fudge sundae."

"Was it the truth, Alex? You weren't scared?"

"Petrified! But I wouldn't show it. I knew Lansky was a tough guy." Castiel handed back the clipping. "I wanted to be just like him."

53 A Pay-or-Die Deal

"I love you," Ziegler said.

Melody Sanders laughed. "Pillow talk, baby. All pillow talk."

True enough, they were in Melody's bed. They had just had sex, and Ziegler was still basking in the glow, feeling as if he were floating on a raft in a warm, calm sea. But that wasn't the reason his emotions were gushing. He'd had these feelings for a long time. This was the woman who understood him, who accepted him just the way he was.

Melody's bed was his sanctuary from an increasingly cruel and heartless world. But today he couldn't stop thinking about that prick Alex Castiel.

"There are only two people who could have killed Max. Amy Larkin and you, Charlie. It's completely up to you who goes down for it."

"Mel, I want to take you to Buenos Aires," he said.

"Really?"

"Or Rio. I think I meant Rio."

Argentina or Brazil? He could never remember which one refused to extradite fugitives to the United States.

"Or Casablanca." He was pretty damn sure there was no treaty with Morocco.

"What are you talking about, Charlie?"

"I can sell the cable channel. Fox is always in the market for more sleaze. And Rodney Gifford would buy the porn distribution business if the price was right."

Melody propped up on an elbow, her face close to his. When she frowned, her nose wiggled like a rabbit's. She was so all-fire cute Ziegler wanted to kiss her from head to toe and frequently did.

"A fresh start for both of us." A youthful bounce to his voice.

"What about your wife?"

"She's not invited."

"Slow down, Charlie." She traced figure-eights on his chest with an index finger. "You're under a lot of stress."

"Damn straight."

"It's not the time to make major decisions."

She was right, Ziegler knew. So damn smart. And supportive. Not just a good lay. His relationship with Melody had always been more than just sex. As the years went by, he relied more on her for advice and counsel. If he had a problem with cable operators or DVD distributors, he'd discuss it with her. She was also the only person in the world Ziegler trusted completely.

"Alex is threatening me and Tejada's strong-arming me." He took her hand in his and kissed her fingertips. "A man can't live like that. Not for long."

"Running away? It's not like you, Charlie."

"I'm talking about a new life. Right after the trial, let's do it."

"Not until you have some breathing room, some time to think. Maybe a couple weeks in the islands, let you unwind. You might see things differently then."

Right again, he thought.

"I have some new toys we can bring along." Showing her salacious smile.

"You're on." Lately, he'd ceded the dominant role in the bedroom to Melody. As he got older, he took pleasure in surrendering power. Ball and gag, rubber mask, clothespins, he loved it all. Who knew that ass beads could add twenty megatons to his orgasm?

"Did you want to talk about the trial?" she asked, gently.

He knew that was her sweet way of saying, "We have to talk about the trial."

"Sure."

"I'm worried, Charlie."

"I screwed up that night, but I can make it right."

"So you've been thinking about what you're going to say on the stand."

"Constantly."

"And . . . ?"

He sighed. "Gonna say I couldn't see who fired the shot."

Worry clouded her face. "Are you going to tell Castiel you're changing your testimony?"

"The opposite. I'll tell him I'm on board."

"Are you sure that's the way to do it?"

Her concern had dug little creases in her forehead. Ziegler loved that look, a mixture of vulnerability and caring.

"I'll let Castiel tell the jury I'm his star witness, then sandbag the fucker."

"How do you think he'll react?"

"Shit his pants in the courtroom, I'm hoping."

"Just be careful, Charlie."

"No worries, Mel."

Ziegler lifted the sheet and buried his head between her breasts. He didn't want to talk about Castiel. Even years ago, when the prick came around sniffing after pussy, he always acted superior, like he was slumming. Ziegler blamed Perlow for spoiling Castiel when he was a kid, telling him he was so damn special. What a crock.

"What are you thinking about, Charlie?"

"It's winter in Rio, hon," Ziegler whispered. "Buenos Aries, too. I love winter."

Nestor Tejada, bodyguard of the late Max Perlow, took the Copans Road exit and headed east toward the town of Lighthouse Point. Nearing the harbor, he parked in the scant shade of a stubby palm tree, got out of the car, and walked to the pink condominium building.

Fucking Ziegler.

Once Tejada had threatened to reveal what he'd seen—Ziegler finishing off poor old Perlow—the weasel had changed his tune. All of a sudden, the reality show idea, "Gangbangers," was a high-concept, dead-solid hit. Ziegler had agreed to terms. But ever since, he'd been stringing Tejada along. Refusing to put anything in writing, saying that's how deals were done in television.

"My word is my bond, amigo. You've got a play-or-pay deal."

Bullshit, Ziegler. You've got a pay-or-die deal.

It was time to let Ziegler know that. Saturday morning. A man of habit, Ziegler would be curled up with his honey. Always best to catch a man with his pants down.

Tejada took the elevator to the fourth floor and headed toward the corner apartment. He hadn't decided whether to ring the bell or kick in the door. When he got to the apartment, the decision was made for him. The door was open. He walked inside. The smell of fresh paint was in the air.

No furniture.

No nobody.

"You're so tense, baby," Melody said.

His back oiled, Ziegler was facedown on the bed, Melody straddling him. She dug her thumbs into the muscles along the shoulder blades. *Pain.* Then slid forward, letting her nipples trace circles in the massage oil. *Pleasure.*

"Relax, baby," she said. "Let the tension drain out."

"Give me five minutes, I got something that'll shoot out."

He could see the bay through the floor-to-ceiling glass. He'd bought the apartment for Melody after realizing Tejada had followed him to the Lighthouse Point condo. So here they were on the seventeenth floor of a Brickell Key high-rise just south of the Miami Avenue bridge. This part of his life had to be kept away from Tejada and Castiel and anyone else who could do them harm.

Her hands felt warm, and his eyes fluttered shut. As he drifted off, he thought again of Rio, and the "The Girl from Ipanema" floated through his dreams.

54 An Army of Assassins

"Oye, oye, oye. The 11th Judicial Circuit is now in session. Judge Melvia Duckworth presiding."

Everyone scrambled up, and Her Honor breezed through a back door, robes flying like an untrimmed sail. Judge Melvia Duckworth was an African-American woman in her fifties who had been an army captain, handling court-martials as a JAG lawyer. I liked her, mainly because she let lawyers try their cases without too much interference, and she hadn't yet said the magic words: "Mr. Lassiter, you are hereby held in contempt. . . ."

The judge wore a white, filagreed rabat at her neck, giving her the appearance of a member of the clergy. She wished everyone good morning and instructed the bailiff to bring in the jurors.

Next to me, Amy had the pallor common to inmates and barflies but did not seem nervous or agitated. Going on trial for murder apparently agreed with her. She wore a prim little business suit. Charcoal gray. White blouse with a little bow. The outfit shouted "innocent." I always want my clients well dressed and well groomed. I could have walked Charles Manson if he'd had a haircut and a Band-Aid covering the swastika on his forehead.

Sometimes I use props. Bibles and rosary beads are my old reliables. I'll put a wedding band on a male client to create the impression that *someone* loves him. I'll take a wedding band off a female client if someone on the jury might want to bone her.

It was time for opening statements. The lawyers' first speech is a window into the way two officers of the court can take the same facts and draw opposite conclusions. If Castiel were trying Goldilocks for burglary, he might tell the jury: "The defendant, with callous disregard for the property rights of others, sneaked into a private home, and, like the gluttonous hooligan she is, ate all the porridge, leaving the rightful owners to go hungry."

Whereas I might say: "A desperate and hungry little girl, intending no harm, sought refuge and sustenance in an open and inviting house."

It had taken four days to pick a jury, a dozen citizens, good and true. Castiel gave them his trial smile and intoned, "First, I want to thank all of you for coming down here and devoting your time and effort to your community."

Because if you ignored the jury summons, I'd have you arrested.

He spent three or four precious minutes waving the flag and telling the jurors how wonderful they were. True blue Americans and all of that.

"What I'm about to say to you is not evidence," Castiel continued.

A lot of lawyers start that way. I don't know why. It's like telling the jurors they don't have to listen. I wondered if Castiel might be a little rusty. These days, he only prosecuted a couple cases a year, attaching himself to high-publicity trials like a lamprey to a shark.

"The evidence that you will consider," Castiel was saying, "will come to you from the witness stand and in demonstrative exhibits from the crime scene. What I'm doing now, and what Mr. Lassiter will do when I sit down, is give you a preview of each of our cases."

Thanks, Alex, but I'm not gonna give them a "preview." I'm gonna start indoctrinating them with the theme of my case.

What's a theme? Lawyers used to say it's a telegram, the short, punchy summary of your case. No one uses telegrams anymore, so I suppose it's a twitter, or a tweet, or whatever you call it. To construct your theme, you *de*construct your case. Pull it apart brick by brick until you're left with the barest structure. The marketing whizzes who write movie taglines know how to do this.

"Houston, we have a problem."

Or . . .

"Just when you thought it was safe to go back into the water."

Castiel stood three feet in front of the jury box. Close enough to de-mand their attention without spraying the front row with spittle. "This case involves an obsessed woman who stalked a man she wrongly believed had harmed her sister, then in an attempt to kill him, shot and murdered another man."

"Obsessed." "Stalked." "Shot." The thematic words Castiel would ham-mer throughout the trial.

I patted Amy on the arm just to let her know nothing Castiel said con-cerned me. To let the jury know, too. In reality, the State Attorney had everything he needed for conviction. Eyewitness testimony. Fingerprints. Ballistics.

What did Amy have? An ex-jock mouthpiece who didn't necessarily be-lieve her story.

"You will hear from an eyewitness, Charles Ziegler, a respected busi-nessman and philanthropist." Castiel was rolling now. "Mr. Ziegler was the intended victim, and he witnessed the shooting. He will tell you under oath that he saw this woman, Amy Larkin, fire the fatal shot."

Castiel pointed at Amy, as prosecutors are inclined to do. *J' accuse!* Amy didn't blink and she didn't turn away. She didn't look angry and she didn't look scared. She merely stared back at Castiel, her head cocked a bit, as if listening to a fairly interesting discussion that did not involve her person-ally.

"You will be presented with evidence that the defendant stalked Mr. Ziegler. You will hear from a fingerprint expert who will identify conclu-sive matches, placing the defendant at the scene of the shooting. You will see cigarette butts bearing the defendant's DNA that were found on a con-struction site adjacent to the crime scene. And you will hear from a ballis-tics expert who will testify that . . ."

While Castiel pounded away, I took inventory of the jury. I was reason-ably happy with our Dirty Dozen. I landed five women, three in their twenties, a pedicurist, a homemaker mother of twins, and a colon hy-drotherapist. I didn't ask the last one any detailed questions about her work.

Another woman, a pharmaceutical rep, was a striking redhead in a short skirt. Drug companies like their salespeople young, female, and pretty. The final woman wore safari khakis and worked as a python wrangler, clearing the snakes out of neighborhood canals.

The seven men included two retirees, a guy who drove a Doritos truck, two wannabe actors, both waiting tables. One man was unemployed, and another said he was a life coach, a term neither Don Shula nor Joe Paterno ever used.

Castiel picked up steam, repeating his key words, "obsessed," "stalked," and "shot" a few times. When I got my turn, I would talk about Amy as little as possible and the two pals, Perlow and Ziegler, a lot. My key phrase would be "an army of assassins," which I hoped would perk up the jurors' ears.

"Enemies, criminals, and assassins. That's who could have lurked outside Charlie Ziegler's windows that fateful night. Max Perlow was a lifelong gangster with deep connections in organized crime. Charles Ziegler spent years as a pornographer, a world crawling with crime and corruption. These men made enemies. Yes, there could have been an army of assassins lurking in those bushes that night."

Before I could give that spiel, Castiel had to finish, and he seemed to be having too much fun to stop.

"Remember that no one piece of evidence is conclusive of guilt or innocence," the State Attorney was saying. "Think of your favorite recipe."

Gin, vermouth, olive . . . if you're talking to me.

"Take strawberry shortcake. If you just eat the dry cake, it's not all that tasty. Add the strawberries and we're getting there. But it's the whipped cream that ties it all together. Please wait until the whipped cream is on top before reaching any conclusions."

Castiel sat down, and the judge said, "This seems like a propitious time for our lunch recess."

55 Clay Pigeons

A criminal trial is not the last half of a *Law & Order* episode. It does not sail along with pithy questions, furious objections, and searing answers. A criminal trial is a slog through the mud, boring and repetitious, with fits and starts and endless downtime. It is played out in an arena cold enough to preserve fish—and hopefully keep jurors awake—under yellow fluorescent lighting that makes even the robust and hearty appear jaundiced and sickly.

The days crawled by as Castiel methodically put on the state's case. An assistant medical examiner with a Pakistani accent testified as to the autopsy results.

Max Perlow, deceased. Death classified as a homicide. Gunshot wound to the chest. Cause of death, exsanguination. The decedent bled to death.

The bullet tore a wide path through bone and tissue and blood vessels. The M.E. explained that the bullet's kinetic energy slowed down when it crashed through the solarium window. A slower bullet causes *greater* tissue damage. He used a blackboard to describe a mathematical equation.

"Kinetic energy equals the weight of the bullet times its velocity squared," the M.E. said, "divided by gravitational acceleration times two."

I wouldn't have cross-examined that, even if I knew how.

The mention of the bullet's weight segued smoothly to the ballistics tech, who testified that the slug pulled from Perlow was a .38 caliber. He compared the striations of that spent bullet with those of the two slugs pulled from the tires of my Eldo. Yep. All three were fired by the same gun.

The state didn't have the murder weapon but didn't need it. The day after the M.E. testified, two witnesses from the gun range told their stories. Both said they saw Amy Larkin slay my innocent Michelins with a weapon they recognized as a Sig Sauer .380. The logical paradigm was simple and straightforward:

Amy Larkin shot my tires with a .38 caliber gun.
The same gun was used to kill Perlow.
Therefore, Amy Larkin killed Perlow.

Then came the physical evidence I'd been expecting. Amy's fingerprints were on two panes of glass in the solarium windows. A scrap of fabric taken from the jagged leaves of the bayonet plants matched a unitard seized in Amy's motel room.

On cross, I got both the experts to admit that the prints and the cloth could have been left several nights earlier. That's what defense lawyers do. Wait for the state to launch a clay pigeon, then try to blast it out of the air. What makes it tough is when the state has more pigeons than you have ammo.

Sitting next to me at the defense table, Amy remained composed. When I glanced at her profile, I sometimes saw her sister. The same angular jawline, the same girl-next-door quality.

I had told Amy that I was still looking for Krista and that I'd found Snake, the biker-turned-reverend. I expected the news to excite her, but she expressed little curiosity, even after my telling her that Snake placed Krista at Ziegler's party.

I gave Amy a legal pad to make notes. Clients sometimes come up with better questions than lawyers. But Amy didn't give me any help. She doodled. She drew pictures of a house with four people standing out front. Mom, Dad, and two daughters, a bright sun in the sky. It reminded me of the artwork in the women's jail, cheerful paintings mocked by the grimness around them.

At one lunch recess, I joined Amy in her cramped holding cell, just down a corridor from the courtroom.

"What's Ziegler going to say on the stand?" I asked, yet again.

"What did he say when you took his deposition?"

"You know damn well. He saw you outside the window."

"So . . . ?"

"So I'm wondering if he had a change of heart."

She was tying the bow on her silk blouse, fumbling a bit without a mirror. "If you must know . . ."

"If I must know! I'm your lawyer, dammit! When Ziegler came to the jail, what did he say?"

"That he was going to do what's right."

"What the hell does that mean?"

"I don't know. I didn't ask."

"The son-of-a-bitch told the cops you were the shooter. He signed an affidavit to that effect for Castiel. In deposition, under oath, he repeated the same thing to me. It's a big deal to recant. But you didn't ask?"

"It's in God's hands."

"Let's hope He doesn't have butterfingers."

"Don't be blasphemous."

Playing the religion card. It could have been an act. But with Amy, who knew?

We had about two minutes before court would reconvene. For weeks, I'd been pressuring her to tell me what Ziegler had said during his jailhouse visit. This *do the right thing* bit was the first crack in her *can't tell you* armor. I decided to stay quiet a moment. In court, it's a trick I use to keep a witness talking. Give the room a moment of silence that demands to be filled. I looked into Amy's green eyes and waited.

"Charlie's different than I expected."

"Yeah?"

C'mon, Amy. Talk to me.

"He asked for my forgiveness."

"For what?"

"For taking advantage of Krista all those years ago. For my being in the situation I'm in now. He blames himself and he's looking for redemption."

Ziegler had talked to me about redemption, too. But talk's cheap, and the man was a born bullshit artist.

"He had tears in his eyes," she continued, "and seemed truly repentant."

What's next? I wondered. Amy and Ziegler as Facebook friends?

She grabbed one of my hands and clutched it in both of hers. "Charlie told me that after all this time, he's almost certain Krista is dead."

"Sounds like he might feel guilty about that."

"I think so, too. But not in the way you mean."

"How, then?"

"Looking at him, listening to him, I don't think Charlie had anything to do with Krista's death. In a strange way, that brought me peace."

She managed a small, soft smile. Placid and accepting. I tried to measure her sincerity. It's what I do for a living, but if I had to deal with Amy every day, I'd go broke. From day one, the woman has been a mystery.

"I don't want you at peace, Amy."

"Why?"

"To help me at trial, I need you alert and wired. Not in some Zen state. Not the president of the Charlie Ziegler Fan Club."

"I can only be who I am, Jake."

Just who the hell that was, I still didn't know.

56 The Portable Vagina

Kip promised to clean his room, do all his homework a week in advance, and never talk back for the rest of his life . . . if only I would take him to the erotica convention.

I turned the kid down.

"C'mon, Uncle Jake. Why should you have all the fun?"

"I'm gonna interview Angel Roxx. It's strictly business."

I knew Angel had a special relationship with Charlie Ziegler. She's who he sent to my house that first night, and she was at his place when he invited me over for sushi and tough-guy talk. Now I wanted to see what the porn actress knew about her boss's relationship with my client.

"You took me to the gun and knife show," Kip said, pouting. "You let me watch *Reservoir Dogs* on DVD."

"So?"

"Violence is okay for kids, but sex isn't? That what you're saying, Uncle Jake?"

Where in the world did he learn the art of cross-examination?

"I make the rules, Kip. Deal with it."

"That's so arbitrary!"

"So's life. Deal with that, too."

I try to be a good surrogate dad. I really do. But sometimes Kip can be a real pest. How do parents handle it? The ones with three or four kids, always yapping, always wanting something. Where does that patience come from? Only this morning, I got a phone call from Commodore Perkins at school. My latest request for a continuance was denied. I'd have to show up for Kip's official disciplinary hearing next week.

"Jeez, I did all that work for you and this is how you treat me," my nephew whined.

"You researched a porn star. It wasn't like digging ditches."

Kip spent last night happily downloading material from Angel's fan sites. He also printed out several photo sets. Some were highly educational. *101 Positions to Try at Home* illustrated the difference between reverse cowgirl and rodeo, something that had always puzzled me.

I skimmed Kip's research and learned that Angel grew up in horse country in Central Florida. "I was just another little cocksucker from Ocala who decided to get paid for it," she was quoted as saying. "Charlie Ziegler discovered me. One day I was doing *Stable Girls in Heat,* and the next I was a legit personality on reality TV. I even have health insurance!"

The convention center was mobbed. Young guys in University of Miami T-shirts and shorts; bikers with multiple piercings and body art; some old hippies, ash-gray hair tied back in ponytails, some with their old ladies along. Booths ran along narrow aisles, like any trade show. But these were staffed by young women in micro-minis, leather corsets, and all manner of see-through teddies, baby-dolls, and assorted *come fuck me* attire. Under the bright lighting, it was a pretty bizarre sight, even by Miami standards.

I passed the Titty Tattoo booth, the Penile Cosmetic Surgery Center, the Sin Toy Shoppe, and a fetish place called "Fluffy Bunny Whips." The biggest crowd—a bunch of young guys cheering and high-fiving—gathered around the Anal Ring Toss competition.

A newspaper ad had alerted me that Angel Roxx would be working the Dip-Stick booth. The business had nothing to do with oil changes. Dip-Stick was a patented plastic cylinder about the size of a flashlight with a pink foam top. A slit ran through the foam with puffy lips on each side and a little clitoral button inside, like the prize in a Cracker Jack box. Basically, a portable vagina. Pussy to go.

The sales hook was customization. The foam receptacles were created from molds of various porn stars . . . including Ms. Angel Roxx.

"Hey, big fellah, how 'bout some MILF pussy?" a woman said, as I approached the booth.

"I beg your pardon?"

The woman wore a peekaboo pink teddy and knee-high, fleece-lined boots. Underneath sheer lingerie, her breasts were a matched set of dirigibles. A muffin top of jelly fat spilled over the elastic top of her thong. She'd had some work done, her nose a thin wafer. Her skin—as tight as the head of a drum—shined with an eerie waxiness, as if buffed by a floor polisher. I pegged her age at somewhere between 40 and hell.

"Anyone ever mention you look a little like Studley Do-Right?" she said.

"All the time. You know the old Studster?"

"Know him? I've blown him. We costarred in *Splendor in the Ass.* I was just a kid, and he was on his farewell tour." She gave a little curtsy. "I'm Cherries Jubilee. I won the Golden Dildo for best girl-on-girl with Bananas Foster back in the eighties."

"Congrats."

"Here's my beav." She handed me a Dip-Stick, vagina-side up, then stuck her index finger between the foam lips, exposing a bulbous little button. "Have you ever seen anything like that?"

In fact, I hadn't. "A clit like a cornichon," I said, agreeably.

"On sale for eighty-nine bucks, and we throw in a tube of lube and batteries for the vibrometer. You can take her for a test drive if you want."

"Can't. Got a suspended license. Is Angel Roxx here?"

"She's in the back, giving hand jobs to guys in uniform."

I was wearing my old Dolphins jersey but figured that didn't count.

"Vets in wheelchairs get priority," Cherries said. "Angel's the most patriotic porn star I know."

I waited five minutes until Angel emerged from behind a black velvet curtain. She wore a red, white, and blue bikini with cowboy boots and a matching cowboy hat.

A close-cropped, square-jawed young man in a wheelchair rolled out just behind her. He wore a U.S. Marines T-shirt, and his body was bulked up, but his legs were twigs poking out of camo shorts.

"Bye, hon," Angel said, kissing him on the forehead. She saw me standing there and said, "You had your chance, big guy. I don't give rain checks."

We sat at a plastic table in the lunchroom, off the main floor of the convention. "Charlie's been good to me," she said. "I'm not gonna stab him in the back."

"Not asking you to. Just trying to find out why he's gotten friendly with my client."

"Didn't know he had. I thought she tried to shoot him."

"Did you know he visited her in jail?"

"No way! Why would he?"

I shrugged. "My client won't tell me, and I can't talk to him."

"Cool. A mystery."

Angel seemed to loosen up. Everyone, it seems, loves a good mystery.

"Ziegler ever mention my client's sister? Krista Larkin, the girl who went missing?"

"Not to me."

"Any changes in his mood lately?" I asked.

"Charlie's always been weird. When your client started stalking him, he got freakier than usual."

"In what way?"

"Nervous. Noises spooked him. Like if he didn't see you and you said something, he'd jump."

"Anything else?"

She adjusted the strap on her bikini, and her right boob did a little dance. "He hasn't been focused on work, I can tell you that."

"How do you mean?"

"We were supposed to shoot a pilot for my new show, *Who Wantz to Do a Porn Star?* Charlie never hired the director, never did location scouting. Time came and went. No show."

Men streamed by the lunch area, carrying souvenir T-shirts, bumper stickers, and mouse pads, some affixed with photos of their favorite porn stars.

"Does Ziegler ever talk to you about what's bothering him?"

"Not to me."

"Not even in intimate moments?"

She laughed. "I'm not fucking Charlie."

"When I saw you at his house that night, I just assumed..."

"Charlie likes having girls around. But he doesn't do them. I doubt he even does his wife. He only does his girlfriend."

"Melody Sanders."

"Yeah. How'd you know?"

"It's my job, and every once in a while I do it. What's Melody like?"

"Never met her. But she must be something."

"Why?"

"Charlie *listens* to her. I've overheard him on the phone. He talks business."

"And this surprised you?"

"Yeah, I figured he'd be shouting at her, 'I'll be over for my blow job at seven,' but it's not like that. His voice gets all quiet and he reads her the overnight ratings and asks her advice, which he doesn't do with anybody, even his corporate officers." Angel checked her watch and rubbed her hands together, maybe to warm them up. "If you want to know what makes Charlie tick, ask Melody. I'm betting she knows him better than anyone in the world."

57 Too Many Questions

It was Monday morning, the start of another week of trial. I planned on a breakfast of toasted Bimini bread, Cuban coffee, and Haitian fried bananas. Hey, it's Miami. We're not a cornflakes town.

Althea's Taco Truck is my office when I'm in trial. It's parked each day in front of the Justice Building, so it's equally convenient for cops, defense lawyers, and home invasion robbers. The owner/driver/cook is Althea Rollins, a Sequoia-size woman in her late sixties who's partial to Caribbean and Hispanic food.

A dozen years ago, one of her sons was picked up for supplying half the senior class at Killian High with weed. I got the kid into pre-trial intervention and the arrest was expunged. He straightened out, went to college, then pharmacy school, and now he's dispensing legal drugs at a chain store in South Miami.

I have long relied on Althea for advice, insight, and breakfast. She provides another valuable service, too. She eavesdrops on prosecutors and jurors as they have lunch, then spills the frijoles to me. Folks say the darnedest things in front of her.

"Nothing so invisible as a black woman in an apron," Althea told me once, after she revealed the state's strategy in a money-laundering case.

After meeting with Angel Roxx on Saturday morning, I had driven to Lighthouse Point, hoping to drop in, unannounced, on Melody Sanders. I was unannounced all right. The condo was empty. She'd moved and left no forwarding address with the management office.

I told Pepito Dominguez to tail Ziegler so he could lead us to wherever Melody was now hanging her negligee. This morning, he was supposed to meet me with a progress report.

As I walked up to the truck, I saw two men leaving. One was Nestor Tejada, no mistaking the shaved head with the crown tattoo on the back of his skull. He wore a gray suit that bunched up at his bricklayer's shoulders. The other man was older, an Anglo with gray hair in a tailored, pinstriped suit. He carried a soft leather briefcase the color of butter. My insightful powers of reasoning told me the guy was a lawyer.

"Hey, Jakey!" Althea greeted me. "Coffee or pineapple nog."

"Coffee, thanks. Say, do you know those two guys who just left here?"

"Gangbanger and a fancy mouthpiece," Althea said.

"I never saw the lawyer before. You?"

She shook her head. "Polished fingernails. And did you see his eyeglasses?"

I shook my head. "Too far away."

"Expensive. Gold frames with a turquoise inlay."

Althea would make an excellent crime-scene witness.

If neither one of us recognized the lawyer, he was either an out-of-towner or a downtowner. I didn't care so much who he was as *why* he was here.

Nestor Tejada had about ten minutes of noncontroversial testimony to deliver. No reason he should need a lawyer in the gallery.

"What were the guys talking about?" I asked.

"My Cuban coffee. Hispanic guy said it tasted like motor oil."

"He's an asshole. Anything else?"

"They were talking real low. Either that, or my hearing's going straight to Hades."

Just then, Pepito walked up in that easygoing gait that said he had a lot of time to get wherever he was going. He ordered a *coco frio*. Althea lopped off the top of a coconut with a machete, stuck a straw in the hole and handed it to him.

"Did you find Melody Sanders?" I asked.

Instead of answering, Pepito handed me a wad of crumpled American Express receipts.

"What's this?" I asked.

"My expenses."

I looked at the first one. Il Gabbiano, a ritzy restaurant downtown. "Two hundred thirty-six dollars! What the hell."

"You told me to follow Charlie Ziegler. He had dinner."

"If he goes into a rest room, that doesn't mean you have to take a piss." I glanced at the restaurant receipt. "You ate veal stuffed with foie gras? Wait a second. There are two entrées here."

"I had the filet mignon. My girlfriend, Raquel, had the veal."

I felt the first hints of indigestion and I hadn't even eaten Althea's fried plantains simmered in wine.

"Don't worry. You're getting your money's worth, boss," Pepito said.

"So you found Melody?"

The kid pulled a little notebook out of his cargo shorts and flipped a few pages. "Ziegler had the mista salad and veal piccata."

"Why didn't you give me his check? It would have been cheaper."

"And Alex Castiel ordered a bottle of red wine. Châteauneuf-du-Pape."

Castiel. That stopped me, but just for a second. Nothing wrong with the State Attorney dining with his chief witness. Had there been, they wouldn't have met in public.

"What were they talking about?" I asked.

"How should I know?"

"You could read the wine label, but you couldn't get close enough to listen?"

"The State Attorney toasted him with the wine. Then, at the end, they shook hands. One of those four-handed deals, you know, hands on top of each other's."

"Then what? Please tell me you followed Ziegler to Melody's."

"First, Ziegler got his car from the valet. While he's waiting, he's talking on the cell phone, and I'm standing right behind him."

"Yeah?"

"He's talking real sweet, 'honey' this and 'honey' that."

"Jeez, Pepito, cut to it."

"He says, 'Honey, I'll be there in ten minutes.' So I figure, she lives close."

"Good figuring. Keep going."

"Then his Ferrari came up. He got into the car and I had to run to get mine from a meter on Biscayne Boulevard."

"So you followed him to Melody's place?"

"I tried. I was four cars behind him when we got to the Brickell Avenue drawbridge. He went across as the yellow light was flashing. The arm came down right in front of me. So I got hung up and lost him there."

"Shit."

"I'm sorry, *jefe*."

"It's okay, Pepito. You did great. Sometimes I'm too hard on you."

I checked my watch. Five minutes to get to court. So much happening. Tejada had a lawyer for reasons unknown. Ziegler and Castiel were best buds. Somewhere out there, presumably ten minutes from downtown, sat Melody Sanders, keeper of Ziegler's secrets. Then there was Amy Larkin, my tight-lipped client. Where was she the night of the murder? Who was she with? What's going on between Ziegler and her?

Some days, I feel in control of my life and my surroundings. But today I felt I was the butt of some cosmic joke in the legal universe. If a meteorite sped across the vastness of space and entered our atmosphere, I had no doubt it would make a beeline straight for my head.

58 The Rat

The man with polished fingernails and the turquoise glasses sat in the back row of the gallery. I gave him a little lawyer nod, but he didn't acknowledge me. I kept my eyes on Tejada during his direct exam and caught him flashing looks to the guy, as if seeking approval.

When Castiel informed me that the witness was mine, I patted Amy Larkin on the shoulder, stood up, smiled pleasantly at the jury, and said, "Good morning, Mr. Tejada."

"Yeah. Morning."

He looked sullen. Fine with me. Jurors like their witnesses to be neighborly and good-humored, not cheerless and sour.

Tejada had walked through Castiel's direct exam, the State Attorney his usual brisk and efficient self. Now I had a clear-cut task. I wanted to point a finger at this jailbird, and while I was at it, smear Ziegler, too.

"Let me get a few things straight, Mr. Tejada. When you heard the gunshots, you raced around the house to the pool deck and straight to the solarium, correct?"

"Yeah."

"How'd you know to run there?"

"That's where the shots seemed to come from."

"Seemed to? Do you have experience with gunshots?"

He gave a little smirk. "Some."

"You're not on the Olympic biathlon team by any chance, are you?"

"Nope."

"And you're not a veteran of Iraq or Afghanistan, are you?"

"No."

"Ever serve in uniform? Other than in prison?"

"Objection!" Castiel fired it off so quickly, he didn't even have time to stand.

"Mr. Lassiter, you will stow the sarcasm in your rucksack," Judge Melvia Duckworth said, employing a term she must have used in court-martials back in JAG.

"Thank you, Your Honor," I said, in the time-honored tradition of accepting criticism with dignity and respect.

On direct exam, Castiel smartly brought out that Tejada had several criminal convictions. Under the rules of evidence, I then couldn't ask anything about his crimes.

"Mr. Tejada. When you reached the pool deck, the first thing you saw was a broken window in the solarium. Is that correct?"

"Yeah. Like I already said to the prosecutor."

"And when you looked inside, you saw Charles Ziegler bent over the body of Max Perlow?"

"That's right."

"Did you see my client anywhere?" I nodded toward Amy, sitting placidly at the defense table, a nonhomicidal look on her angelic face.

"No."

"If she shot Mr. Perlow, how do you suppose she got away?"

"Objection!" Castiel bounced to his feet like a fighter coming off the corner stool. "Calls for a conclusion."

"Sustained," Judge Duckworth said.

"Let me ask it this way. Mr. Ziegler's house sits right on the water, correct?"

"Yeah. The pool deck runs to the seawall."

"Did you see anyone fleeing by boat?"

"No."

"When you were running from the north side of the house, did you see anyone running toward the south?"

"Nope."

"Did you hear any car engines starting up or driving off?"

"No."

"So the only person you saw was Charles Ziegler, who's bent over the victim?"

"Yeah. Said it a couple times now."

"Was Mr. Ziegler trying to stop the bleeding?"

"Not that I saw."

"Was he performing resuscitation?"

"Don't think so."

"So, what was Ziegler doing? Just watching Max Perlow die?"

"Objection, Your Honor." Castiel again. "Argumentative."

"Overruled. You may answer, Mr. Tejada."

"Ziegler was kind of paralyzed. In shock, like."

"Maybe he'd never seen anyone shot before?"

"I'm sure he hadn't."

"But you have, correct? You've seen men shot."

At the prosecution table, Castiel stirred but didn't stand up. He could easily object. But Castiel knew which hills to defend, and which ones to give up without losing any troops.

"I've seen a couple dudes shot, yeah."

Tejada glanced toward the man in the last row.

"Let's step back for a minute. Just why was Mr. Perlow visiting Charles Ziegler that night?" I asked.

"To collect money."

I liked the answer. "Collect money" had a seedy sound.

"You had a business deal of your own with Mr. Perlow, didn't you?" I already knew this from taking Tejada's depo.

"Slot-machine contract. We serviced Indian reservations."

"What were the terms between you and Mr. Perlow?"

"I had a third of the business. When Mr. P died, I got the rest."

Bingo.

"So you stood to gain financially on Mr. Perlow's death?"

"I see where you're going, but I was happy working for Mr. P."

"Really? Driving his car was better than owning his business?"

"I wasn't in a hurry. The old dude was like family."

"Weren't you getting tired of waiting for the old dude to die?"

"Nope. I enjoyed his company."

I was out to collect a string of "no"s. Get enough negatives, they sometimes turn into a positive.

"So that wasn't you on the pool deck with a gun . . ."

"No way, man!"

" . . . purposely making a noise to lure Perlow into the solarium . . ."

"Hell, no!"

" . . . where you could shoot him through the glass?"

"Screw you, Lassiter! That's crap."

His face had heated up with a look that was positively murderous.

"The witness will keep his voice down," the judge instructed.

"So now, Mr. Tejada, you're the proud owner of one hundred percent of the slot-machine business, correct?"

He answered softly. "As soon as the legal papers are done, yeah."

I decided to throw a Hail Mary, see who would catch it. "Is that why your lawyer is here today?"

Tejada's eyes flicked again to the man in the last row of the gallery. "That's not why he's here."

Okay. I was half right. At least, the guy was his lawyer.

I took another chance. "Are you currently charged with a crime, Mr. Tejada?"

"Downtown. The feds indicted me for money laundering."

"Is the charge related to your slot-machine business?"

"That's what they say. My lawyer's gotta talk to the U.S. Attorney about my plea deal."

His plea deal. Oh, shit.

If Tejada had been indicted for the slots business, Perlow was likely to be charged, too. The old mobster was the bigger fish, so Tejada had some leverage in a plea deal in which he cooperated with the feds. Meaning . . .

Tejada didn't want Perlow dead. Perlow was Tejada's ticket out of jail.

I had fallen into a gator hole, and I needed to get the hell out before I got my leg chewed off. "Your witness," I told Castiel.

The State Attorney gave me a snarky smile and said, "Mr. Tejada, let's tidy up a bit."

Translation: The defense lawyer took a dump on the floor. Let's rub his face in it.

"Did you become a cooperating witness after your indictment?"

Tejada looked down as he answered, "Yeah, I did."

"What were the terms of your cooperation?"

"If I testified against Mr. P, I'd get a reduced sentence. Maybe no prison time."

"So did you have a motive to see Max Perlow dead?"

"*Todo lo contrario.* The opposite, man. With him dead, I got no deal with the feds."

"Thank you, Mr. Tejada." Castiel slid back into his chair.

Two tons of sand weighted me down, but I still managed to get to my feet. There was no reason to flail away any longer, but I always prefer going to the lunch break with my words in the air, rather than the prosecutor's. "Your Honor, just a couple questions."

"Quickly, Counselor."

"Are you what's called a rat, Mr. Tejada? A snitch?"

"That and a lot worse names."

"Max Perlow was good to you, wasn't he?"

"He was the best."

"And you turned on him?"

"He wouldn't look at it that way," Tejada said. "Mr. P used to tell a story. Two men are walking through the woods and come across a big bear. The bear starts chasing them, and one guy says, 'You think we can outrun this bear?' The other guy says, 'I only have to outrun you.' It's what Mr. P taught me. When the shooting starts, put someone between yourself and the shooter. Save yourself first. Worry about others later. I was just doing what the old man taught me."

59 The Dark Side

Amy was back in her holding cell, probably gagging on her lunch. Two slices of bologna on white bread with a packet of mustard, a half pint of milk, and a small bag of potato chips. Yeah, I hate how we pamper our prisoners.

Judge Duckworth was off to the Bankers Club, sliced tenderloin with a tangy horseradish sauce, a Caesar salad, and a martini, straight up. The jurors were downstairs in the cafeteria, escorted by the bailiff.

The courtroom abandoned, I sat alone at the defense table, surveying the wreckage of my case. Basically, I had a client who wouldn't level with me, and she had an incompetent lawyer.

I was riffling through my file folders, as if I could find a scrap that would win the case. There was nothing in the paperwork. There seldom is. I opened Kip's research files, pulled out the forty-year-old photo of Max Perlow and Meyer Lansky walking into the very courtroom where I now sat brooding. Then another photo, an aged Lansky, in dark slacks and light sweater, walking a little dog on a leash.

"Bruzzer!"

The voice from over my shoulder startled me. I turned and saw Castiel.

"Lansky's dog was named 'Bruzzer,'" he said. "Spelled with two 'z's."

"I know. Max Perlow told me that. Said he used to go with Lansky on his dog walks."

Castiel eased into my client's chair, propped his feet on the defense table, and leaned back, both hands behind his head. "Not like you to skip lunch, Jake."

"Not like me to step on one of your land mines, either."

"You're overly aggressive. Sometimes it works. And sometimes..."

His shit-eating grin made me want to slug him. "Tell me the truth, Alex. Did you tell Tejada to stop by Althea's truck with his lawyer this morning?"

"I might have mentioned something about Althea's high-octane Cuban coffee."

"Shit. You suckered me."

"I've been watching Althea feed you plantains and state secrets for a dozen years." He gave me his politician's laugh. "I know you too well, amigo."

Funny thing was, I didn't know Castiel at all. Until Amy Larkin came to town, I hadn't known just how closely my pal had been tied to shady characters like his Uncle Max and the Prince of Porn.

"Is Tejada really gonna do time?" I asked.

"Doubt it. He's a professional snitch. He's got others to rat out."

Other bears to outrun, I thought. "Dammit, Alex, you played me."

"Coming and going." He whipped a Cuban Torpedo out of his suit pocket and grabbed his gold lighter, that fancy gift from General Batista to Bernard Castiel. "Just wanted you to know I'm a better trial lawyer than you. Always have been."

"Should I drop my shorts? 'Cause I didn't know we were having a dick-measuring contest."

"No need. I've got a slam-dunk case, old buddy."

Oh. I hadn't seen this coming.

When a prosecutor turns boastful, he's worried about something. The whole Tejada shtick was a misdirect, like a play-action fake on a passing play.

"So what are you offering, old buddy?" I asked.

"Your client gets convicted, she's looking at life. But I've been doing some soul searching..."

"Let me know when you find it."

He flicked the lighter, watched the orange flame, then snapped the top shut. "I'd be amenable to Manslaughter, seven to ten years."

That caught me by surprise. I wondered what happened to: *"I'm taking her down, and I don't give a shit if I take you down with her."*

"Strange, you making this offer right before Charlie Ziegler is gonna testify."

"Got nothing to do with him."

"Sure it does. He's out of control."

"I met with him last night. He's strong and steady. Sticking to his testimony."

"That could have been the Châteauneuf-du-Pape talking." I was showing off, letting him know I wasn't clueless about his dinner date.

From the door behind the bench, the bailiff poked his head into the courtroom, checked us out, and said, "Mr. Castiel, if you're gonna smoke that thing, I'll get the air freshener."

"It's okay, Oscar." Castiel slipped the cigar back into his pocket. The bailiff left and Castiel turned back to me. "Charlie feels remorse for whatever happened to Krista Larkin. Amy showing up brought it all back to him. Messed him up."

"Why not just admit it, Alex? You don't trust Ziegler. You're scared shitless of what he's gonna say."

"The matching bullets are enough for conviction. I don't need Charlie."

"Fine. Don't call him."

"You'd like that, wouldn't you, old buddy?"

"You bet. In closing argument, I'd remind the jury that you promised an eyewitness. Or maybe I'll call Ziegler on my case. Helluva chess match, Alex."

"What about it, Jake? Will you recommend your client take the plea?"

"Amy swears she didn't shoot Perlow. Whenever I can avoid it, I try not to send innocent people to prison."

Castiel sighed and looked genuinely sad for his old buddy, namely me. "So many bad choices."

"Maybe, but they're *my* choices."

"You're gonna lose, and Larkin's gonna get new lawyers. They'll file an appeal claiming ineffective assistance of counsel, and you'll be in the papers."

"My clients don't read the papers."

Another click of the lighter, the flame dancing. Castiel's pyromaniacal habit was getting on my nerves. "Just looking out for you, Jake. Didn't expect you to listen."

"You're saying I should learn from Perlow? First, save myself."

"It's not bad advice. Uncle Max started telling me that when I was nine years old. Lansky had been telling him that for thirty years."

I pondered his words. The me-first philosophy had been passed from gangster to gangster to prosecutor. Nothing out of line about that in Castiel's world. He's the one who believed that life is a constant struggle of the valiant side versus the dark side. Ever since that first day in his office, I'd been wondering which team was winning in the battle for Castiel's soul.

60 Living a Lie

Castiel wished me bad luck and left. In a few minutes, the courtroom would be open for business. Nothing good would happen this afternoon. It seldom does on the state's side of the case. One of Ziegler's employees would take the stand. She was yet another "stalking witness," having seen Amy lurking in his office building lobby a few days before the shooting. Then a lab tech would testify that shoeprints in the mud of a construction site next to Ziegler's house matched the running shoes found in Amy's motel room. Finally, a cop would tell the jury about Amy's stunt outside the Grand Jury chambers. The maraschino cherry on top of that sundae would be her threat: "Charlie Ziegler killed Krista! If you won't do something about it, I will." Like I said, not a great day for the defense.

Tomorrow, the courthouse would be dark. Budget woes stopping the wheels of justice two days each month. The following day, Charlie Ziegler would say his piece. When he finished, the case would either be won or lost.

I started cleaning up the defense table, returning useless papers to their folders. That's when I spotted Castiel's solid gold cigarette lighter. He'd left it on the defense table. I flipped it open. Inside was an inscription:

"Para el Judio Maravilloso, del Mulato Lindo."

"To the marvelous Jew, from the pretty mulatto."

The pretty mulatto was General Fulgencio Batista, a nickname he'd acquired in his playboy youth. The marvelous Jew was Lansky.

Castiel had lied to me.

The lighter was a gift to Meyer Lansky, not to Bernard Castiel, Alex's father.

It made sense. Batista, the Cuban strongman, would be more likely to honor Lansky, the casino owner who split profits with him, than Lansky's hired help, the guy who delivered the cash. But why would Alex lie about it? And how did he end up with Lansky's cigarette lighter?

I remembered something Castiel told me. Lansky promised him a hundred bucks if he proved he was a brave little boy.

"He told me to carve my name under the judge's bench."

I pictured nine-year-old Alex Castiel, his face scrunched in concentration, both hands on the Swiss Army knife, gouging at the wood, making his mark, a sacred secret between himself and the most notorious gangster of his time. But was it true?

I scurried to the front of the courtroom, hopped the three steps to the judge's elevated throne, and pulled back her chair. I ducked under the bench and flicked on the lighter so I could see. I brushed away cobwebs and swept dust off the wood.

There it was, in the corner, carved with a surprisingly steady hand. As I read the name, I felt my stomach heave as if an elevator plunged several floors. A sense of embarrassment, too, as if I were a Peeping Tom.

I looked hard at the letters etched into the mahogany, believing that some of my questions about Alex Castiel had just been answered. Then I ran a finger across the torn wood and said the name aloud: "Alex Lansky."

61 Family Ties

I headed out the courtroom door and down the corridor. Castiel was huddling with a homicide cop near the elevator. He looked up and I tossed the lighter to him. He nabbed it in one hand, then caught the look on my face. He shook hands with the cop, then joined me in an alcove where the phone booths used to be located in the days before cellular.

"After all these years, Alex, finally I understand you."

"Meaning?"

"I always thought we had something in common. I lost my father very young. You never knew yours. Everything I know I learned from my granny, who's not really my grandmother. You got your lessons from your uncle Max, who's not really your uncle."

"So?"

"You weren't a fatherless, penniless little boy who grew up seeking justice. You had a Mafia scholarship from the day you were born."

"What the hell are you talking about?"

"Meyer Lansky is your father, and when he wasn't being chased around the world by the feds, he was mentoring you. When he was gone, Max Perlow pinch hit for him. Perlow set you up with people who could get you elected. He wanted you to do for him what Batista did for Lansky. Or maybe he had bigger dreams."

Castiel shot me a wry smile. "All this figuring, Jake. It's above your pay grade."

"I keep thinking about that photo in your office."

"Careful, Jake..."

"Your mother standing between Bernard and Lansky. She was a beautiful woman who gets hit with this double tragedy. All hell breaks loose with Castro taking Havana, and then Bernard is killed. She must have been devastated. But there's Meyer Lansky, rich and powerful, with a finely tailored shoulder to cry on. Who can blame her for falling for the guy? Unless..."

Something was nagging at me, an itch in the back of my brain. In the corridor, the bailiff was leading the jurors back into the courtroom. We had just a couple minutes.

"Unless that story about Bernard's heroic death was total bull," I said.

"You gonna crap on his memory, too?"

"What do you care? He's not your father. Maybe your mother was already having an affair with Lansky, and Bernard found out. In some Jewbano rage, he confronted Lansky. Threatened him. Whatever he did got him killed. I'm betting Lansky ordered it and Perlow carried it out."

"*The Havana Post* said Bernard was bayoneted by the rebels. I have the clipping."

"Batista propaganda. If I'm right, your mother continued her affair with Lansky and got pregnant. Or she was already pregnant when Bernard was killed. Either way, that's when you come into the picture. Castro confiscates the Riviera. Lansky gets out of Dodge, and Perlow puts you on a Pedro Pan flight to Miami. Your mother is supposed to join you, but she's dying of cancer. Lansky was married and had kids of his own. He also didn't want you carrying the weight of his name. Helluva lot better to be Alex Castiel, son of a supposed martyr, than Lansky's kid. So Perlow arranges for a sham adoption with a nice family in Coral Gables, all the while keeping your real father, Lansky, behind the scenes."

Castiel was quiet a moment, then spoke softly. "If I had a time machine, I'd go to Havana, hang out with Meyer at the Riviera."

I understood. If I could travel through space and time, I'd go shrimping with my old man. Spend as much time with him as I could.

"I'm not ashamed of being Meyer's son," Castiel said. "I loved the man, and he loved me. I like to think he'd be proud of me."

That hit me hard, and I wondered just what Castiel would do to earn that love and respect. And looking back, what had he already done?

62 Lawyers, Guns, and Money

The next morning, I was cruising north on I-95. No court today. I had twenty-four hours until Charlie Ziegler appeared as a witness for the prosecution. I still wasn't sure what he would say when Castiel asked the magic question: *"Can you identify the shooter?"*

Traffic slowed near 125th Street, where a refrigerated truck had overturned, spilling several tons of Florida lobsters onto the pavement. The critters scrambled across the expressway into the high-occupancy lane. Unless they'd purchased SunPasses, they'd likely get tickets.

Cars crunched the crustaceans. A few drivers hopped out, trying to corral their supper. I swerved through the traffic and made it to a warehouse district near the Broward County line. Last night, as I was eating Granny's deep-fried frogs legs, Pepito Dominguez had called. He'd been tailing Ziegler. The idea had been to find Melody Sanders, but Ziegler had a different destination. His old porn production facility, now owned by Rodney Gifford.

Pepito told me that Ziegler and Gifford drove to Morton's in North Miami Beach where they ate steaks and drank martinis, Ziegler picking up the tab. My semi-pro P.I. took a table nearby but couldn't hear their conversation. That didn't keep him from ordering double-rib lamb chops and faxing me the bill. At the end of the meal, Ziegler and Gifford hugged. Pepito couldn't be sure but he thought he saw tears in Ziegler's eyes.

What the hell was that about?

Today's job was to find out. I guided the old Eldo into the parking lot beneath the sign that said, *Gifford Worldwide Productions.* On the radio, Warren Zevon was gambling in Havana, where he had gotten into trouble. The solution seemed to be "lawyers, guns, and money," which in my experience often make things worse. With that thought, I killed the ignition and headed inside.

A heavily tattooed young man with a pimpled butt was having sex with a life-size silicone doll named Candy. I knew her name because young Olivier kept grunting "Fucking you good Candy; fucking you good, Candy," as if reviewing his own performance. Candy kept quiet, except for an occasional silicone squeak.

"In the second act, the doll comes to life and kills him," a production assistant told me.

They were shooting *Killer Candy 8,* a video about homicidal love dolls. The tattooed guy made some disturbing guttural sounds of distress, like a boar in cardiac arrest, then spritzed his money shot all over Candy's 38-DDD boobs. Rodney Gifford yelled, "Cut," called for the Windex guy, and gave cast and crew a ten-minute break.

I walked up to Gifford as he was thumbing through a script. He was a trim, khakied man in his fifties. Khaki slacks, khaki safari vest, khaki chest hair.

"I'm Jake Lassiter. Can we talk?"

"How big's your dick?"

"What?"

"Does it take two hands to handle your whopper?"

"You start all conversations this way?"

"You're here for the casting, right? *White Men Can't Hump.*"

"I'm a lawyer."

"No shit. You look a little like Studley Do-Right. Guy had a helluva wad."

"I've got some questions about Charlie Ziegler."

"You got a subpoena?"

"Nope."

"So why should I talk to you?"

"Why wouldn't you? Do you have something to hide?"

"Doesn't everyone?" Gifford rasped a smoker's laugh and squinted at me through eyes the color of snot. "C'mon, Studley. You got ten minutes, not a second more, unless I find you fabulously entertaining."

We walked up a set of steel stairs to his office, a cluttered rat's nest just off a catwalk, overlooking the production set. He offered me lukewarm coffee and a chair with torn, upholstered arms. I took the chair, declined the coffee, and asked why Ziegler came to see him yesterday.

"None of your business, Stud-bug." He drummed his manicured fingernails on his desk. On the wall were a pair of movie posters. *Don't Ask, Do Tell* showed women in military uniforms, tunics open, breasts exposed. *Saving Ryan's Privates* showed men in unzipped combat fatigues. Apparently, Gifford also made patriotic films.

"The way I hear it, Ziegler screwed you on the sale of the business," I said.

"Old news."

"Stole your girlfriend and married her."

"Lola? His loss, not mine. Monogamy is overrated, don't you think?"

"Not compared to celibacy."

"Touché," he said, waving an index finger like a saber.

"Then yesterday, you and Ziegler are seen eating steaks and hugging."

"Charlie's going through some changes, okay? Trust me, it has nothing to do with your case."

"Ziegler expressing remorse for his past, is that it?"

I was just repeating what Castiel had said yesterday. Ziegler, too, had used the word the night I ate sushi at his house. *"Looking back now, I've got a lot of remorse."*

"Any law against being sorry for the shit you did?" Gifford asked.

I hope not, thinking of myself.

"If the shit includes murder," I said, "that's pretty much against the law."

"Ziegler's a prick. But he's not a killer. If you must know, yesterday he apologized for screwing me over. He's sorry, sorry, sorry."

Ziegler apologized to Gifford, and to Amy at their jailhouse visit. He was on an apology tour. I tried another angle.

"A few before Perlow was shot," I said, "my client came around and asked you some questions."

"Lovely woman—but so filled with anger."

"You lied to her. You said Krista wasn't at the party, but I have a witness who places her there."

"I told your client I saw Ziegler with three or four girls, and Krista wasn't one of them. That's as far as I went."

"You chose your words carefully."

"As I do my lovers." His smile showed me two rows of ultra-white crowns.

"Tell me who Krista was with," I ordered.

"Why should I?"

I bounded out of my chair, grabbed the collar of his safari jacket, and jerked him to his feet. "Because I'll toss you through the wall and off that catwalk."

"You wouldn't."

I lifted him off his feet. "You better hope you land on silicone tits instead of a concrete floor."

"Why not spank me instead?"

I wheeled him into the wall so hard, the poster of *Booby Trap XXIII* crashed to the floor. "Bumper cars!" he yelled.

It occurred to me that he was enjoying this.

"Spanky, spanky, spanky!" he said.

"I don't spank. I punch."

I wrapped my hand around his throat. "What'd you see that night at Ziegler's?"

A croaking sound came from Gifford's throat and his eyes bulged.

"Tell me!" I said, loosening my grip just a bit.

"A man asked for some ludes. Krista was with him, half-zonked already."

"Who was he?"

"I gave him a handful of pills, and he carried her to the Fuck Palace."

"Who? Give me a name."

"He's scary. Scarier than you."

I grabbed a handful of mousse-slicked hair and yanked him away from the wall. Headlocked his skull with my right arm, then pasted my big left mitt over his mouth and nose, pinching his nostrils shut. I waited until he started bucking. "Who was he! Who took Krista to the Fuck Palace?"

His cheeks were turning crimson. Then I let go with my left hand and let him suck in a breath.

"More," he begged me. "More, sir."

"I don't have time for this shit." I propped him up with my left arm and threw a short, right hook into his gut. Solid, but not a pile driver calculated to make him expel his breakfast onto my shoes.

His knees buckled and he dropped to all fours. He looked up with dancing eyes, a horse awaiting a rider. "The man..." He gasped. "The man with Krista was Alex Castiel."

63 Playing Hooky

Granny was frying a big-mouthed, pink hog snapper, head and all, in her largest cast-iron pan. Kip was in the kitchen, grating cabbage for cole slaw.

"What's with the sunburn, kiddo? Did you play hooky today?"

"You used to cut school to work in a bar."

"Who told you that?"

"I'm standing on the Fifth Amendment," Granny said, flipping the fat fish with a spatula. "Snapper was running off the reef, so we took the dinghy out."

"Kip, until we get past your disciplinary hearing, you can't cut school," I said.

"We're past it, Uncle Jake."

My look shot him a question, and Kip explained. The Commodore had called him into the office. The esteemed State Attorney and distinguished alumnus Alejandro Castiel had placed a call. Vouched for Kip. Charges dismissed.

"That really pisses me off," I said.

"Why, Uncle Jake? We won."

"I don't want to owe Castiel any favors."

"Why not?"

"Because I have to do something really shitty to him."

This time, *his* look asked the question.

"I have to destroy him."

64 Never Let Them See Your Fear

The next morning, I drove north on 27th Avenue and passed under the Dolphin Expressway, headed toward the Justice Building. Robert Plant and Alison Krauss were pounding out "Gone, Gone, Gone," and the world was tilted crazily on its axis.

"Because you done me wrong."

At precisely ten A.M., the bailiff escorted Charlie Ziegler from the corridor to the witness stand. The saddlebags under Ziegler's eyes seemed puffier today, and a mini-bandage on his chin looked like the aftermath of a shaving accident. Sleepless night? Shaky hands?

He avoided my gaze on his walk past the bar. I wasn't offended. He didn't look at Alex Castiel, either. But he shot a glance at the jury.

Next to me, Amy Larkin seemed composed, her hands folded primly in her lap. I had never encountered a defendant so damned placid when facing life without parole.

Castiel took his star witness around the track slowly at first, establishing his background in the "adult entertainment industry," so that my cross-exam would not come as a dirty little surprise to the jury.

Then Castiel moved to the stalking and the threats. Yes, Ziegler had observed the defendant on a neighbor's property, watching him. Yes, he had seen her in the lobby of his office building. "Loitering and surveilling," in Castiel's words.

"Do you recall an occasion on which you received a phone call from Mr. Lassiter concerning his client?" Castiel asked.

"If you're talking about the incident at the gun range, yes, I do," Ziegler said.

"What occasioned that conversation?"

"I had made a proposal to Mr. Lassiter to set up a fund to search for Ms. Larkin's sister."

Sounding noble, indeed.

"So you thought that's what he was calling about?"

"Yes, but he said—"

"Objection, hearsay," I called out.

"May we approach?" Castiel said.

Judge Melvia Duckworth waved us forward, and we trekked to the bench for a sidebar, out of earshot of the jury. "Your question clearly appears to call for a hearsay answer, Mr. Castiel."

"I'd submit that Mr. Lassiter's response was an 'excited utterance' and therefore an exception to the hearsay rule."

"Let's hear a proffer," the judge ordered.

"Mr. Lassiter replied that Ms. Larkin would rather, quote, 'empty a clip into your gut than take your money,' close quote," Castiel recited.

The judge raised her eyebrows and turned to me.

"I wasn't excited," I said.

"Your Honor," Castiel hopped in, "the defendant had just shot out all the tires on Mr. Lassiter's car."

"Three tires," I corrected him.

"Mr. Lassiter immediately called Mr. Ziegler to warn him that Amy Larkin was armed and coming after him. The evidence code defines an 'excited utterance' as one immediately following a startling event in which the declarant is under stress and is excited. Clearly, this falls under the rule."

"I wasn't excited," I repeated, drily. "I was calm and rational. As I recall, I was thinking about whether I should buy four new tires and not just three. It seemed a prudent thing to do, given balancing and rotation and tread wear."

"Objection overruled," the judge declared.

We resumed our places, and Ziegler repeated my regrettable words:

"Mr. Lassiter said, 'She's got a gun, and she's headed your way.' Or something to that effect."

The jurors' eyes switched from the witness to my client. Grave looks. I didn't like that. Not one bit.

Castiel moved to the night of the shooting. An assistant handled the projection gear, showing the solarium, the broken window, and what would be the grand finale, the body of Max Perlow. Castiel methodically paced Ziegler through the moments leading up to the murder. A noise outside. The two men walk into the solarium. Perlow waddles up to the window, approaches the glass, and *ka-boom, ka-boom*. Then the money question.

"Did you, Mr. Ziegler, see who fired the gunshots?"

The jurors leaned forward in their chairs. I clenched a pencil.

Ziegler spoke clearly into the microphone. "I saw a figure outside."

"Can you identify that figure?"

"Not really," Ziegler said.

Castiel's eyes flickered. "Not really?"

"It wasn't the woman sitting next to Mr. Lassiter," Ziegler said. "It wasn't Amy Larkin. I can tell you that."

I'll be damned. Just as Amy said, Ziegler was doing the right thing. Assuming it was the truth.

A ripple of murmurs moved through the gallery. Jurors exchanged looks.

Castiel fixed his face into a mask of Zen-like equanimity. He knew the first rule of trial work: Never let them see your fear. "Now, Mr. Ziegler, do you recall giving a statement to homicide detectives?"

"Amy Larkin is tall and thin," Ziegler said, ignoring the question. "The shooter was bigger, stockier. It was definitely a man."

A couple jurors exchanged whispers.

"So that it's clear, Mr. Ziegler, your testimony directly contradicts your statement to the police, isn't that correct?"

"I'd just seen Max shot and was very upset."

Castiel stayed calm and did not raise his voice. He'd been doing this too long to pee his pants over a recanting witness. "When you gave your statement to homicide detectives at the scene, the shooting was fresh in your mind, was it not?"

"With Amy Larkin stalking me, there was some sort of mental sugges-tion that it must have been her."

" 'Mental suggestion'?" Castiel sounded amused.

"Like if you know someone has a green car, if you see a green car, you think it must be them."

"Was this mental suggestion, this green-car syndrome, still preying on your mind when you repeated your identification in a written affidavit?"

"It must have been."

"And when you and I met prior to your deposition, you again con-firmed your earlier statements, correct?"

"Yes, sir."

"More green-car syndrome?"

"I guess I'd convinced myself."

"When Mr. Lassiter deposed you under oath prior to trial, what did you say then?"

"Same deal. But I was wrong."

Ziegler was trying to exonerate Amy, I thought. Only problem, he *looked* like he was trying. There was something artificial and pre-packaged about the recantation.

Castiel picked up the wooden pointer he'd used to highlight diagrams of the house and pool deck. He might have wanted to flail his witness with the pointer, but he merely wagged it like a parent scolding a child. "You've been upset ever since Ms. Larkin came to town and made those accusa-tions against you, haven't you?"

"She accused me of a crime I didn't commit, so yeah, I was steamed. Probably the way she feels right now."

That zinger brought a sharp look from Castiel, but he kept his voice even and untroubled. He made a show of looking at the clock, then at the jurors, and finally at the judge. "Your Honor, perhaps this would be a good time for the lunch break. As you might expect, I am not finished with this witness."

Translation: I'll spend the next hour sharpening my scalpel and the afternoon removing his liver.

The judge turned to me for my assent. "Mr. Lassiter?"

"I could eat a bear," I said.

"Done. We stand in recess for one hour."

65 The Alibi

I had lied to the judge. I wasn't hungry. My stomach was filled with razor blades.

An aging sheriff's deputy swung open the steel door, and I joined Amy Larkin in the windowless holding cell behind the courtroom. We were deep in the bowels of the Justice Building. I made a mental note to spend the next hurricane here.

When the door clanged shut behind me, I must have been frowning because Amy said, "Smile, Jake. We had a great morning."

I sat down on a steel bench bolted to the wall. "Think so?"

"C'mon, Charlie was terrific."

"Only if you like circus tricks. Now cut the bullshit and tell me what's going on."

"What do you mean? Charlie said he was going to do the right thing, and he did."

She seemed almost giddy.

"You're playing me, Amy. You and your new best friend. *Charlie.* And you're playing the court. Problem is, you're both amateurs."

"C'mon, Jake. Charlie torpedoed the case."

"What makes you think so?"

"There's no eyewitness testimony."

"Sure there is. Ziegler I.D.'d you half a dozen times before he recanted. You think the jury slept through all that?"

"Why would they believe a story he says is no longer true?"

"Because Castiel did a good job impeaching him, and he's not done yet. Plus all the circumstantial evidence. The matching bullets. The prints. The stalking. The threats. Not to mention my call from the gun range."

"You're saying I'll still be convicted."

"Bet on it."

Her smile vanished. "Charlie said this would work."

"He's a better pornographer than lawyer."

"And there's nothing you can do?"

"Give me your alibi. Unless that's bullshit, too."

"It's real!" Her face heating up. The anger looked sincere.

"A name. Give me a name."

She toyed with a thought before speaking. "I need to make a call."

I handed over my cell, and Amy dialed a number. "Hi. It's me. Can you come to the courthouse right away? Jake says he needs you."

A pause. She listened.

"I know, but things have changed." Her eyes flicked toward me. "Jake says Charlie changing his testimony won't work with the jury. He accused me too many times before. Jake says today was just a circus trick."

Amy listened some more, then laughed. "I'll tell him you said that."

"Said what?" I asked, but she waved me off.

"An hour, then," Amy said into the phone. "Thanks. I knew I could count on you."

She hung up and her face was once again beatific. Not a care in the world.

"Who the hell was that?"

"Melody Sanders."

That rocked me. "Ziegler's girlfriend is your alibi? No way."

Amy shrugged. "It's true."

"What were you doing with her? And what did she say just now that's so damn funny?"

Amy gave me a little smile. "That the circus hasn't even started yet." The smile turned into a full-tilt laugh, and I got the feeling the joke was on me.

"You lied to me. You said you were with a man that night."

"A little white lie."

"You said it was too dangerous for him to testify."

"That part was true. Melody could be killed."

"By whom? And why? And how do the two of you even know each other?"

Amy rolled her eyes at me. "Frankly, Jake, I thought you'd figure it out before now."

"Figure what out?"

"There's Charlie. Melody. Me." She gave me a cutesy little smile. "And me. Melody. Charlie."

"Yeah, I get it. Melody's the linchpin between the two of you. She's . . ." *Holy shit.*

Suddenly, it all came into focus. There it was, right in front of me. Where it had been all the time.

66 A Courtroom Visitor

Thirty minutes later, I was hustling into the courtroom when my cell phone buzzed. Pepito Dominguez.

"Quickly, kid. I'm in court."

"Melody Sanders is a dead end, Jake."

"Thanks, Pepito, but I'm not gonna need any Melody info."

"But get this, *jefe*. She's really dead. Melody Sanders from Sarasota. Died fifteen years ago in a head-on crash on Alligator Alley."

"Got it, Pepito."

"You're not surprised?"

"You did good work, kid. I'm gonna tell your dad that. Gotta go."

Moments later, all the players were in their places. Judge Duckworth reminded Ziegler that he was still under oath and told the jury she hoped they hadn't tried the eggplant parmigiana in the cafeteria, because she'd lost a couple jurors to it last week. Half a dozen spectators were scattered throughout the gallery, on hand for the free entertainment. A lone reporter from the *Miami Herald* was slumped in the front row.

As soon as he was on his feet, Castiel launched his counterattack. Again, he held the wooden pointer as if it were a riding crop.

"Have you been under a lot of stress, Mr. Ziegler?"

"My business, it's always stressful."

"Drinking a lot?" A little wave of the pointer, Esa-Pekka Salonen conducting his orchestra.

"Enough."

"The defendant showing up in town. Did that bring memories back of her sister, Krista Larkin?"

"Sure did."

"The young woman you had employed who'd disappeared."

"That's right."

"Even though you had nothing to do with her disappearance, did you feel badly for her family?"

"Of course."

"Is it possible that your testimony has changed because you don't want to see Krista Larkin's sister also meet an unhappy fate?"

"That's not it. Amy wasn't the one outside the window." Hanging tough.

The courtroom door opened with its customary squeak. I turned. A tall, attractive woman in a gray business suit walked in. Limped in, actually. She had a noticeable hitch in her gait. She wore sunglasses, and her reddish-brown hair was tied back in a bun. Her overall appearance was that of a mid-level executive at a local bank.

I turned back and saw Ziegler lift out of his seat. He was caught in an awkward half crouch, his mouth open, trying to form the word "no."

Melody Sanders. Or so she called herself. He had no idea she was coming. He didn't want her here.

She walked up to the front row, wincing just a bit as she sat down. A pinkish scar ran from her left ear diagonally across her cheekbone, stopping just short of her mouth. She removed her sunglasses. Smiled at me. She mouthed a greeting, "Hello, Jake."

I thought I was ready for this moment, but I wasn't. The last time I had seen her, she was flipping me the bird and hopping into Ziegler's Porsche, headed for some porn shoot. My throat was parched, and my voice wobbled. "Hello, Krista," I said.

67 The Damn Ugly Truth

Alex Castiel had been watching Ziegler. Then he swiveled toward the gallery. For a second, no sense of recognition, but as he focused on Krista Larkin, Castiel's face fell into slack-jawed disbelief.

He looked back at Ziegler, then his eyes returned to Krista. Yep, still there. Finally, his look turned to me. He seemed to be asking how much I knew.

A lot, old buddy. I know what happened after you carried Krista into the Fuck Palace all those years ago.

I'd had everything wrong. I'd mistaken the dragon for the knight, and vice versa. Charlie Ziegler was gruff and profane but ultimately had a heart. Alex Castiel polished his exterior to a fine gloss, but inside he was the beast.

And me? I was the guy who failed to rescue a girl eighteen years ago but had a chance to make amends today.

That's right, Alex. It's fallen on me to save my client and ruin your life.

Castiel was glaring at me. In just a few seconds, he had gone from confusion to fear to blinding hatred. Suddenly, the wooden pointer in his right hand snapped in two, the *cra-ck* as loud as a gunshot.

"Mr. Castiel, anything further?" the judge prompted.

"Not at this time, Your Honor." Castiel dropped into his chair and struggled to keep his emotions in check.

On the witness stand, Ziegler kept a grip on the rail. I got to my feet and approached. I could let him go. The state would rest. I'd tell the judge I had a newly discovered witness not on my list. An alibi witness. Krista Larkin. Castiel would object, but the judge would allow her testimony. It would almost certainly be reversible error not to.

Or . . .

I could take a shot at Ziegler first. Krista's existence was no longer a secret. What did he have to lose by confronting Castiel with his past?

"Mr. Ziegler, first I want to thank you for the courage to correct your earlier mistaken testimony."

"Objection!" Castiel snapped, letting me know that he hadn't left the building. "This isn't an awards banquet."

"Sustained," Judge Duckworth agreed. "No speechifying, Mr. Lassiter."

I turned sideways to the witness stand and looked toward the gallery. My granny taught me it was impolite to point, so I merely nodded my head in that direction. "Do you know the woman who just walked into the courtroom?"

He didn't answer. I listened to the whine of the ancient air conditioner. A spectator coughed. A juror's swivel chair squeaked.

Finally, Ziegler said, "Melody Sanders."

"Has she ever been known by another name?"

He was barely audible when he said, "Krista Larkin."

"For the record, just who is Krista Larkin?"

"Your client's sister."

Several jurors gasped. The mystery woman—the presumed deceased mystery woman—was in the room. The jurors stared intently at her, aware she must play an important role in the shooting of Max Perlow, but not knowing just what.

"Obviously, my client was wrong," I said. "You didn't kill her sister."

"Obviously."

"Did there come a time that my client learned her sister was still alive?"

"Not from me."

"How, then?"

Another pause. He still hadn't made up his mind how much to tell.

"Mr. Ziegler," the judge said. "There's a question pending."

"Krista went to her sister's motel. They had a reunion, you might say."

"Did you approve of this get-together?"

"I didn't have a vote. Krista never asked my opinion."

"Would you have said no?"

"Probably. When Amy came to town and started making accusations, I told Krista to let the dust settle before reaching out to her."

"When did this happen, the reunion at the motel?"

"The day before Max was shot."

A soft murmur floated through the courtroom.

"So, take us back there. It's the day before Max was killed. The sisters are at Amy's motel. What happened next?"

"Krista brought Amy back to her apartment."

"How long did my client stay?"

"Two nights."

"How do you know that?"

"Both women were in the apartment when I called Krista to tell her that Max had just been shot. That's when I learned the girls had gotten together."

He wasn't there, so it wasn't a complete alibi. Maybe half-a-bi. Krista could lock it down when her turn came to testify. Equally important, Ziegler's testimony destroyed motive. Once Amy learned that her sister was alive—the day *before* the shooting—she'd have no desire to kill Ziegler. If anything, she would shower him with kisses. At least, that's what I planned to tell the jury in closing argument.

"Over the years, did you ever tell Alex Castiel that Krista was alive?" Relying now on what Amy had told me before I left the holding cell.

"Objection!" Castiel bounced to his feet and took a position between my table and the bench. "Irrelevant and immaterial. These supposed facts involving the defendant's sister have no nexus to the shooting of Max Perlow."

I ran a curl pattern around the defense table and ended up alongside Castiel. "Your Honor, the prosecutor opened the door when he asked whether the witness felt guilty over Krista Larkin's disappearance."

"I agree," the judge said. "Door open. Horse out of the barn. Overruled."

Castiel didn't take his seat. He seemed unable to move.

"Mr. Ziegler?" I prompted. "Did you ever tell Mr. Castiel that Krista was alive?"

"No. I told him the opposite."

"That Krista was dead?"

Ziegler hesitated. Once he started down that road, there was no turning back.

"Mr. Ziegler," the judge said. "Do you understand the question?"

"Yes, ma'am." He looked at Castiel head-on, and suddenly, I knew he could do it. "I told Mr. Castiel that I'd buried Krista in the 'Glades."

I shot a look toward the jury box. No one was sleeping. Number three, the colon hydrotherapist, had one hand fluttering over her heart.

"Did you tell anyone else?"

"Max Perlow. Told them both that I'd finished off Krista by suffocating her, then burying her out by Shark Valley."

This time the murmurs in the gallery became a drone, and the judge banged her gavel. At the defense table, Amy sat paralyzed, tears tracking down her cheeks.

"That sounds like the tail end of a story," I said. "Please tell the jury what happened that night that would cause you to concoct such a terrible lie."

Ziegler's face seemed to draw itself tight. He looked old and tired and beaten. I tried another way to get it out of him.

"Mr. Ziegler, have you achieved redemption?"

"What?"

"That's what you talked about when I came over to your house one rainy night. But you can't buy redemption. You have to earn it. Mr. Ziegler, why not begin by telling your part in all of this?"

He looked toward Krista, whose eyes were wet. She nodded at him, and he began to speak. "There was a party a long time ago to celebrate a win in court. I'd been charged with obscenity up in the sticks. Suwannee County. We'd shipped maybe half a dozen videos into the county and some ambitious D.A. up there indicted me. I asked Alex Castiel for a favor and he helped me get the case dismissed."

"How'd he do that? Wasn't Mr. Castiel a prosecutor in Miami at the time?"

"Alex drove up to East Jesus and talked to the D.A."

"Talked to him?"

"And left him a briefcase with fifty thousand dollars of my money."

"Objection!" Castiel bounded out of his chair and took a step in front of me, as if blocking me out for a rebound. "Move to strike. This is a blatant attempt to smear my reputation and has nothing to do with the guilt or innocence of the defendant."

I leaned close and whispered in his ear. "Relax, Alex. I haven't even begun to smear your reputation."

"Sustained. The jury will disregard the witness' last statement. Mr. Lassiter, I'm allowing you leeway to inquire into events concerning the party, but if you stray afield again, I'm cutting you short."

"I understand, Your Honor. Now, Mr. Ziegler, please tell the jury what happened at your victory party."

"It was Max Perlow's idea. He said we had to do something for Alex, and that's how the whole godforsaken thing started."

"Alex has a hard-on for your new girl," Perlow said.

"Fuck him." Ziegler saw where this was going and wanted no part of it.

They were standing on the pool deck. Porn videos were being projected on a screen anchored to a pair of royal palms in the yard. On the speakers, Color Me Badd was singing "I Wanna Sex You Up."

"C'mon, Charlie," Perlow said. "One night. Let him get it out of his system."

"He plays too rough."

"Alex promises he'll behave."

"I gave him that girl from Alabama. She couldn't work for a week. Kid's a freak, Max."

"He comes from good stock. Your little girl will be fine."

Ziegler knew it was more than a request. You didn't say no to Max Perlow. Krista had shown up early in a silver mini and high-heeled sandals with straps that tied at mid-calf. Sunburned and mellowed from smoking weed at the beach. Ziegler told her what she had to do, and she got all pouty and whiny. She'd heard stories about Castiel from the other girls. He liked pain. Inflicting it, not suffering it.

"Why you doing this to me? He's a sick fuck, Charlie."

"One little favor. I'll make it up to you."

"How?"

"Paradise Island. We'll laze around the Ocean Club, eat stone crabs and drink piña coladas all weekend. Whadaya say?"

She smiled, pecked him on the cheek, and pranced away on long colts' legs.

An hour later, the place was mobbed. The usual night crawlers, SoBe scuzzballs, club-hoppers, and wannabe players. He'd caught sight of Castiel, scoring some ludes from Rodney Gifford on the pool deck. Then Castiel took Krista to the cabana, the Fuck Palace. Ziegler had a momentary thought of intercepting them, stopping the whole thing. But he didn't do it.

It would be nearly dawn when he next saw Krista. Naked, legs splayed across the bed at an unnatural angle. Unconscious. Face caved in. Blood leaking from an eye. A gym bag of toys spilled across the floor. Handcuffs and whips and dildos. Castiel sat on his haunches in a corner of the cabana, a sheet wrapped around him, muttering gibberish, sucking on his swollen knuckles.

Ziegler dropped to his knees and vomited. He shouted for help.

Perlow hurried in and began barking instructions. He would clean up Castiel and drive him home. One of Perlow's men would get rid of Krista's car.

"She was never here tonight, Charlie. You got that?"

"Jesus, Max. You can't sweep this under the rug."

"Shut up, you pussy! Bury her."

"What?"

"You heard me. Bury her, now!"

"She's still breathing, for Christ's sake."

"Alex is important to us," Perlow said.

"Not to me, he isn't. Jesus, Max, look what he's done."

"She's nobody. Who'll even miss her?"

Ziegler was frozen in place, paralyzed.

"It's not just his cock on the chopping block, Charlie. You been fucking an underage girl, using her in porn, giving her drugs, pimping her to your friends. Maybe you and Alex can get adjoining cells."

Ziegler didn't move, didn't speak. Perlow slapped him across the face. "Goddammit, Charlie! Finish her off. Bury her in the 'Glades. And let's get on with our lives."

Perlow helped Castiel out of the cabana, and Ziegler sat there for several minutes looking at the girl, listening to her moan. Then he took a washcloth and tried to clean her face.

———

Ziegler told the story softly and sadly, stopping twice to dab at his eyes and once to blow his nose. Not a person in the courtroom thought he was lying.

As he spoke, something was happening I'd never seen before. No one was watching the person asking the questions, me. Or the person answering, Ziegler. Everyone—judge, jurors, clerks, bailiff, defendant, every spectator and journalist—was watching Castiel. Looks of shock, horror, and disgust.

Castiel sat stiffly at the prosecution table, hands clenched in front of him. His face frozen. Maybe he'd found the time machine that would let him hang out with Meyer Lansky in Havana.

I turned toward the gallery and discovered I had been wrong. Not *everyone* was staring at Castiel. In the front row of the gallery, Krista Larkin kept her eyes on Charlie Ziegler, tears streaming down her face.

I took two steps toward the witness stand and said, "Mr. Ziegler, now I want to bring you back to the night of the shooting."

Looking exhausted, Ziegler simply nodded his head.

"On direct examination, you stated that Amy Larkin wasn't the shooter, is that correct?"

"Yes, sir."

"Were you telling the truth?"

"Yes, sir."

"The whole truth?"

"What do you mean?"

The courtroom had been nearly empty when Ziegler had testified before lunch. But the beehive that is the Justice Building had begun buzzing, and now the place was filled. Lawyers. Cops. Office workers. A TV crew belatedly set up a camera. Each time the door opened, I could hear the commotion in the corridor. Lights were turning on, camera crews setting up to pounce on Castiel when he exited. Circus Maximus.

"You said the figure was a man, correct?"

"That's right."

"Did you clearly see this man?"

He shot a look at Krista, gave a little shrug that seemed to say, "*What can I do?*"

"Clear enough," he said.

"Who was it?"

Ziegler sighed, a long whistling breath. He'd come this far. He'd scorched the earth behind him. Why stop now?

"It was Alex Castiel."

A hundred gasps seemed to suck all the air out of the courtroom.

"Alex Castiel shot Max," Ziegler continued.

"That's a lie!" Castiel on his feet now. "That's a goddamn lie and you know it!"

The judge banged her gavel. "Sit down, Mr. Castiel."

The State Attorney slumped back into his chair.

"Were you finished with your answer?" the judge asked.

"Alex killed the guy," Ziegler went on. "That's all I was going to say, Your Honor. Then Alex blamed it on the sister of the woman he tried to kill. That's the damn ugly truth."

68 Suitable for Framing

"We stand in recess." Judge Duckworth banged her gavel. "Counsel, my chambers, now! Bailiff, please summon two sheriff's deputies."

The judge stood and disappeared through the door behind the bench.

I had failed to get to my feet when the judge rose. I was still reeling.

Alex Castiel killed his surrogate father.

There was a certain logic to it. Perlow was about to be indicted on the slot-machine case. All his life, Castiel listened to his uncle Max telling him to be ruthless, to save himself first. So Castiel figured the teacher would do what he taught. Perlow's get-out-of-jail-free card was his ability to bring down the State Attorney. Tell the feds about Alex being a bagman for a porn producer, then beating a girl to death, and who knows what else over the years? Maybe Castiel was wrong; maybe Perlow never would have talked. Now we'll never know.

Amy squeezed my arm and breathed, "Thank you," into my ear.

Krista stepped through the gate and joined us at the defense table. The sisters hugged, and Krista said, "Is the case over, Jake?" Hope rippling her voice like a stream over rocks.

"Not quite yet. Let's see what the judge has to say."

"Whatever happens, you were wonderful, Jake."

That gave me the chance for a long overdue apology. "Krista, I'm sorry I didn't step up when I had the chance. Sorry I didn't keep you safe."

Krista gave me a soft, rueful smile. "Don't sweat it, Jake. In the shit storm of my life, you weren't even a drizzle."

I wasn't willing to be let off the hook so easily. "If I knew then what I know now, I would have been a better man."

She laughed and gave me a knowing smile. "Amy's told me all about you. You're a better man now."

"You sure about that?"

"You've proved it by helping Amy."

I started for the judge's chambers, but Amy grabbed my sleeve. "Do you think the jurors believe Charlie?"

"I do."

"About everything? Not just that it wasn't me. But that Castiel shot Perlow with my gun."

I recited the evidence of what I figured would become the second trial: *State v. Castiel.* "Once Castiel had the bullets you fired into my tires, all he needed was to get the gun from your motel. He had evidence of your stalking, your threats against Ziegler, and now the forensic evidence. By making it look like a botched attempt to kill Ziegler, you were just like Castiel's law school diploma."

Her look shot me a question.

"Suitable for framing." I stuffed my briefcase and headed for the door behind the bench. Her Honor was waiting.

69 Breaking the Conspiracy

Judge Duckworth's chambers were a quiet place with the scent of leather furniture and old books. A pair of sheriff's deputies guarded the door, one on the inside, one on the outside.

Her Honor wasted no time. As soon as the court stenographer had set up her little machine, the judge started in. "Mr. Castiel, do you have anything to say about the accusations made against you under oath in my courtroom?"

Stone-faced, the State Attorney said, "Not until I speak to my lawyer."

"Fine. You are hereby removed from this case. I'm declaring a mistrial on my own motion. I expect the Governor will suspend you, *instanter*, pending an investigation. I'm ordering the defendant released from custody and strongly recommending to your replacement that charges be dismissed with prejudice."

Yes! That's what I wanted to hear. The case was won, or nearly so.

"In the meantime, I am instructing the county sheriff that you be barred from the State Attorney's Office. All files of this case will be sealed until an acting State Attorney is appointed. Do you have any questions?"

"May I be excused to call my lawyer?"

"Not yet." The judge turned to me and left her smile at home. "Mr. Lassiter, I have never been a fan of your courtroom methods."

Ouch.

"But today, you really showed something in there."

Oh.

"Thank you, Your Honor."

"You've come a long way. Since that time you scored a touchdown for the wrong team, I mean."

"Safety," I corrected her.

"That's it, then. We're in adjournment." She rose and flew out of her chambers, robes trailing, looking like a nun on her way to Mass.

Castiel and I got to our feet at the same time. He seemed to stumble a bit. I didn't know if his knees buckled, if he tripped on the chair leg, or if he was having a stroke. I caught him by the elbow, and he yanked away from me. We stood there a moment, eyeing each other. His complexion had gone all sallow under his tan, and his eyes were blank and bottomless.

"Go ahead, Jake. Say it."

"Okay. You turn my stomach. You want me to go on? Because that's just the tip of the iceberg."

"I didn't kill Max."

"Like they say, tell it to the judge."

"Max Perlow did everything for me that Meyer couldn't do. To think that I'd kill him because I was afraid he'd flip on me, it's crazy. I loved the man."

"It's a good argument. I'll try to be in the gallery when your lawyer makes it."

"Goddammit, Jake. I'm being framed, can't you see that?"

"I doubt Charlie Ziegler is smart enough or tough enough to do it."

"He had help from Krista. I figure her for the shooter."

"You're pissing upwind, Alex."

I started to leave, and this time, he grabbed my arm. "Ziegler's the way in, Jake. He's the weak link."

"In where? Link to what? What the hell are you talking about?"

"Breaking the conspiracy. Proving they used you and framed me."

"Good luck with that, Alex. Let me know how it turns out."

"A long time ago, you had a dirtbag client and you did the right thing."

"A wire? That's what you want me to do?"

"Your brethren hated you for it, but you didn't care. You wear your cynicism on your sleeve, but deep down, you believe in the system. You believe in justice." His voice dropped to a whisper. "I've always admired that about you, because I don't believe in anything."

"So you admit you're corrupt?"

"Maybe it's in the Lansky genes, but yeah, I'm dirty."

"You can't blame your old man for this. It's *you*, Alex."

"Okay, I'm corrupt. Through and through. Happy now?"

"And you admit you beat Krista within an inch of her life?"

"I was strung out on meth and coke."

"So now you're blaming the drugs?"

"I nearly killed her. It's on me, I admit it, okay?"

"So why would I help you?"

He spoke through gritted teeth. "Because they used you, Jake. Krista's grand entrance into the courtroom. Charlie all shocked. The phony alibi. You think that wasn't planned?"

"No idea. All I know is that you're a worthless piece of scum."

"But I didn't kill Max, Jake. I swear to God I didn't."

70 Rough Justice

Three days after the precipitous end of the murder trial, I was invited to dinner at Ziegler's house. A foursome. Charlie and Krista. Amy and me. We could have played bridge.

Earlier that day, the Governor appointed an acting State Attorney, who immediately dismissed all charges against Amy on account of prosecutorial misconduct. I gave her the news by phone, and she whooped with joy. Her tone of voice had become free and uninhibited. A new woman.

The acting State Attorney immediately announced a Grand Jury would hear evidence against Alex Castiel for Perlow's murder. Ziegler was delighted with that news. On the home front, Lola had moved out of Casa Ziegler, Krista had moved in, and Amy was set up in the guesthouse.

A happy family.

Of murderers, according to Alex Castiel.

I promised I would take a shot at them. Not because I wanted to help Castiel. I believed what I said in the judge's chambers. He wasn't worth the effort. But a piece of Ziegler's testimony didn't hold up, and it nagged at me. I would confront him with it. If I had been used to frame a man for murder, I was going to do something about it. Not for Alex Castiel. But for me.

And so just like old times, I wore a wire.

We ate squab in a sticky sweet sauce, and Krista told me about her life.

When she was near death, it was Ziegler who quietly got her to a private hospital, then flew her to New York for facial reconstruction, and finally five months in a rehab facility.

"Charlie helped me walk again. Worked with me on speech therapy. When I was better, he got me a job in a casino in Tahoe, but I couldn't stand on my feet all those hours. I got messed up with painkillers and attempted suicide. Charlie put me into therapy, got me straightened out again."

Ziegler was her common denominator. He'd been there—for better or worse—since she was seventeen. A few years ago, he'd convinced her to move back to Florida so they could be together.

All told, she had been in hiding eighteen years. Castiel thought she was dead. A living, breathing Krista Larkin could ruin him. I understood all that. But something puzzled me.

"Why didn't you contact your family all these years?"

"I tried! I called my father when I was still in the hospital. By then, he'd found out what I was doing in Miami. He told me I was a slut who was being punished by God, that I would be better off dead."

I remembered the photo from Bozo's that Sonia Majeski had given Krista's father. He'd written on the back: *The Whore of Babylon.*

"He said if I tried to talk to Amy, he'd tell her all about me," Krista continued. "He made me feel so ashamed. After a while, I told myself Krista Larkin was dead, so I buried her. I was Melody Sanders, a new person with a new life."

But that was years ago and raised another question. "When Amy came to town, why did you wait to reach out to her?"

"Charlie asked me to chill for a few days, so he could figure out the situation. He was worried about Amy's reaction if I told her the truth about Castiel. What if she went after him with a gun?"

"But then she comes after Charlie with a gun," I said. "Or threatened to."

"Which is when I contacted Amy without telling Charlie."

"After Amy was charged, you could have come forward with your alibi."

"I told her not to," Amy said, "because Charlie said we could win without exposing Krista to the world."

"The world" meaning Castiel.

I didn't like the story, but so far, I didn't have any evidence to contradict it. Of course, I still hadn't questioned Ziegler.

After dinner, the sisters were floating on rafts in the swimming pool, gabbing and laughing and catching up on all those years apart. Ziegler and I sat in his study, my host in a fine mood. I was eyeing the artwork and an impressive gold-plated statuette of a naked woman. It was the People's Porn award for one of Ziegler's classics: *Driving Miss Daizy Crazy*.

"I'd like to pay Amy's attorney's fees," he offered, agreeably.

"Nothing to pay. I told her I'd handle her case pro bono."

"Doesn't seem right. I'd feel better if I paid you."

"I'd feel better if you didn't."

"Suit yourself. My life's fine either way."

Yes, it surely was. At least until I was through with him tonight.

Ziegler hauled a bottle of cognac out of a cabinet so we could toast the legal system and justice for all. We'd had frosty martinis before dinner. We'd moved on to that pricey daiginjo sake Ziegler liked so much, and now we were hitting the cognac. I wanted to loosen Ziegler's tongue, preferably without having to yank it out with my hands.

"A Léopold Gourmel," he said, pouring the cognac into a snifter, "aged thirteen years. I think you'll catch a whiff of almonds and orange zest."

He swirled, sniffed, and sipped, quite pleased with himself.

It seemed to be a good time to start asking questions. "What I still don't get, Charlie, is why you I.D.'d Amy the night of the shooting."

"Told you before, Castiel pressured me."

"Yeah, but this is your lover's sister we're talking about."

"Half sister," he said. "Someone she hadn't seen since she was a kid. Besides, I pretty much assumed it *was* Amy shooting at me, and since she missed, I thought she might come back for a second try."

"So you didn't get a good look?"

"Well . . ."

"Because in court, you I.D.'d Alex Castiel."

"It sort of came back to me later."

"Really? How's that work?"

"I thought it through, afterward. You gotta remember, Max recognized the shooter. He said 'You?' sounding real surprised—hurt, even. I looked up, saw this figure I later realized was Alex."

"Later?"

"Yeah. Combining all the factors."

"With all due respect to a fine host . . ."

"Yeah?"

"That's a load of crap."

Ziegler held his look for a moment, then burst out with a laugh. "Aw, what do you care, Lassiter? Castiel's a fucking lowlife."

"Agreed." I laughed, too, rough and hearty. I thought it best to let that issue go for a moment. Our conversation was being recorded. I had a good start and didn't want to spook him by hitting too hard too fast. "We've come a long way, you and me, Charlie."

Ziegler's voice was wet and boozy. "You mean the day you busted into my office and called me a sleazebag."

"There was something I didn't realize back then."

"What's that?"

"That you really loved Krista."

"Damn straight. From day one."

"Which made it easier for you to commit perjury for her."

His head snapped back as if I'd just stung him with a jab. "Jeez, Lassiter. Just when we were getting along."

"Relax, Charlie. I'm trying to help you here. There's a bit of testimony you might want to fiddle with before you testify to the Grand Jury about Castiel."

That seemed to settle him down. "I'm listening."

"You said both sisters were in the apartment when you called to tell Krista about Max getting shot. You gave Amy an alibi, so I wasn't gonna challenge you on it, but Castiel's lawyers will."

"How?"

"Castiel will subpoena your phone records just like I did. You called twice. The first one was made to the landline in Krista's apartment and reached voicemail. I figure Amy was there but was under instructions not to answer the phone. After hanging up, you immediately called Krista's cell phone. This time, you reached her and spoke for eight minutes."

He showed me a sloppy smile and bought time by taking a long hit on the cognac. "Landline. Cell phone. What's the big deal?"

"The cell tower records show that Krista's phone was in Coconut Grove when she answered. Meaning she was in her car, headed back to her apartment."

"From where?"

"From your house, where she'd just shot Max Perlow with Amy's gun."

It was a bluff. The part about the cell tower was true, but I had no idea where Krista had been a few minutes before taking the call.

Ziegler didn't reply immediately. Instead, he opened a fancy thermidor and pulled out two fat Cuban cigars. I shook my head, and he put one back inside. He used his guillotine clippers to behead the stogie, French-kissed the tip, and with a wooden match put a blue flame to the tobacco. Finally, he said, "You've got Krista all wrong. Murder isn't in her nature."

"Don't attribute your characteristics to her. Murder isn't in *your* nature."

Ziegler had his cigar in one hand, his cognac in the other. "If Krista was gonna kill anyone, it would be Alex for raping and beating her. Or hell, even me, for letting it happen."

"I'm not a shrink but I think I know how she handled her conflicting feelings about you."

"Then tell me, 'cause I never figured it out."

"She loved you when she was still a kid, and you betrayed her. She didn't want to stop loving you, so she transferred her anger to someone else. Perlow's the one who coerced you into giving Krista to Castiel. You got the pass, Perlow got the bullet, and Castiel got framed. It fits very nicely."

"So she waited all these years to kill Perlow?" He blew smoke into the air. "Not buying it, Lassiter."

"Something new had happened. Perlow had you tailed. He started asking questions about Melody Sanders. I'll bet you tensed up every time he mentioned her name. The old bastard sensed something, and you knew it. You also knew he'd kill Krista to protect Alex. Hell, he'd already tried."

"Keep going. This is a good story."

"I'm betting you told Krista you wish you had the guts to kill the old hood."

"So what if I did? Idle chat."

"Not to Krista. She hatches a plan to get rid of Perlow, so you two can live sexily ever after. And I gotta admit, it was a pretty good plan. Best part was not telling you. Krista figured you'd either put the kibosh on it or screw it up."

Ziegler tapped cigar ashes into a carved glass bowl on his desk and shook his head. "You got a great imagination, Lassiter."

"I figure Krista parked in the construction site next door, then walked along the seawall onto your property. Once on the pool deck, she purposely knocked over a planter to make a noise. You and Perlow come into the solarium, and Krista plugs him through the window, the same way Bugsy Siegel got his. You reach Krista on her cell to tell her what happened. Only she already knows. And guess what, you *did* screw it up. You'd already told Castiel that Amy was the shooter, just one sibling away from the truth. But then, you thought it *was* the truth."

"A man could sprain his brain, thinking the way you do."

Ziegler poured himself more cognac and tipped his glass to me. "All this speculation of yours. You gonna take it to Castiel?"

"And let him go free? No way!"

He looked puzzled, so I explained. Castiel can't be prosecuted for assaulting Krista. The statute of limitations expired years ago. So, unless Castiel took the fall for the murder of Max Perlow, he'd get off scot-free.

"Like you said, Charlie, Castiel is a lowlife. And like I always say, rough justice is better than no justice."

I could tell from Ziegler's look that he didn't know if I was playing him. His voice turned skeptical. "So it doesn't bother you if Krista gets off, even if she aced Max?"

"I shed no tears for Max Perlow."

"No?" Studying me.

"Eighteen years ago, Perlow stood in your cabana, looking down at Krista's naked body. She'd been choked, raped, and beaten into a near-coma. Her face was busted up, her pelvis broken. And Perlow told you to finish her off. Am I right about all that?"

"'Bury her'!" Krista's voice, coming from behind me. "Perlow told Charlie, 'Bury her.'"

I turned and saw Krista walking into the study. She was barefoot and wore a white terry-cloth robe, her wet hair wrapped in a towel.

"I must have been semi-conscious," Krista said, "because when I came to, I remembered hearing Perlow's voice. 'Goddammit, Charlie! Finish her off. Bury her in the 'Glades.'"

Amy followed behind Krista, similarly dressed. They'd come in from the pool by way of the solarium, scene of the crime.

"Helluva memory to carry around all these years, Krista," I said. "You must have really hated the man."

Krista's tone turned suspicious. "Why are you two talking about this, anyway?"

Ziegler straightened in his chair. "No reason, hon. We're just shooting the shit." He gave her his *you know me* smile, with just enough lubrication to prove he was drunk.

"Charlie, I told you not to open up to Jake."

"Aw, c'mon, hon. He knows you shot Max."

"He knows shit! Unless you told him."

"What are you up to, Jake?" Amy demanded. The sisters were flanking me.

I gave my palms-up sign of peaceful coexistence. Three sets of eyes looked back. "Krista, you did what had to be done. I have no beef with that. Like I said to Charlie, rough justice." I glanced at my watch, got out of my chair, and said, "Well, I've got court in the morning. . . ."

I wanted to get out of there. Slowly and casually and without any fuss. Not that the three of them could stop me.

"I need to frisk you," Krista said.

"Oh, c'mon, hon," Ziegler said.

"Jesus, Charlie. You're the one who told me Lassiter wore a wire for Castiel."

"Long time ago," I said. "Got nothing to do with you guys."

Krista took a step toward me. "Then prove it. Take off your shirt and loosen your belt."

Getting out of there would not be difficult. I would pivot, grab Ziegler by the scruff of his neck, and slam him, nose-first, into his desk. I would gingerly pick up Krista and deposit her in a chair, and if Amy stepped in my way, I'd knock her aside and head out the door. Who says there are no gentlemen left?

"I don't have to prove anything, Krista," I said.

"Charlie!" Krista shouted.

Ziegler popped open his desk drawer, pulled out a handgun, and pointed it at me. "Do what she says, Lassiter."

Oh, shit.

"Put the gun down, Ziegler, before you blow your dick off." Trying to sound as if I were in control.

"Keep the gun on Jake while I search him, Charlie," Krista ordered.

I was glad she wasn't the one holding the gun. The fabric of Krista's being was sinewy rawhide. If each of us is the product of the significant events of our past, the sum total of this woman's life was survival. She'd already shot and killed a man. I had no doubt she could kill me without blinking. But the *pistolero* was Charlie Ziegler, a guy with a spine made of noodles. Problem was, cowards can pull triggers, too, and even a lousy shot can hit a target five feet away. I felt a sense of dread that turned my legs into iron pilings.

"Ziegler, you're not gonna shoot me, so just put the damn gun down." Still trying to sound confident.

The shot—snapping like the crack of a whip—made me jump. Ziegler had fired into a marble sculpture across the room—a ballerina with her left arm above her head, right arm curled around in front, as if playing an imaginary bull fiddle. The slug caught the ballerina squarely between the eyes, splintering her marble head.

"Strip, Lassiter," Krista said.

"Do as she says," Ziegler ordered, "or I'll put the next one in your thick skull."

"Don't think so," I said. "It's not in you, Ziegler."

Krista walked over and faced me squarely, standing so close I could feel her breath. Her jaw was set, her greenish eyes colder than ice. I could see the power of the woman's will. Doctors say broken bones heal even stronger. The woman before me had been forged, like molten steel, from her own crushed bones. She looked at me, not with hatred, but with fearless determination.

"Start with your shirt," she said.

It was time to act. It would take only a second for me to grab her by the shoulders, toss her into Ziegler, and make my way to the door.

We were standing so close I never saw her good leg jerk upward.

She kneed me in the groin.

A solid hit. The pain pitched me sideways. I gasped for breath, my eyes tearing. Amy joined the fray. She caught me alongside an ear with a karate kick and I staggered sideways. Women nowadays, with their pilates and kickboxing and martial arts, are all aggression and attitude.

A second kick caught me just above the knee, and I toppled to the floor.

Amy hopped onto my back, raked her fingernails across my forehead, then reached under my shirt and grabbed for the wire. Her fleecy robe had come open, and underneath, she was naked and still wet from the pool. I turned and grabbed at her, but it was like trying to catch a fish in my bare hands. She kept wriggling and I couldn't get a grip.

"You bastard!" she shouted at eardrum-breaking decibels.

I struggled to my feet and tried to shake her off. She bit my right ear. Chomped down hard and drew blood. I was already bleeding from the gouges in my forehead. Krista grabbed the front of my shirt and yanked, popping most of the buttons. Then she reached into my pants, searching for the recorder, finding something else.

"Ouch!" I yelled, twisting away.

Ziegler vaulted from behind his desk, screaming, "I'll shoot you, I'll shoot you!"

Amy was still riding my back, the shell to my tortoise. "I've got it!" she shouted.

Her hand came out with the battery pack that had been taped to the small of my back. The recorder was still on my thigh. I shook from side to side, like a wet dog, and she flew off me.

"I'll shoot!" Ziegler repeated, in case I'd forgotten.

Blood flowed into my eyes from my forehead, and I could barely see. I wheeled toward Krista and saw the blur of movement. The People's Porn statuette, coming at my head. Krista with a death grip on the naked woman's torso. I raised an arm and caught the blow, the statuette breaking in two at the woman's hips. An electric jolt, a stinger, shot through my shoulder.

Krista tried to slash me with the jagged bottom half of the statuette. I slid to one side, dodging her. She came at me again, but I grabbed the collar of her robe and tossed her to the floor. "Shoot him!" she yelled.

Amy came at me, arms flailing. I caught her wrist in one paw and twisted until she cried, "Ow," then spun her into the credenza.

Ziegler moved between the door and me, holding the gun in two hands.

"I'm out of here, Ziegler."

"Give it up and I'll let you go."

"You'll let me go now."

I took two steps toward him and he raised the gun to chest level. "Don't make me."

"Kill him!" Krista screamed, from the floor.

"I'll do it. I swear I will!" Ziegler's arms trembled.

"You're a better man than that, Charlie. That's the damn irony. Compared to these two, you're the Humanitarian of the Year."

I wrenched the gun from his hand. A Sig Sauer .380.

Amy's gun? The murder weapon? I'd bet on it.

71 The Old Fumblerooski

The next morning, my forehead was stitched, my knee wrapped, and my ear bandaged. Other than a crushing headache, I felt damn good.

As I swung the old Eldo into the Justice Building lot, I listened to Johnny Cash sing about that old "ring of fire."

"And it burns, burns, burns . . ."

The acting State Attorney was a silver-haired woman in her fifties named Cheryl Halpern. A lifer in the U.S. Attorney's Office, she ran the Public Corruption Unit and had earned a reputation as a smart, tough prosecutor. Today, having been convinced by the Governor to give up her federal paycheck, she sat in Alex Castiel's old high-back leather chair.

She hadn't had time to either unpack her boxes or move Castiel's possessions out. The photograph of Bernard Castiel, Meyer Lansky, and Rosa Castiel looked at us from the credenza.

Seated next to me were Castiel and his lawyer, a silver-haired Brooks Brothers mouthpiece from Palm Beach. His wingtips were highly polished, and he eyed me with outright hostility. He didn't offer his name and I didn't take it.

I had asked for the meeting, so State Attorney Halpern told me to say my piece. I spent ten minutes telling them everything I knew. I handed over the Sig Sauer, which I'd put in a kitchen plastic bag and labeled, as if I were a crime-scene tech. Then I asked if they'd like to hear the audiotape.

"You wore a wire?" Cheryl Halpern said. "Again?"

I shrugged. I've lived in South Florida practically my entire life, yet was known for only two things. I'd once toted a football to the wrong end zone, and I'd once blown the whistle on my own client. Okay, make that twice.

As I played the tape, Mr. Palm Beach stopped giving me the evil eye and began bobbing his head, as if keeping time to a pleasant tune. When I clicked off the recorder, Ms. Halpern said, "Illuminating." She also had a reputation for brevity.

"Thank you, Jake," Castiel said. "Thank you."

"Didn't do it for you," I said, not looking at him.

"It seems clear that there's no case to take to the Grand Jury concerning Mr. Castiel," Mr. Palm Beach said. "I'd suggest the state build its case against Krista Larkin."

"She's already lawyered up," the new State Attorney said. "Kevin Moore called me this morning."

"Did he sniff around about a plea?" I said.

"Hardly. He says you're wrong about the phone calls and you've got the wrong shooter."

"Yeah?"

"Moore says Krista never left her apartment that night. She had some wine, turned off the phone, and went to bed early, which is why Ziegler's first call went to voicemail. Then he called her cell phone, which the lawyer claims Amy answered while driving Krista's car."

Uh-oh. I saw where this was going.

"I don't get it," Mr. Palm Beach said. He might charge six hundred bucks an hour but still was a step too slow.

"The old switcheroo, the fumblerooski," I interjected.

"How's that?"

"They're saying that Amy was driving back from Ziegler's house, where she'd just shot Perlow. *Amy.* Not Krista. And because the case has already been dismissed with prejudice against Amy . . ."

"Double jeopardy!" Mr. Palm Beach brayed, as if he had known it all along. "Double jeopardy bars a second prosecution against Amy."

"Not that we would charge her," Halpern said, "if Krista is the shooter, and this is just a ruse."

"The perfect defense," Mr. Palm Beach said, a bit wistfully. "Blame the murder on a person who can't be tried."

Castiel leaned forward in his chair and wagged a finger at his replacement. "You can't let them get away with it. If I were still State Attorney—"

"You're *not,* Mr. Castiel," Halpern said, "and with good reason."

Mr. Palm Beach put a gentle hand on Castiel's arm and turned to the new State Attorney. "No need to be testy with my client, Ms. Halpern."

She ignored him and looked at me. "Mr. Lassiter, thank you for your efforts, but unless you have a suggestion, I think we may be at the end of the road here."

"There's one thing you might want to consider," I said. "Charlie Ziegler testified that Alex was the shooter and now admits on tape he was lying. You've got him dead to rights on perjury."

"I see where you're going with this," Halpern said. "Charge Ziegler with a felony and offer him a deal. But will he turn on his mistress?"

"He's the weak link," Castiel said. "I'll bet he goes for it."

"I'd bet against it," I said. "He loves Krista, really loves her."

The air went out of the room with that assessment.

"So, what, then?" Halpern asked. "We put Ziegler away for a few years and the killer goes free?"

"There's still a way you might convict Krista Larkin."

"How?"

"Krista loves Ziegler, too. Give her the choice which one goes to prison. Indict her for Perlow's murder, plead it down to manslaughter. Give her a chance to spend a few years locked up in return for not charging Ziegler with perjury."

"Horse trading," Halpern said. "It's not perfect."

"Justice seldom is," I replied, as if she didn't know that.

"And if they both hang tough?"

"Ziegler goes away for a bit, and Krista pines for him. Either way, I'm not gonna lose any sleep over it. Like I told Ziegler, Perlow getting aced is rough justice. The guy ordered Krista's execution."

"Jesus, Jake!" Castiel exploded. "We adhere to the rule of law. We don't countenance vigilantes."

"The rule of law?" Halpern said. "How dare you even use the phrase!"

Castiel looked away. Defiant, not ashamed.

"I agree with Mr. Lassiter," Halpern continued. "I can think of worse things than Perlow's murderer not being convicted. You going free, Mr. Castiel, comes to mind."

"I have a thought on that subject, too," I said. "Alex suborned perjury and obstructed justice by browbeating Ziegler into fingering Amy as the shooter."

"Jake, what the fuck!" Castiel was glaring at me.

"Ms. Halpern, I think you can put him away for a while. Again, it's not perfect but it's better than nothing."

"You bastard," Castiel said.

"Mr. Lassiter, my esteem for you keeps rising," Halpern said.

"Thank you."

"'Rough justice,' you called it." She sighed. "I've been doing this twenty-five years, and now I wonder if that's all we can ever expect."

"We can always aim higher, but I never like to get my hopes up."

She gave me a rueful smile. "That reminds me of what the Attorney General told me when I was sworn in."

I seldom speak to an Attorney General, so I listened, figuring I might learn something.

"He said, 'Cheryl, put your ideals in the desk drawer with the rubber bands and paper clips. Just work hard to do the right thing and hope for the best.'"

That sounded about right.

I said my good-byes and headed out, thinking about the law and justice, and the tenuous relationship between the two. I found my old Eldo in the steaming parking lot, a snowy white egret perched on the hood like a feathery ornament.

I keyed the ignition and listened to the giant V-8 sputter to life. The skinny-legged bird turned its pointy beak toward me but didn't move.

"What do you want from me?" I asked.

No answer. Its beady yellow eyes seemed accusatory.

"Hey. I do the best I can."

The egret squawked twice, crapped on my hood, spread its wings, and took off.

"Okay, okay! I'll try harder."

I watched the bird dip, then soar, heading toward the river and disappearing into the glare of the morning sun.

Acknowledgments

I gratefully acknowledge the assistance of Randy Anderson, Angel Castillo, Thomas Douglas Engel, John Schulian, John Macaray, Paul Basile, Ed Shohat, Maria Shohat, Judge Stanford Blake, James O. Born, and Carmen Finestra.

As always, I am indebted to my agent Albert Zuckerman at Writers House and my battalion at Bantam/Random House: Randall Klein, Kate Miciak, Kim Hovey, Lisa Barnes, and Sharon Propson.

ABOUT THE AUTHOR

PAUL LEVINE is a former trial lawyer and an award-winning author of legal thrillers, including *Illegal, Solomon vs. Lord* (nominated for the Macavity Award and the James Thurber Prize), *The Deep Blue Alibi* (nominated for an Edgar Award), and *Kill All the Lawyers* (a finalist for the International Thriller Writers Award). He won the John D. MacDonald Award for his critically acclaimed Jake Lassiter novels, which are now available as ebooks. He's also written more than twenty episodes for the CBS military drama *JAG*. Paul Levine lives in Los Angeles, where he is working on his next Jake Lassiter thriller.

ABOUT THE TYPE

This book was set in Monotype Dante, a typeface designed by Giovanni Mardersteig (1892–1977). Conceived as a private type for the Officina Bodoni in Verona, Italy, Dante was originally cut only for hand composition by Charles Malin, the famous Parisian punch cutter, between 1946 and 1952. Its first use was in an edition of Boccaccio's *Trattatello in laude dei Dante* that appeared in 1954. The Monotype Corporation's version of Dante followed in 1957. Though modeled on the Aldine type used for Pietro Cardinal Bembo's treatise *De Aetna* in 1495, Dante is a thoroughly modern interpretation of that venerable face.